D0978042

SUBMIT
Book Two in the Surrender Series

By

MELODY ANNE

SUBMIT
Book Two in the Surrender Series

Copyright © 2013 Melody Anne

All rights reserved. Except for use in any review, the reproduction or utilization of this work in whole or in part in any form by any electronic, mechanical or other means, now known or hereafter invented, including xerography, photocopying and recording, or in any information storage or retrieval system, is forbidden without the written permission of the author.

This is a work of fiction. Names, characters, places and incidents are either the product of the author's imagination or are used fictitiously, and any resemblance to actual persons, living or dead, business establishments, events or locales is entirely coincidental.

ISBN-13: 978-0615822990
ISBN-10: 0615822991

Cover Art by Edward
Edited by Alison
Interior Design by Adam

www.melodyanne.com

Email: info@melodyanne.com

 /MelodyAnneAuthor  @AuthMelodyAnne

First Edition
Printed in the U.SA

DEDICATION

This book is dedicated to my Aunt Linda. Thank you for always being such a wonderful person. You have been there for me since I was a young child. To this day I can't listen to the Top Gun soundtrack without thinking of you. I love you!

OTHER BOOKS BY MELODY ANNE

Billionaire Bachelors:
*The Billionaire Wins the Game
*The Billionaire's Dance
*The Billionaire Falls
*The Billionaire's Marriage Proposal
*Blackmailing the Billionaire
*Run Away Heiress
*The Billionaire's Final Stand

The Lost Andersons:
*Unexpected Treasure
*Hidden Treasure
*Holiday Treasure
*Priceless Treasure

Baby for the Billionaire:
*The Tycoon's Revenge
*The Tycoon's Vacation
*The Tycoon's Proposal
*The Tycoon's Secret
*The Lost Tycoon

Surrender:
*Surrender - Book One
*Submit - Book Two
*Seduced - Book Three
*Scorched - Book Four

Forbidden Series:
*Bound -Book One
*Broken - Book Two
*Betrayed - Book Three
*Burned - Book Four

OTHER BOOKS BY MELODY ANNE (CONT.)

Unexpected Heroes:
*Her Unexpected Hero
*Who I am With You - Novella
*Her Hometown Hero
*Following Her - Novella
*Her Forever Hero - (February 2016)

*Safe in His Arms - Novella - Baby, It's Cold Outside Anthology

The Apocalypse Series:
*Midnight Fire
*Midnight Moon
*Midnight Storm
*Midnight Eclipse

Becoming Elena:
*Stolen Innocence

NOTE FROM THE AUTHOR

I can't believe another book is done and ready for publishing. I've thanked you all over and over, and I can't say it enough. Thank you to my fans, my family, and my wonderful friends. A new person I want to acknowledge is Alison! You are amazing. Thank you for the time and effort you put into editing and for the fabulous job you do. You don't allow me to be less than the best and I appreciate it so much!

Thank you again to my fans, especially those on my street team, Melody's Muses. You truly inspire me and I love the amazing effort you put out each and every week to promote my books and to encourage me. Thank you!

Thank you so much to Jack, who goes above and beyond the call of duty and makes changes for me, encourages me and deals with my millions of e-mails. You are a rock star!

I hope you're enjoying this newest series. I hope you all forgive me for the end of this second book. This is something I've wanted to do for a while. It's such a thrill having a job doing what I absolutely love. Thank you!

Melody Anne

CHAPTER ONE

RAFE SAT THERE, unmoving, as Ari continued toward the open door of his jet. A chill traversed the length of his spine and his throat tightened — surely the thudding of his heart couldn't be fear. He stiffened slightly, but only to keep his body from betraying his reaction. If she were to walk out the door, onto the tarmac, and out of his life, he wouldn't stop her.

He knew she wanted him, knew it wouldn't be a hardship for her to stay. Any use of force was out of the question. Much as he wanted her submission, he'd gone as far as he ever would with this game; the chase was over.

Ari held all the cards — she just didn't realize she was in control. He wouldn't keep her mother's home or business from her. They were just bargaining chips.

Rafe's only real power was in Ari's not knowing if he was as ruthless as he'd claimed. He'd proved himself a callous adversary — he only hoped she didn't call his bluff.

When Ari suddenly stopped, Rafe's heart skipped a beat. Slowly, she turned, flames leaping from her eyes. She was stunning in her fury, and his body awoke with the overwhelming need to take her, claim her as his own.

Did she really have a choice?

No — and now they both knew it. They both knew that Ari couldn't let her mother down. If Sandra left the hospital only to find that she had neither a home nor a business, that Ari had been compelled to sell them during her mom's long and terrible illnesses, both women would be devastated.

"You realize I will forever despise you, right?"

"I don't need your affection — only your submission," he replied with the slightest tilt to his lips. Confidence now emanated from his whole being as he watched her make her decision.

She was his!

Without another word, Ari lifted her head high and began the short walk to the back of his jet — straight to his bedroom. Excitement pooling inside him, Rafe rose from his chair, his senses tuned in to the soft sigh of her shoes as she moved before him.

He turned to tell his pilot they were ready — the doors could now be shut — then he followed Ari into his room.

Anticipation made him almost unsteady as he circled her. They had only a few things to settle and then she was his for the taking. The long anticipated wait had been worth it, if his body's reaction was any indication. Her eyes caught his every movement and he liked the uncertainty she was trying so valiantly to hide.

"Come here and sit," he commanded her.

A slight smile lifted the corners of her mouth as she began her slow approach. Yes, he'd always known she'd make a good

2

submissive. Still, disappointment filled him at how easily she was bending to his will. If he managed to break her so soon, would he enjoy her nearly as much? Part of her appeal was her defiance.

Ari moved to the other side of the chair he was holding out, then lifted her arm and let her hand trail along the backrest just inches from where his hand rested. Oh, the anticipation of sinking inside her was burning through his veins.

"You might as well wipe that victorious smirk off your face, Rafe. This is a power game to you; you wield your business agreement and your Snidely Whiplash words like a sword and shield. But it *is* only a game and I refuse to play. I said I'll stay — and I will. You've obviously managed to get the upper hand, but that doesn't mean you will own me."

"I don't understand." A rush of adrenaline almost made him light-headed as he looked at the fire flashing in her eyes. Joy coursed through him. She was in no way defeated — not even close. They had only a few minutes before they'd have to go back out front and sit for takeoff. He'd been hoping to get the formalities out of the way and then relieve the ache in his body.

This was better.

"I won't be on a leash. I'll be your mistress, but I have my own conditions. If you don't like what I have to say, then turn this jet around and let me leave. My mother would rather lose everything than lose me. I may not want her to go through the pain of knowing she has nothing left — but she'd never forgive me if I gave up my soul."

"What are your conditions?" Rafe was surprised by her words — even more surprised that he was entertaining the idea of allowing provisions. He didn't allow his mistresses to make demands. He certainly didn't allow them to speak to him this way. Any other woman would have been banished from his life on the spot. Ari wasn't just any woman, though. She was his obsession.

"First off, I want to keep my job. I won't accept a salary for doing nothing other than bending over the back of your desk. Secondly, I get one day a week off — one day to do with as I like, such as visit with my mother or my friends. I've sacrificed too long, and I won't have you telling me I can't spend time with my mother — after all, she's the reason I'm degrading myself this way in the first place."

He beheld the passion in her eyes, heard the slight quiver in her tone. She wasn't bluffing. If he refused her, she'd walk. Would that be so bad? Quite honestly, he just couldn't tell any longer. The only thing he knew for sure was that he couldn't seem to let her go.

"Mr. Palazzo, we're cleared for takeoff. Will you please return to your seats?" Rafe glared at the small sidewall speaker. Walking over, he pressed the intercom button.

"I need ten more minutes."

"Yes, sir."

Rafe returned to Ari and the two of them stood motionless in a face-off. He knew it was critical not to cave to her demands. It would set the bar for their relationship. Being a master at negotiation, Rafe weighed his odds. If he called her bluff, yes, she'd walk away. His other option? Make a few concessions, but still keep his unbendable rules intact.

What was most important to him? His fixation on her could very well undermine every defense he had put in place over the last few years.

Was she worth it?

*****

Ari didn't know how she was keeping her knees from knocking together. What if he'd simply had too much and decided to throw her out? Was that what she wanted? She hated him in these moments, but there was no doubt she desired him, too.

It wasn't such a hardship to imagine sharing his bed. She just couldn't turn herself into a whore. She refused to be one of those women who were nothing more than candy for their man.

Keeping her heart from being affected shouldn't be a big deal. When he bullied her, treated her like nothing but another member of his staff, she had no problem despising him. The hard part would be in not needing him. Rafe was powerful, someone she could easily imagine leaning on. And that was something she absolutely couldn't ever do.

The seconds passing by seemed more like minutes. Ari didn't know how long the two of them stood staring at each other, neither wanting to blink first, but finally she couldn't take it. Her anger was evaporating, and she needed to sit. Breaking their deadlock, she moved to the bed and sat on the edge.

Rafe spoke after a brief pause. "You take a lot for granted, Ari. One of these times, you'll push me too far and lose everything. Being with me isn't such a hardship. I treat my mistresses well."

"I have no doubt you treat them exceptionally well. I just don't understand your desire to be with me. I've fought you from day one. Sure, the sex was good, but I imagine you've had a lot of good sex. I don't really see the appeal in all of this for you."

"You'd be surprised how hard it is to find someone who's truly compatible sexually. The sex isn't just good, Ari — it's extraordinary. I will give you your one day off per week. Of course, that will be void if we're out of the country. That's something I can't help."

"If that happens, then when we get back, I can take two days the week after, and so on until I am paid the days off that are owed to me," she broke in. By the flare in his eyes, she knew she was pushing her luck.

Too bad. He needed to be defied. Obviously, not enough people refused the all-powerful Rafe Palazzo.

"We can negotiate that point when the time comes. Under no circumstance is your day off an excuse to see other men. While you're with me, you are exclusively mine. Do you understand?"

"Yes."

"Good. As for the employment, that's not up for negotiation. You can't carry on full-time work, or even part-time, and be committed fully to me."

The arrogance in his tone made her skin crawl. How could she submit to him? She'd never been the sort to cave in to anything. This wasn't going to end well.

"Then you will just have to find me a position at your offices. I won't be paid to be your mistress. I don't care what the job position is. I'll file mail, copy documents, fetch coffee for people — *I do not care.* I absolutely won't do nothing more than sit around a paid-for home and wait for your call — this isn't negotiable."

Ari hadn't realized how much she was revealing to him with her words. She needed this job to be more than just her being his personal sex slave — she needed to earn her paycheck through actual work, not on her back. If she'd known the desperate sound of her voice, she would have put her armor back in place. In no way did she want him to see her as weak, show him a soft spot for him to sink his fangs into. She felt her best defense was to have an impeccable offense and show not one iota of weakness to him.

Her small moment of vulnerability is what gave her power, though, even if she didn't realize it. Seeing her so exposed ate away at Rafe's conscience — much as he fought the idea of even having a conscience.

"Fine. I'll find a position in the Palazzo offices that will allow you to be available to me at all times. I'll have to speak to Mario about it."

Ari was surprised at how willing he was to compromise. When she looked up, she was expecting to see victory in his dark eyes, but she was greeted only by a blank stare. What had she gotten herself into? In what universe did she believe she could come out the victor in a battle against Rafe?

He might be allowing her some concessions, but he was the champion of their match. His quiet arrogance left no doubt about that. Ari might hate him, but she was reminded in this moment of the thin line between love and hate. This man had the power to break her in two. It would take everything inside her not to allow that to happen.

CHAPTER TWO

"WE NEED TO get seated. We'll discuss this more out front." Rafe didn't wait to see whether Ari would follow him. If he hesitated, he would show her a crack in his armor. He'd already given in too much today.

Making his way to his seat, Rafe heard the gentle sound of Ari's breathing as she followed behind. His afternoon hadn't gone the way he'd planned, but then again, he really hadn't known whether she would stay or go. Not knowing the outcome of a situation he was going in to was new for him. Feeling the anticipation of awaiting her answer was a shocking exhilaration. He couldn't deny, even to himself, that he was grateful she was still there.

"I'll serve drinks once we're safely in the air," the flight attendant said after making sure that he and Ari were belted in, and then left them to their uncomfortable silence. After the jet started moving down the runway, Rafe turned to gaze at Ari as she looked out the windows. Her shoulders remained firmly back, her head high.

"We'll go over my expectations of you."

Warily, Ari turned and looked at him. Then, when the jet began its ascent, she glanced back out the small window as if she were considering escape. Soon they'd be high in the air, with the only way down a long, long jump.

Rafe penetrated her thoughts, and satisfaction filled him at knowing he had her right where he wanted — at least for now.

"I think that's a good idea," she finally answered.

"Good. There's no use in sidestepping the issues, so we may as well get right into it. I've already made concessions for you. There are certain areas in which I'm unwilling to compromise. You should consider yourself lucky that I've been as lenient as I have."

"Are you kidding me? If this is you being lenient, I'd really hate to learn what *strict* means in your vocabulary."

"Can you for once engage in a rational discussion without a smart-ass response?" he asked in frustration. If he'd been the type to pull out his hair — no, he didn't want to think about it. At least Ari kept quiet for the moment, but the searing look she sent Rafe's way didn't escape his notice. If ever a woman needed to be tamed, she was it. Now *that* was something he'd like to think about.

"Fine. I'll listen, but I just want to say it's under duress. If you were a decent man, you'd let me go and forget all about this."

It was a good thing he'd never claimed to be a white knight. He'd been up-front from the beginning about who he was and what he wanted. The only way he'd departed from his normal routine was by chasing after her.

"Of course you can go. All you have to do is tell your mother that when she finally leaves the hospital next week, she won't have a home or a business to return to." Why let Ari know that he liked Sandra and would have given both to her no matter what Ari chose to do now? "You and I both know that I'm not letting you go, so let's not waste our time discussing it. Most of all, I expect obedience. I'm not a selfish lover and you'll be highly satisfied — you already know that quite well. I also have a healthy appetite — probably more than you do — and will expect you to be prepared for that, day or night."

"Please! Do you have to talk like that?"

Rafe lifted an eyebrow, smirked briefly, and then continued in a businesslike tone. "I've promised never to hurt you, and I won't, but I've discovered in the last few years that I like... more. Seeing you strapped down to my bed thrills me; taking complete control of your body until you're begging me for release sets me on fire. I will take you higher than you've ever been — and in order for me to do that, you'll have to relinquish your control to me."

"And if I don't?" she asked, slightly out of breath.

A smile spread across his face as he firmly held her gaze. His lifestyle excited her. She wanted him to own her — pleasure her — make her scream. She'd also rather suffer the tortures of hell than admit to it.

"Then I'll *still* take control — I'll *still* find great pleasure... but *you* won't."

As Ari's eyes widened, Rafe wondered how much she would fight him. He enjoyed the fight, loved the chance to battle her. What he didn't like was withholding pleasure from her. Not many of his mistresses had fought him — and the few who had, had done so only once. When they defied him, he easily walked away.

Ari was a first for him in many respects. He didn't want to leave her unsatisfied. He loved the way her face glowed as she cried out his name, and the way her body pulsed around his throbbing manhood. Her response to him was so spontaneous and real that it sent him into an unknown, unmapped, mind-bending realm of desire.

He wanted her to fight him — he just didn't want to withhold anything from her. But they'd discuss that more when the time presented itself.

"I won't throw everything at you at once, Ari. I'm not the monster you think I am. I've been open and honest about what I expect. I'm not asking you to do anything you will later feel shame over. If you can't live with this, then we really have nothing else to discuss."

Challenging him — he wanted that, but having a complete lack of respect for him? That he wouldn't tolerate. He knew they were compatible, as they'd already had better sex than he could remember ever having before. She just had to get over her preconceived notions of right and wrong.

Sex was about pleasure, not love. The sooner she accepted that fact, the better off the two of them would be.

"I'm not making promises, but I'll give it a try, Rafe." At least she was no longer fighting his orders on how to address him. He loved the sound of his first name on her lips.

"Fine. We have gone over employment, which will get straightened out next week, and my expectations for you sexually. Of course, as soon as we return, you will move into the condo I have waiting for you."

"Why can't I just stay at my mother's? She needs someone to take care of her until she's healed fully. I can still be at your beck and call, and meet you at the condo."

"No. This isn't up for discussion. I'll have a care provider for your mother, and if anything happens to her, I won't keep you away — but I want you in that condo. Family...complicates things, and I don't want her with you when I speak to you on the phone. I also want you available to me even if it's at three in the morning. You *will* stay where I want you."

Rafe waited as she considered his words. He knew she was trying to decide what to say next, but his temper began fraying at her slow response. He'd been very generous in his compromises. She needed to accept some things without questions or objections; it would be a good test of what was to come.

"Fine, but if it ever gets to the point that I can't take it, then I walk. Also, I want there to be a time frame for my prison sentence with you — I'd say three months is sufficient."

They were now in the air, but the seat belt signs weren't off yet. Rafe didn't care. She had a way of pushing him further than she should be allowed to. He swiftly unbuckled and stood before her, delighting in the quick intake of her breath and the way her pulse quickened as he grabbed her wrist.

"If you want this to feel like a prison, I can make it that way, Ari. I have no problem with chaining you to my bed..." At her gasp, he paused while his fingers caressed the smooth skin of her inner arm. Then, kneeling before her, he leaned in, bringing his mouth to her ear.

"Don't pretend you aren't getting wet right this minute. I already know your body, know what makes you hot and moist. I can make you orgasm with the barest of touches. You can cry wolf all night long — and I am one — but the reality is that if you were so averse to being in my presence, you would have stepped straight out that door. You may not like that I make your body sing, and you may even despise the power I hold over you — but you don't hate the act of sex with me."

In between his words, Rafe's tongue traced the edge of her ear; his hand moved up her arm to her shoulder and then began a downward motion. As soon as he finished speaking, he bit down on the lobe of her ear and his hand squeezed the soft swell of her breast, her nipple hardening in his palm.

She wanted him — but she hated herself for it, and she spoke with contempt both for herself and for him.

"Fine. You've easily proved that you make me want you. None of that matters, though. This is business — that's all. When it comes to an end, I'll walk away without ever looking back," she almost panted out, her back arching.

Rafe laughed as he moved his lips across her cheek, then traced her jaw before moving to her mouth. She had the most delectable pink lips — he could play with them all day. He sucked her bottom lip into his mouth, then ran his tongue along the smooth surface before she opened up to him.

Her legs spread apart as he slid to the edge of the chair, Rafe's frustration mounting when he couldn't press against her. He tried telling himself that wasn't what this was about, but in devouring her mouth he was quickly becoming lost in her essence.

Steadily pursuing a single goal, his hand moved to her leg and slipped under her skirt, his fingers gliding along her smooth thighs as he reached inexorably for her heat. Her small wisp of lace didn't stop him as he reached inside her panties and touched her hot core.

Ari groaned into his mouth and twisted in her chair, trying desperately to get closer to him. Rafe slid two fingers inside her heat and began pumping his fingers while his thumb moved in a circular motion over her swollen pink bud.

It took only a few short minutes for her to shatter, her cries swallowed by his hungry mouth. With supreme effort, Rafe pulled his hand from her still quivering body and leaned back to look. Ari's flushed face and shocked expression almost made up for the fact that he was now rock-hard and hurting.

"You may hate me, but you fall apart in my arms," he whispered as he brought his finger to his lips and licked the taste of her from his hand. Her eyes widened, making his erection jump with unfulfilled desire.

He'd been planning to prove something to her, but his lesson had royally backfired on him. He needed a minute to pull himself together. Just as she got her clothing straightened out, the flight attendant entered their cabin, and Ari jumped. He knew she was mortified at how close the two of them had come to getting caught with her half-naked. Her face heated as Rafe stood up.

Ari was offered a drink and something to eat, but she didn't seem able to speak as his efficient staff member waited patiently. Rafe sent the middle-aged woman off to start their meal before throwing one more scorching look Ari's way. When she refused to meet his gaze, he turned around.

Without saying another word, he walked to the bathroom and splashed cold water on his face. After about five minutes he was calm enough to join Ari again, but he knew if he didn't take her that night, he might suffer permanent damage to his nether regions.

As Rafe leaned back in his chair, Ari's gaze strayed to his, fear and excitement mingled in her eyes. He knew she was unsure of what was to come, and that was a good thing. It was best to keep her slightly out of control.

The less time he gave her to dwell on their situation, the more likely they both got something they wanted from each other. She needed him — he just had to make her realize that.

For the next fifteen minutes, the cabin remained uncomfortably silent as Rafe pulled out his laptop and checked through his e-mail. Ari's gaze didn't stray from the window, and as their meals were brought out, he had had enough.

"Why do you continue blaming yourself over your mother's accident?" He wasn't accusing her of anything; he truly didn't understand it. For a moment, he thought she was going to refuse to answer him, but then he saw a sigh escape as she turned in his direction while picking up her fork and toying with the food in front of her.

"I was the one who called her out that night. She never would have left the house if it wasn't for me."

"You didn't cause the accident. You didn't cause her cancer. She had many unfortunate incidents occur in a row that were no one's fault. As for selling the property, you had little choice. The medical bills had to be paid."

"I would think you of all people would understand this, Rafe. You may despise women, but you obviously adore your parents and siblings. It doesn't matter how much you or my mother or anyone else tells me that it's not my fault, I still feel responsible. I can't seem to make that feeling go away."

"Would you be here now if you didn't feel responsible?" He held his breath as he waited for her answer. She looked at him as if truly considering her words.

"Yes. I'm not here because I feel guilt over causing the wreck. I'm here because whether it was my fault or not, I have the chance to make my mother's life a little bit better. She always sacrificed everything for me, and now it's my turn to do the same for her. This has nothing to do with whether I'm responsible or not; this is about making my mom's life a little bit better."

"And if I tell you I want your total submission?" He felt himself holding his breath as he waited for her response. When a genuine smile flitted across her face, he fought not to join her with his own grin.

"Then I'd tell you that you'll be sorely disappointed."

Ari took a few bites of her meal, but when his attendant came back, she gave her the tray, then leaned against the seat and looked back out the window. It didn't take her long to fall asleep, her features relaxing as she involuntarily let down her guard.

Rafe found that he could gaze at her for limitless amounts of time and be perfectly content. Frustrated with himself, he opened his laptop back up and forced himself not to think about Ari for the next couple of hours. He had her where he wanted her — now he needed to focus on other priorities in his life.

It was easier said than done.

CHAPTER THREE

"ARI, WE'RE HERE. Ari?"

Startled awake, Ari opened her eyes to find Rafe peering down at her. Darn, his little foreplay on the jet had zapped every ounce of her energy. She moved her neck, then winced as she felt the pinch. Sleeping while sitting up in a seat — even a chair as comfortable as the one on Rafe's jet — was murder on the muscles.

"We're in New York?"

"Yes, we're pulling up to the hangar now. It's seven, so I thought we'd grab a bite to eat before reaching the hotel."

Ari's nerves twisted into a tight coil when he mentioned the hotel. She knew what he expected, and it wasn't a cold night in their room. What in particular was on the horizon? She had a suspicion that her obedience training would begin without delay.

Excitement wasn't what she expected to feel coursing through her, but that's exactly what it was. Rafe had a way of turning her body to jelly; say what she would, being with him wasn't the end of the world.

Ari's biggest fear in these precious last moments of freedom was of falling in love with him. He'd been more than honest in setting forth his feelings about their relationship. It was about sex and *only* sex for him — nothing more. Yes, she'd be a fool to fall for him. If he continued acting like an irredeemable jerk, it would be much easier for her to despise him. It was the moments of kindness he exhibited that scared her. She couldn't resist his tenderness.

"I'm going to use your bathroom for a minute," she said as she stiffly rose to her feet, grabbing her clutch before making her way to the back of the jet. As the large aircraft cruised to a stop, she had to hold on to the counters as she moved. She was thankful the jet stopped as she closed the bathroom door. She understood now why you weren't supposed to leave your seat until the aircraft had come to a complete stop — it was difficult to remain standing.

Taking her time, Ari knew Rafe was probably glancing at his watch every fifteen seconds, but she didn't care. She needed to pull herself together, so she washed her face and reapplied her makeup before choosing to join him again.

As she made her way out front, she was impressed that he didn't seem irritated. The jet's door was already open and he waited there at the top to escort her down. She could refuse the arm he was holding out to her, but that seemed petty, so she accepted it and walked down the steps, feeling the warmth of his side so close to hers.

Immediately, the biting wind of New York sneaked up her skirt and sent shivers through her body. It was much colder in the Big Apple than back home. She was wishing she'd packed warmer clothing, but she'd been given no time before leaving to check the weather on the East Coast. How could she be expected to know what it would be like? She'd never been out of California. She hated nylons and never wore them, but as the wind continued whipping, she regretted not wearing a pair to protect her naked legs.

Rafe escorted her to the waiting limo, and then quickly followed her inside the large car. She scooted down the seat, unsure of how she was supposed to act. When the newness of the situation was over, this would doubtless be a lot easier.

"Come here, Ari." It wasn't a request. The low timbre of his voice made her stomach quiver, though the soft command irritated her. She thought about ignoring him, pretending she hadn't heard, but she needed to pick her battles.

To scoot or not to scoot closer to him in a car? That wasn't a match worth fighting. Much larger skirmishes loomed on the horizon, she was sure. Moving more slowly than usual, just to prove a point, she wriggled toward him.

When she was within easy reach, Rafe gripped her underneath her arms and hauled her onto his lap. Before she had a chance to catch her breath, he pulled her face to his and kissed what little air she had left in her lungs right out of her.

His unique smell invaded her senses — an intoxicating mixture of hot spices and clean sweat. She'd never taken time to appreciate a man's smell before, but with Rafe, she could find him by scent alone. It was raw power — the embodiment of masculinity — and pure seduction.

She whimpered into his mouth as his hands traveled up and down her spine. Pushing his tongue forward, he demanded a response from her and she could resist him no longer.

Each time she was with Rafe, he owned another piece of her, possessed her body just a little more. She knew she should care, but as his tongue swirled around the contours of her mouth, she couldn't find the will to protest.

With total submission, she melted against him, their bodies almost one. His hand moved to push her skirt further up, exposing her thighs and making it easier for her to spread her legs and settle more fully against his stiffening erection.

When his teeth grazed across her bottom lip before sucking it inside, then nipping it, she shuddered in his arms. He pulled back to look into her half-closed eyes as he raised his hips and pushed his hardness against her heat. Ari pulled back, the emotions coursing through her too much for her to handle.

"Quit trying to retreat from me. When we're together, I want to touch you, run my hands along the silky skin of your thighs, feel the curve of your breasts against my arm, and take your lips with mine, knowing they're swollen from our kisses. You are *mine* now, Ari. I'll prove that to you over and over again," he whispered, making her body throb.

"Tell me you understand." This he said as his fingers moved her skirt fully out of his way, exposing her barely covered bottom to his hands. He squeezed her behind and pulled her more firmly against his erection.

"I understand," she groaned as she moved her hips, seeking relief. How could she have any desire to come again when she already had a very few hours ago? Never had she imagined having such an appetite for sex. But hey, since she had no choice but to be in this messed-up game with Rafe, she might as well quit complaining and enjoy the sexual delicacies he offered.

"See, Ari, it's not so hard to be agreeable now, is it?" he asked as his lips nuzzled her throat. How she wished she could feel nothing.

"It will always cause me displeasure to agree so readily to anything you ask," she said, her insult not having nearly the impact with her voice so low and breathy. To her surprise, instead of being offended, Rafe laughed.

"Your words and your body say two different things to me, Ari. Even though you protest with your mouth, your eyes beg me to take you."

"Believe what you want," she said through gritted teeth as she fought the heat building inside her. She thought for a moment that she'd won their little argument as he pulled back. Then he spoke.

"We're here now, so we'll have to continue this tonight — and, Ari, it will be a great night."

Rafe removed her from his lap, and she angrily straightened her skirt. She was in a world of hurt. The only consolation was knowing he was in the same state as she was.

"There won't be any interruptions once I get you into our room," Rafe promised as the door opened and he stepped from the limo, then held his hand out to her.

With his voice echoing in her head, Ari grasped his hand and exited the car. As much as she'd protested to Rafe, she couldn't wait for their meal to end and for them to arrive at the hotel.

The next hour crept by as Ari only nibbled, too nervous to force much of the delicious meal into her mouth. She couldn't say what she'd eaten or if it was any good, but after enough time passed, she needed to take a moment to herself.

"Excuse me." Rafe stood as Ari rose and walked from the table. Making sure to keep her pace steady, she weaved around the other diners and walked to the bathroom.

Looking in the mirror, Ari hardly recognized herself. Her cheeks were glowing a slight pink, her eyes were glazed, and her skin felt as if it were on fire. A few glances, stolen touches, and some indecent acts and her body was going through a total transformation.

She'd gone into this situation thinking she would hate every minute of it, but the emotions she felt right at this moment were anything but hate. She felt passion — need — excitement. She felt…alive.

Was it so bad being with Rafe, really? What was he asking of her? Sure, he wanted control over every aspect of her life — but he wasn't enforcing that. He'd made a lot of demands of her, but then he'd backed down when she refused to settle.

She was too tired and too confused to think much more about it right at the moment, but she wished she had more time before their night ended in the way it inevitably would. Rafe was going to have sex with her — and she wanted him to. She would only have liked to have had more warning, more time to strengthen the armor around her heart. With him in her life, she knew time wouldn't be something she'd get a lot of.

When Rafe made a decision, it was set in stone — at least in his eyes. All she could do at this point was try her best to keep up with him instead of being dragged along behind.

*****

As Ari walked back toward the table, Rafe stood, as good manners and her beauty demanded. She took his breath away. Even after a day of traveling and dealing with a less-than-pleasant situation, she held her head up high, and her face glowed.

He pulled out her chair, then leaned down, trailing his fingers along the bare skin of her neck as he whispered in her ear.

"I sometimes forget to breathe when you enter a room."

Ari tensed in his arms, but then her shoulders went limp and she leaned back against him. This is what Rafe wanted. He needed her to trust him — allow him to show her he wasn't the monster she believed him to be. He would take care of her — she just had to allow him to do so.

Walking back to his seat, their eyes connected, and the passion blazing in her expression made his decision. Dinner was over. It was time to show her what their time together would be like over the next few months.

"Check!" he called to the waiter. Anticipation burned as he stood again and took her arm. Suddenly, the hotel seemed all too far away.

CHAPTER FOUR

Shane

"THIS HAD BETTER be good!"

"Shane? Is that you?"

Apprehension filled Shane as he sat up in bed, instantly awake upon hearing the fear in Lia's voice. He glanced over at his clock, noting that it was three in the morning. Something had to be terribly wrong.

"Lia! What's going on? Where are you?" he asked as he slid naked from his bed and strode to his walk-in closet to grab the first set of clothes he came to.

"My car broke down at this rave party way out of town in an abandoned barn. Things got…well, it just got scary and I don't know who else to call. Rafe's in New York and Rachel will kill me if she finds out…"

"Give me the address. I'm on my way." Shane finished dressing in a pair of jeans and his favorite sweatshirt, then grabbed his wallet and keys as he made his way down the stairs.

"I don't know the address, but I have directions. You take the old mill highway out of town about ten miles and then turn onto a gravel road. There will be an orange spray-painted keg letting you know where to turn. Follow that out another ten miles and you'll be able to find me."

"Okay, I'll be there in less than twenty," Shane said as he jumped in his car and revved the engine. If he drove a hundred miles an hour, he might make it there that quickly. He'd certainly give it his best effort.

"Don't hang up!"

Lia's panicked voice made Shane gun the gas as he pulled from his garage and out onto the deserted streets. He didn't like the thought of her being at some ecstasy party in the middle of nowhere.

"What in the hell were you thinking, Lia? Do you know the kind of crap that goes on at those parties?"

"I've never been to one. I just wanted to do something fun."

"Lia, you aren't a teenager anymore. You're a twenty-six-year-old woman with a family that cares about you. You can't do stupid things like this," he lectured.

"I didn't call you to gripe me out, Shane."

"Great. Now you're even *sounding* like a teenager."

"Dammit! *Listen* to me! I called because I know I can count on you to be there for me when I need it. Can you please just help without making me feel worse than I already do?"

Before Shane could respond there was a banging sound, like someone pounding on her windows, followed by Lia's scream, and then the line went dead. Shane immediately re-dialed but the phone just rang until it went to voice mail. The sound of her sweet and cheery recorded voice quickly soured his stomach as visions of what could be happening to her clouded his mind.

Terror engulfed him as he pushed the gas to the floor and sped from town. He almost passed the gravel road, and then nearly spun into the ditch when he yanked his wheel to the right and took the corner at ninety miles an hour.

His car would never again be the same after the way he flew down the gravel road, destroying his shocks. He couldn't care less. The car was replaceable — Lia wasn't.

It felt like forever before Shane found the dilapidated barn with screaming music filtering through its shabby walls. Throwing his car into park and jumping out, he was overcome with anxiety as he eyed the place, unsure of where to start his hunt for Lia. She could be anywhere.

Hoping for a miracle, he barreled through the seemingly endless miles of empty vehicles, his ears not missing a single sound around him as he dialed Lia's number again and again. The farther he was from the barn, the easier it was to hear. He kept hitting resend when his call reached voice mail, hoping Lia still had the phone on her even if she couldn't answer.

With every minute that passed, his stomach tightened further at the thought of what might be happening to her. His mind perversely recalled many horrifying stories he'd watched on crime shows, and he grew even more frantic in his pursuit. When he thought he'd searched everywhere and was just getting ready to call in the cavalry, he heard a slight chirping noise like that of a ringtone, and then he picked up voices. What they said lashed him into a fury.

"Come on, baby. You know you want to. Everyone comes to these parties to get high and get laid."

"If you don't stop now, my boyfriend is going to pound the crap out of you when he gets here!"

Shane rushed in the direction of Lia's voice just in time to see her head whip back as some asshole slugged her. She slumped over and another guy reached for his pants. Her clothes were ripped and Shane prayed she hadn't been raped already.

Rage leading him, Shane rushed forward and knocked two of the four guys out before they even knew he was there. When the other two saw his face, they immediately retreated, leaving their friends to take their punishment.

As much as Shane wanted to bloody the two remaining guys and go after the would-be-rapists now scurrying away, he couldn't fight the innate urge to help Lia first. Her body lay crumpled on the ground and blood was seeping from her cut lip.

His anger fought to be released, but Shane tucked it away as he gently lifted Lia in his arms and began moving toward his car.

"Shane? I knew you'd come," Lia whispered as her eyes cracked open. Her hand lifted to his face and rubbed his prickly stubble.

He knew her faith in him was unwarranted — he wasn't the hero she thought he was. Too many dark secrets from his past still haunted him. He acted carefree most of the time — it was how he survived.

"Take it easy, Lia. I don't know what you've ingested. We're going to the ER."

"No. Take me home, Shane. You can give me your own special tender loving care," she pleaded as her hand moved down to his neck and rubbed the top of his chest.

How much was he supposed to withstand? Shane had to remind himself that this wasn't just any woman; this was his best friend's sister. Rafe had already been betrayed by one of his best friends. Shane was worried that if he fooled around with Lia, Rafe would never trust anyone again.

"I can't, Lia. Rafe would kill us both."

"I really don't want to hear my brother's name when I'm picturing you stripping my clothes off," she replied with a flirtatious giggle.

With tremendous relief, Shane reached his car and carefully placed Lia in the passenger seat. While bending across her to secure her seat belt, she reached out and grabbed his head, catching him off guard and pulling until her lips whispered over his.

Shane tried to pull back, but the sweet taste of Lia's mouth on his tongue melted his resolve. He pressed harder against her until she let out a cry. Only then did he remember her cut and bruised lip.

"I'm sorry, Lia. That shouldn't have happened."

"Much more should happen, Shane. I know you want me, and I — it's just that my lip is throbbing, and my head is about to explode," she responded, cringing.

Shane gently shut the door, hoping to minimize the sound, and rushed around to the driver's side. Jumping into the car, he started the engine and made his way more carefully back down the gravel road. He wanted to get her to the hospital as quickly as possible, but didn't want the jarring road to make her feel worse.

Halfway down the road, Lia's hand crept over to his thigh, making him hit the gas too hard and causing him to swerve into a bush before he managed to gain control over the vehicle again.

"If you want us to make it to town in one piece, don't do that, Lia," Shane groaned through his tightly locked jaw.

He was worse than slime to be lusting after his best friend's sister, especially when she was not only hurt, but also obviously drugged. Shane figured there was a special place waiting for him in the depths of hell if he didn't pull himself together.

He didn't want to ask, but he needed to know whether the men had done anything other than rip her clothes and slug her in the face. Trying to hold back the bile rising in his throat, he looked over before speaking.

"Lia, did they...um, did I get there in time?" he asked hoarsely, unable to say what he feared.

It took a moment for her to understand, then her eyes widened as she seemed to realize the amount of danger she'd placed herself in.

"Yes, you did, Shane," she whispered before turning away. The fear in his gut wouldn't dissipate. What if she was lying to him out of embarrassment?

"You know you can tell me the truth, right?"

When Lia didn't respond, Shane looked over and found her passed out against his seat. With new urgency, he floored the gas as soon as he was on solid pavement again. He couldn't reach the hospital fast enough.

CHAPTER FIVE

ARI DIDN'T WANT to feel the sweet anticipation of what was to come, but she couldn't control her hormones. She wanted to hate Rafe, she even *planned* to hate him, but as he opened the door to their suite, all she felt was lust — pure unadulterated lust.

How far she'd fallen from the prim, repressed, bookish female she'd been not a year ago, someone who'd worried that she might be frigid. He'd opened a door that she couldn't shut no matter how hard she tried, and now it seemed her appetite was insatiable. The clicking of the hotel room door made her jump. They were all alone for the first time since she'd set foot on that jet. Nerves began to take complete mastery over her body as she made her way across the entryway into the huge living room area.

Her tiny apartment wouldn't fill even a quarter of the space of the giant suite. Ari understood Rafe's desire to have the best in life, but wasn't this a bit pretentious for a temporary visit? Sheesh!

Yet the huge windows were calling her name as she made her way across the plush carpet, and she couldn't contain a gasp at the view. Central Park!

Especially after her mother's grave injuries and then near-fatal cancer, this was a place Ari had thought she'd see only in the movies. And yet, here she was, almost in touching distance. She noticed a telescope to her right and quickly put the eyepiece over her eye, clueless to what she'd see, but not caring. She just wanted to feel truly in New York City for the first time.

Ari squinted as she peered out at the park and to her delight saw a few people strolling down the walk, several couples walking hand in hand, and a group of kids with glow sticks all over their clothes performing a dance. She wanted to run down the stairs and join in, but she knew there was no way Rafe was leaving the room now.

*****

Rafe watched with amusement as Ari's enthusiasm for a city he'd been to numerous times practically leaped off her. She pivoted from one foot to the other, and held on tightly to the telescope as she did her best to see everything at once. After pouring himself a glass of bourbon, he sat on the couch and watched her play with the telescope until she was satisfied with the settings.

He found himself smiling when she gasped over something she'd spotted. What was it that she found so fascinating? She had piqued his curiosity, but he stayed seated. He had big plans for them that night, and he needed to take a few minutes to calm himself.

If he took her too soon, his pleasure would end far too quickly, and he certainly didn't want that. Considering how well she responded to him, they could play all night and it still wouldn't be enough. He drank the amber liquid, enjoying the burn as it glided down his throat and entered his bloodstream. But not even the potent liquor was helping him tamp down his raging lust.

His patience was up. He needed to take Ari — and he needed her to know *he* was in charge from here on out.

"Ari." He left no doubt by the command in his voice that he wanted, and *expected*, her attention. Now. Pleasure filled him as she let go of the telescope and slowly turned around, her expressive eyes widening at the unveiled desire in his own.

He had not a single doubt as he watched her quiver before him: she could fight him all she wanted, but in the end she was his to command — and pleasure.

*****

"Come closer."

Everything in Ari told her to resist. She couldn't allow herself to cave in so easily to Rafe, but wasn't that the point? He had to exert his dominance. If she fought him, she'd only lose — and even worse, she'd end up aching.

With a steadying breath, she took a step toward him, and then another. Soon she stood only five feet from where Rafe was lounging on the couch, her nerves stretched thin as she waited for what was to come next.

"I want you to strip for me. Start with your skirt, then your top. Leave on your bra, panties and heels. I want to admire your body with only a few pieces of lace concealing your most feminine areas."

Tremors shook Ari at the husky sound of his voice. An overwhelming shyness fell upon her as she gazed at him. The room was well lit, the curtains open. She couldn't just strip down to nothing in full view. She was horrified at the thought.

"Ari, I don't like repeating myself," he said firmly.

With trembling fingers, Ari reached for the buttons on her skirt. It took a few fumbling tries, but she managed to get the small pearl circles through the holes and loosen the top of the dark blue garment. With no flourish, she released the loose material and it floated down her body to land at her feet. She kicked it away, then reached for the top button on her blouse.

The darkening of Rafe's eyes as she undid that button and the next gave her the confidence to continue. He shifted on the couch as his desire escalated visibly and violently and his body hardened. Her small striptease was turning him on, and that knowledge sent heat flooding to her core.

She shouldn't want to please him, but the look of admiration in his eyes was a huge stroke to her ego. He desired her — wanted *her* — thought her body was something special.

As the trembling in her fingers ceased, Ari dealt with the rest of the row of buttons and parted her blouse, then shrugged her shoulders, letting the light material fall first down one arm, then the other. With a slight tug, she pulled the shirt free and tossed it over her skirt.

Unsure of what she was supposed to do next, Ari waited for Rafe's instructions. As his eyes moved down her body, resting upon her breasts, stomach and thighs, heat continued to build. She felt her nipples harden, the sensitive peaks begging to be touched. Her panties became damp, her core readying itself for his large arousal to fill her once again.

"Very good, Ari. You are flawless in every single respect. The swell of your breasts, the womanly curve of your hips, the roundness of your sweet ass are all perfect. I could take you over and over again and still not get enough."

His words should have offended her, but they were melting her from the inside out. She'd never imagined that someone could so completely desire her, and yet here Rafe was staring at her as if she were the most delectable dish known to man.

"Take off the bra," he said, his voice low and urgent.

Reaching for the clasp in the front, Ari slowly unclipped it, then felt a rush of relief as the bra parted and she felt the straps loosen on her shoulders. Holding the material to her chest with one hand, she reached up and slid one strap down before switching hands and taking down the other side. Never before had the mundane task of unhooking her bra become such an erotic sensation as it was while she was displaying her naked charms to Rafe. When the soft material fell from her body, she was left there shaking as she stood before him in nothing but a small piece of black lace and three-inch black heels.

Though the look in his eyes made her feel sexy, she still had to fight the impulse to lift her arms and cover herself. The longer he gazed at her in silence, the more self-conscious she became. She didn't know how much longer she could just stand there.

"Raise your hands and cup your breasts — feeling their weight."

"What?" She couldn't do *that*!

"Now, Ari! Don't question me. Hesitation is a prequel to punishment. I find satisfaction in watching your hands slide over the mounds of your breasts. I want to see you pinch your nipples between your fingers. Do this while slowly walking toward me. Keep your hands in place while you climb onto my lap and straddle me."

Ari was frozen, her hands stiff at her sides, as she waited for him to tell her he was just kidding. Yet he didn't break the stare as he waited for her to fulfill his command.

With her stomach on fire, Ari timidly lifted her hands, her fingers grazing her quivering belly as they crept upward. When she reached the underside of her breasts, she paused. This was wrong — so wrong. She wasn't supposed to try to pleasure herself.

As her hands started moving up and over the curve of her breasts, his eyes lit, fire practically leaping from their deep purple depths. The look of unadulterated lust in his expression gave her the courage to continue, to reach down and find her inner harlot — something she'd read that all women had buried deep inside, though it took a certain man to bring it out. Rafe was exactly that kind of man. To discover this of herself brought such sexual confidence, she almost didn't recognize who had taken over her body.

She covered her breasts, lifting and squeezing as he'd demanded. Her head tilted back as her palms brushed her sensitive mounds and caused the ache in her core to pulse. A moan escaped her tight throat as desire flooded her body.

Moving her fingers, Ari circled her dusky pink nipples and pinched, sending more heat through her body as she opened her eyes and moved forward. Oh, this felt good. As much as she wanted his hands on her, the feeling of touching herself while he watched was unbelievably pleasurable.

She gently squeezed her breasts and pressed them together as she reached him, her legs bumping his knees. His eyes were dilated and almost black as desire clouded his vision. Without any more hesitation, Ari scooted forward, straddling his lap as she sat down and continued to massage her aching breasts.

"Now, move one hand down and touch your heat. Lean back and rub your very core. I want to look in your eyes as the pressure builds inside you," he whispered, his voice hoarse.

Ari didn't hesitate this time. His hands gripped her back as she leaned into the strength of his arms while she moved her hand down her stomach and inside the lace of her thong. Wetness flooded the area, making it easy for her finger to circle the aching bud where so many nerve endings converged. She rubbed the spot, her pleasure quickly rising, and her hips surged forward, seeking Rafe.

Just as she felt herself nearing orgasm, Rafe gripped her hand and pulled it away. She groaned in frustration — she was so close.

"Very good, Ari. You are supremely sensual. There are many desires in you just waiting to be set free," Rafe said in praise before taking her finger inside his mouth and sucking on it. Ari's hips ground against his hardened arousal, needing this game to stop and for him to satisfy what felt like an unquenchable thirst.

"Please, Rafe. I've done what you asked. Please don't leave me like this," she begged.

Rafe pulled her forward and took her lips. This wasn't a slow, sensual meeting of mouths. It was hunger — possession — greed. He reached down and shifted his clothes, freeing his solid length before rapidly sheathing it, and then quickly ripping away the last barrier of her panties. He surged up inside her as his breath exploded from his lungs.

"Ride me, Ari," he called as his hands gripped her hips.

Ari grabbed hold of his shoulders and her body took over as she began moving up and down on his thick shaft, in and out. She was so close to leaping over the edge. It wouldn't take much at all. She didn't want this to end, but she didn't know how to prolong it.

"Yes, Ari. Faster. You feel so good — a perfect fit." Rafe's voice was strained with need and he lowered his head taking one of her peaked nipples into his mouth, sucking it hard.

"Rafe..." she screamed as the pleasure built higher and higher.

"Let go, Ari," he demanded as he pulled her tightly against his chest, while grabbing her hips and taking over the movement. He thrust hard inside her, pounding her wet heat as he groaned in pleasure.

His moans filled the large room and mixed with hers as they both neared their release.

"Let go, Ari. Come with me," Rafe shouted as he surged upward, his body tightening as she felt his manhood begin to pulse. His cry of pleasure was all it took to send her the final few inches over the cliff, and she gladly fell with him.

After a moment of gasping silence, Rafe gripped her head while looking into her half-closed eyes.

"Thank you for trusting me. That was…beautiful." Rafe's words made Ari's heart skip a few beats.

He doesn't believe in love. It's just sex. Ari rested her head against Rafe's shoulder as she repeated those sentences over and over. She couldn't take his words for more than what they were or she'd get her heart broken.

As he lifted her in his arms and carried her to the suite's bedroom, then carefully laid her down, she knew she could be in trouble. She had to find a way to make it through all this with her heart still intact.

When he returned from the bathroom and lay down beside her, then pulled her into his arms, she felt a stinging in her eyes. She thought he didn't sleep with his mistresses. As if he could read her thoughts, his next words were like cold water, washing away her stupid fantasies.

"The connecting room wasn't available. We normally won't sleep together, but I don't want you in a separate suite, so this will have to do this weekend."

Ari prayed for sleep to come as she fought her tears. After she finally heard the slow and steady breathing testifying that Rafe was no longer awake, she allowed a few tiny teardrops to escape. Tomorrow she'd work on hardening her heart.

CHAPTER SIX

"BLESS YOU," A woman said as Ari sneezed. Ari looked up in surprise and managed to say a quick thank-you before the stranger disappeared among the sea of people passing by.

As she looked out at the children running through the crowd, and at teenagers throwing Frisbees, frustration filled her. This was Central Park in New York City and she was tired of doing nothing but sitting in the grass.

There were so many people out there who said the people of New York were a nation unto themselves, but with the kind words of a stranger she felt welcomed to the city. Wearing a comfortable blouse and capris accompanied by a large hat and oversized sunglasses to protect her eyes, she was ready to explore.

Bless you might only be two simple words, but they were enough to make her feel less intimidated, and ready to take on

New York. She wanted to see all she could before it was too late and they had to return home.

*****

"I think I've figured out why you are so freaking moody."

Rafe looked up in surprise, eyebrows raised. No one insulted him — well, apparently nobody except his new mistress, who was supposed to be more obedient than the rest of the people in his life.

"I'm working, Ari. I agreed to accompany you to the park, but that doesn't mean my workday just stops."

With those few clipped words, Rafe looked back down at his iPad and finished the e-mail he'd been composing. He figured Ari would soon grow bored and their little adventure to Central Park would be over.

Rafe had stayed in the same hotel year after year, but not once had he come down and sat on the grass in this world-famous park. Really, what was the point? He found it almost humorous that Ari and her nonstop pestering had managed to make him do it.

He would have sent any other woman on her way and finished his work in peace, but not Ari, it seemed. He could hardly leave her by herself in the park, where she could so easily be taken advantage of. She'd already proved several times that she was a bit too naive even in her own hometown. He shuddered to think what trouble she could get herself into in a city such as New York. Yes, it was the middle of the day and plenty of law enforcement officers were around, but that didn't help ease his mind.

Back in their hotel suite, before Rafe knew what he was saying, he had offered to take Ari down to the park. When her eyes lit up with excitement and she danced in a circle, he'd pulled back. Had he made the wrong choice? Ari's attractions increased, for some odd reason, when she let down her guard.

"There is no way we're going to just sit in this spot, especially with your nose buried in that stupid computer. If you want to work, I understand that, but I want to play. Why don't you go back to the room and do whatever it is you do so well? *I'm* going to meet people and have a little fun."

"You're working, too, Ari, or have you so quickly forgotten?"

"Nope. There's no way I'm allowing you to be an arrogant prig and ruin my day. It's sunny, there are people everywhere, and I'm in the Big Fat Apple for the first time in my life. You can try being master and commander all you want, but I'm on break right now."

With that, Ari stood up and sashayed away with confidence. Rafe was so stunned by her words and her outright defiance that she made it a good twenty yards before he closed his mouth and climbed to his feet. A smile overtook his features as he watched his prey. He couldn't believe he'd ever imagined breaking her.

Putting his iPad away, Rafe dialed his assistant. "Cancel my meetings for the rest of the day." Without giving Mario time to respond, Rafe hung up, and then took off after Ari, who was now a good hundred yards from him. She was well within his sights, and his true predatory nature came out as he stalked her from behind.

The sound of Ari's laughter filled him with delight. She was so unique — unspoiled. Even though he'd pushed her past the point a normal human being could be pushed, she still smiled, still found elation wherever she could. To snuff out her spirit would be a crime.

*****

The breath rushed from Ari's lungs as strong arms wrapped around her. Fear spiraled inside her for just a moment, until she realized it was Rafe. He spun her in his arms and then she was pressed up tightly against him as his head descended.

Ari was winded and more than a little light-headed when he lifted his head again, his heated gaze aimed directly into her eyes.

"Where do you think you're off to?"

"I don't know yet. I figure once I find something fun to do, that's where I'm supposed to be," she answered. "What happened to your work?"

"I decided I'd take the rest of the day off."

As Rafe released her from his arms only to grab her hand and begin walking with her through the park, Ari didn't know what to think. This was another of those Dr. Jekyll and Mr. Hyde moments. Rafe seemed almost…carefree as the two of them began passing vendors and street performers.

"Just like that, you've decided to stroll through Central Park?"

"Yes, just like that. I *am* the boss, after all. If I want to take the day off, then that's exactly what I'll do," he answered arrogantly.

Ari couldn't find it in her to be even the slightest annoyed with him. She was too pleased to spend a somewhat normal afternoon in his presence.

"Well, then, we're wasting time," she announced as she picked up her pace. Ari was on a mission to experience everything she could during her brief time in what seemed an almost magical place.

Rafe held her hand and she raced down the path, stopping to watch street performers sing and dance, and insisting that Rafe give each of them a donation before the two of them moved on to the next sight. She didn't know how hard it was for him to resist bending to her will when her countenance lit up the entire park as she observed everything she could with childlike wonder and joy.

They reached the Gapstow Bridge and she felt as if she were in a foreign country because of the architecture's pre-World War I feel, and she admired the stunning detail.

"You know, Ari, this was designed to look like the Ponte di San Francesco in San Remo, Italy, a beautiful area not far from my mother's home."

"That's amazing, Rafe. I bet you come here all the time just to feel as if you're back home. How do you stand having two separate places calling to you?" Ari asked as she looked around the park.

"I visit Italy when I get homesick, which isn't too often. My work keeps me very busy. Still, we may need to make a trip there in a couple of months. I have several businesses in my mother's homeland, and it's never a hardship to visit them."

"You want me to go with you?" Ari had long given up imagining she might get to travel around the world. That prospect might not make up for the fact that he liked to hire his women, but it definitely didn't hurt.

"It's business, Ari. Don't get too excited." Rafe's words were like a cold metal snuffer to a single-candle flame.

"I know," she replied as she moved forward, some of the magic from her day stolen away by his insensitive words. Before she managed to get too far, Rafe's hand was gripping her arm.

"Look, I'm sorry. I…I don't really know how to talk to you sometimes. This situation is all new to me. I just want to make sure you aren't getting your hopes up that this may lead into something more permanent. Our relationship is…a temporary thing."

The fact that Rafe wasn't trying to be cruel — that in reality he was trying to make sure she didn't get hurt — didn't keep his words from stabbing her straight in the heart. This was the reason she didn't want to get attached to him, why she couldn't afford to let her emotions get involved.

Her earlier joy crushed, Ari turned away and began walking through the park. She hadn't needed a reminder of their relationship. She'd just wanted one day where none of it mattered. She was simply a normal girl and he was an average guy and they were strolling through a beautiful park like all the other couples around them.

It seemed she wasn't allowed to have even that — not as long as she was Rafe Palazzo's mistress. It suddenly seemed odd that there weren't dark clouds in the sky, she was so filled with gloom.

"Follow me," Rafe said, taking her hand and dragging her forward. She just wanted to go back to the hotel, but she followed him, the nice little obedient mistress, she thought sourly.

But Ari forgot about her bad mood as soon as she looked where he was pointing. There was a large group of people doing something she couldn't quite make out, and as music drifted toward her and Rafe, someone turned up a loudspeaker.

"What's going on?"

"Just wait," he said with a mysterious smile. His grin drove away the rest of Ari's gloom, and she watched as the large group started to break out in a synchronized dance.

"It's a street mob!" Ari shouted as she took several steps forward for a better view of the group. She'd never seen one live before and excitement filled her as she watched the performance and saw that it also stopped other tourists, who seemed as entranced as she was.

After the dance ended, Rafe took her on a lengthy tour of the park. Ari dashed into the beautiful zoo showcasing creatures from tropical, temperate and polar zones from around the world. The human pair wandered around hand in hand, pointing out different animals and their antics, and laughing particularly at the exhibitionist monkey urinating from a tree.

"Oh, Rafe! These are my favorites!" she exclaimed at the pool of sea lions in the center courtyard. The creatures shared their playful mood with onlookers as they performed tricks for snacks, and then spiraled underneath the water. A close second to the sea lions were the penguins. Ari couldn't help but giggle at the way they waddled on land but then dived into the water like bullets fired from a gun. They appeared to be having so much fun, it was difficult not to catch their enthusiasm.

Rafe had to drag her from the zoo, especially after Ari, with her profound love of history, fell in thrall to the Arsenal building at the zoo's edge. She drank deep from its treasure trove of historical memorabilia.

Ari found the day passing by far too quickly as they continued their rambles. "Stop!" she cried when they came upon a hot dog vendor. "We have to have a New York hot dog," she insisted as she saw the look of disbelief on Rafe's face.

"I'm certainly not going to eat those vile animal byproducts," he said as she dragged him toward the cart.

"In all the years you've visited New York City, have you seriously never had the pleasure of partaking of a street hot dog? Look, Rafe. You have your rules, and I have mine. I refuse to leave this park until we each have one. I've heard that there is nothing comparable."

Ari looked him in the eye with her hands on her hips. She meant business. He wanted her to compromise on everything — well, she wanted to see the hoity-toity Rafe eat a hot dog.

Much to Ari's surprise, Rafe stepped forward and ordered them each a dog. He wrinkled his nose as he brought the mystery meat to his lips, but he took a bite and Ari wanted to shout with glee. The sight somehow made him more human.

"What do you think?" she asked after she swallowed. It truly was the best hot dog she'd ever tasted.

"I don't know how you can eat this with a smile, Ari. It's absolutely terrible," he said. The disgust on his face made her laugh.

"If you eat the whole thing, I won't ever complain again about the strange dishes you make me try," she promised.

With raised eyebrows and eyes that lit up, Rafe looked from his hot dog to her face, as if he were really trying to find out if the dare was worth it.

"Why don't we up the stakes?"

"What do you have in mind?" she asked nervously.

"I get a future request."

"What kind of request?" She wasn't going to grant him just anything.

"That's part of the mystery. I eat your horribly fatty and probably diseased hot dog, and I get a teensy little request later on."

"Fine. I really want to see you eat the whole thing."

With a smile on his face, Rafe took his next bite, and another, and another. As he finished the hot dog, Ari realized she'd been hustled, because he walked up to the vendor and ordered a second one. She'd just traded him a to-be-determined favor for something he obviously enjoyed.

Oh, he was so much better at acting than she was.

CHAPTER SEVEN

THE DAY'S LIGHT had faded as Rafe and Ari arrived at the Sea Grill Restaurant. Their table overlooked the many hopeless amateurs skating on the ice rink at Rockefeller Center. She badly wanted to be out there with them, but waited patiently; the meal couldn't last forever, could it?

"Have you gone ice-skating before?" Rafe asked as he held out her chair.

"No, but I've always wanted to, and to do so at Rockefeller Center for the first time would be beyond exciting, even though I'm sure I will make a fool of myself," she replied breathlessly.

"We're lucky it's still open. This is the last day until next winter."

"I'm not very hungry. I can always grab a bite later," she said as she looked longingly out at the white frozen surface. She was afraid that if they waited too long, the rink would close up and she'd miss her chance forever.

"I assure you it will still be open after we've had dinner, Ari," he responded with a laugh.

With reluctance, Ari picked up her menu and looked for something to eat that would take the least amount of time to prepare. The restaurant was crowded, though, so she knew she wouldn't get on the ice for at least another hour.

"Would you like me to order?"

Ari's first instinct was to say no, that she was perfectly capable of ordering herself, but he hadn't steered her wrong so far in his choices of food. She would most likely get something much better if she just let him choose.

"That will be fine," she said, and she went back to watching the many skaters glide across the surface of the well-lit ice.

Just as the waiter was pouring them a glass of wine, the ice was cleared of people except for a man and a woman. Ari watched as the man dropped to one knee and held out something in his hand. He was proposing!

She couldn't hear the two people speak, but obviously she'd said yes, because the crowd around the rink clapped and cheered before they all resumed their adventures on the ice.

"How romantic," Ari sighed without realizing she'd spoken out loud.

"I can think of many more-romantic ways to propose," Rafe scoffed.

Ari whipped her head around to look at him. He didn't seem to be the type of guy to think about such things as marriage proposals. As if he could read her thoughts, he continued.

"I mean that if a man wants to propose — which is foolish, as more than fifty percent of marriages end in divorce — then he could do it a lot less publicly and pleasantly than in the middle of a freezing-cold ice rink."

"The point is that he loves her so much, he wants the rest of the world to know about it," she argued as their appetizers were set on the table. She picked up a jumbo shrimp and dipped it in a delicate horseradish sauce before taking a bite, anticipating his next verbal challenge.

"I suppose you think marriage proposals at ball games are romantic, too? You would want your hoped-for fiancé to splash his intentions on the giant billboard for all to see?"

"It would make me feel special that he wasn't ashamed to have the entire stadium and TV audience see him proclaim his love."

"Women," he grumbled as he picked up a piece of lobster and sank his teeth into it as a distraction.

"There's nothing wrong with being a romantic, Rafe. The fact that you treat relationships like a business transaction doesn't mean the rest of the world should. Most people are looking for love and romance, and they want to be swept off their feet. Someday, love will hit you again and then, you watch! You'll be doing a cheesy proposal of your own," she said smugly as she grabbed another shrimp.

"I can guarantee you, that won't happen."

"The most confident of men are the ones who fall the hardest," she warned.

"We'll just agree to disagree on this point." With that, he closed the discussion.

Ari was grateful, after a moment's thought, because talking about commitment of any kind with Rafe was uncomfortable at best. She knew her place in their relationship.

She directed her eyes back to the skating rink and watched a man and woman start spinning around like professionals. The man lifted his partner up high as he spun around, and then he released her. She twirled in the air and landed gracefully. Their fellow skaters, who had slowed down to watch the show, clapped their approval.

Talk about risk, Ari thought. How frightening it would be to be lifted up high and then released to fall toward the hard ice. And the blades of those skates were thin, and sharp. She just knew she'd trip and end up slicing off a body part. She'd much rather stay safely on her feet.

After she and Rafe got through a meal characterized by incredible food and awkward silence, she prepared to face the rink. Once she'd rented a pair of skates and moved along the wall to enter the arena, excitement took over, making her irritation with Rafe vanish. Her heart thundered as she took her first step onto the glistening ice.

As Ari skated out further on the rink, now moving faster, she felt her arms flail as she began to slip. She was going down and it was going to hurt. Just as her foot began sliding out in an upward arc, strong arms wrapped around her waist from behind and she felt the solid wall of Rafe's chest pressing against her back.

"It's not as easy as it looks, huh?" he said, his laughter pealing softly next to her ear.

"No. It's definitely not," she agreed as she soaked up the warmth of his body. He pushed forward and the two of them slowly began to glide, one of his legs between hers.

The heat of his breath took the chill from her neck as she looked around her, thinking the moment was too romantic. How could he be so hot one moment, and then so cold the next? How was she expected to guard her heart when he literally swept her off her feet?

The two of them laughed as they circled the rink and watched people from beginners like her to experts glide across the ice. When it was time to leave, she did so with an almost childlike reluctance. The night was too perfect and she didn't want it to end.

Rafe helped her off the ice, and then, when they sat down, surprised her by lifting her feet onto his lap and untying her skates. Their eyes connected as he removed her skates and took a moment to rub the sore soles of her feet.

"Your feet will most likely be a little tender after skating for the first time. If you truly enjoy it, we'll have to get you a pair of your own skates so you can break them in. Once you're used to them, it's like wearing a comfortable pair of sneakers."

"How do you know so much about ice-skating?"

"Rachel loved to skate when she was little. I would take her to a rink close to our home, and that little girl could stay on the ice all day and night. She could have pursued the sport seriously, even professionally, had she really wanted to, but it requires a lot of hours and dedication. She never took it beyond a hobby, but I found myself enjoying it with her."

"You really are a good big brother, aren't you?"

Rafe handed over her shoes, then removed his own skates and put his leather dress shoes back on. Ari had never yet heard him acknowledge a compliment.

"We should make our way to the hotel now. It's been a long day," he said as he held out his hand for her.

Ari reached for him without hesitation. Forced, as she was, into a relationship with him, she'd thought she'd be miserable all the time, but being with him wasn't turning out to be a hardship. Yes, misery surely awaited her — she'd grow too attached and Rafe would grow bored — but she hoped she was strong enough when that moment came.

*****

Rafe watched as executives took off in helicopters to get to work. He'd done that himself. He truly loved New York; the bustle of the city seemed never to slow down, not once throughout the day. Even on the weekends, businesses ran, and people worked — as he should be doing.

Instead, he was sitting on the esplanade overlooking Manhattan's Financial District while men and women in business attire rushed to and fro on their way to earn another dollar, give or take a few.

Ari sat next to him as she munched on a pastry and sipped coffee. It was early in the morning and he'd promised her a tour of the city. His business plans had stalled as he took time to entertain his wide-eyed mistress. Normally, he wouldn't have cared what the woman in his life wanted — after all, he was the employer, she the employee. But with Ari, he couldn't seem to say no.

She wanted to see the city, so that's what they were out doing, no matter how hard he tried to talk himself out of wasting his day. Was it really a waste of time? It was certainly enjoyable, and he had devoted himself to the pursuit of pleasure.

When they started a leisurely stroll, a homeless man sitting there against a building caught Ari's eye. Rafe grabbed her hand and tried to usher her away.

"One minute," she said as she pulled away from him. Walking over to the man, she removed a few dollars from her purse and placed it in his cup.

"Bless you," he said with a toothless smile filled with sadness and the look of a hard life.

"You, too," Ari replied in a choked voice. When she turned away, Rafe pulled out a hundred-dollar bill and slid it into the cup. When a tear fell down the man's face and he opened his mouth to thank Rafe, he held his finger to his mouth. He didn't want a big deal to be made out of his gesture, and he didn't want Ari to see.

Though Rafe had grown up more privileged than the average person, he'd never forget how much his best friend, Shane, had gone through. It had changed the way Rafe viewed the world. Rafe felt people should work hard for what they got, but he also understood that sometimes life threw unexpected turns that were hard to recover from.

The man might use the money to buy his next bottle of booze, or he might just use it to go and buy a new pair of clothes and get a shower so he could apply for a job. Rafe chose to believe that his gut always steered him in the right direction. He had to hope that this was a person needing that one small break to pick up the pieces of his life.

Their morning passed quickly as they strolled through the city and entered Times Square. Rafe couldn't take his eyes from Ari's face as she looked all around her at the thousands upon thousands of people pushing past them on the wide sidewalks.

"I've seen this place in movies, but I can't believe how many people are out here. It feels like if I blink, I'll be lost forever. How does anyone ever find their way around this city?"

"Very carefully. You can usually tell the difference between the tourists and the locals by the way they move. Tourists are slower and look in every direction at once, while the locals keep their eyes on target and move swiftly in between people on the street. There's a lot of business in this town and if a person doesn't want to get left behind, he or she had better learn how to adapt."

"I wouldn't want to live here. It's just too fast for me. I do, however, want to try some of the local pizza. I've heard it doesn't get better than here."

Pizza was hardly Rafe's first choice for lunch, but once again he found himself unable to say no, so he found himself at John's Pizzeria. Seeing Ari's eyes light up at her first gooey bite made the extra grease he was ingesting well worth it.

"I don't know how you are so slim with the amount of terrible food you eat," he laughed as he grabbed another napkin to absorb the oil coating his fingers.

"Probably because I don't usually get to eat this well. I survive on a lot of ramen noodles and canned soup. My mom is an excellent cook, but before her accident I was living in a dorm and religiously ate meals that were cooked in a microwave." Ari winked. "Though my mother has always taken great care of me, money was still a concern, and on campus I needed to be careful. It's a real treat having these fancy meals," she said and took a bite, then swirled a long piece of cheese around her finger.

"I wouldn't call pizza fancy," he said, unable to take his eyes from her mouth as she sucked the gooey cheese from her finger.

"That's because you're a snob." The twinkle in her eye let him know she was teasing him, but still, he couldn't let her get away with a comment like that without at least a little retaliation.

"No more pizza for you. It's caviar for dinner." She glared at him as she took another bite and chomped extra hard on her thin-crusted treat.

"I don't know why the egg of a fish is so special. Seriously! That's so disgusting."

"It's an acquired taste," he said with a laugh.

"Yeah, well, I prefer cheese to salty fish eggs. I promise never to call you a snob again if you won't take me to another snooty restaurant that has foods I can't even pronounce," she pleaded.

The utter look of horror on her face had Rafe laughing. The comment was even funnier because of her utter seriousness. Not one of his other mistresses had preferred pizza or hot dogs to Beluga caviar and oysters. Who really had the right idea? Rafe found himself asking.

As they finished their lunch, and once again stepped onto the busy sidewalks of New York, Rafe took Ari's hand and led her on a tour of some of the city's amazing architecture.

"New York is known for its old architecture mixed among the sleek new skyscrapers. There are many hidden treasures in the city and numerous landmarks on almost any block you turn onto. When you add the creativity of the many people looking to break into show business or the art world, this is almost like one giant playground. I can't possibly show you everything in only a couple of days, or even a couple of months, but I can at least give you a small taste of why the locals are so loyal to their home."

"How do you know so much about the area if you grew up in Italy and California?"

"My dad traveled a lot for business and we spent at least a couple of weeks each year in New York. I've spent a lot of time in Chicago, Seattle and Philadelphia, too. By the time I was eighteen, I was a frequent flier," he answered.

"I can't imagine how wonderful that would be. I'd never even left California until this trip. I think you've created a monster, though, because I am enjoying myself tremendously, even if my feet are killing me."

"Do you want to go back to our room?"

"Not a chance. We haven't even visited the Statue of Liberty or the Empire State building," she replied with horror.

Rafe laughed as he hailed a cab and took her on a concentrated tour of the city. He wanted their night to end on top of the Empire State Building, though he called himself a fool for his romantic gesture. Nah; get real — he was doing it only because looking out at the lights of the city at night was an experience everyone should have, not because he wanted to pull her into his arms and kiss her above all the twinkling lights. It wasn't as if he'd become some slobbering love-struck fool who spouted off poetry in one of the many cafés catering to such a crowd.

For all his happily cynical thoughts, Rafe still took her into his arms as they stood at the top of the Empire State Building. His head moved downward involuntarily and he captured her mouth with his. His lips were tender as he caressed hers, coaxing her mouth to open to him so he could taste her on his tongue. His arms wrapped tightly around her waist, and he got lost in her sweetness.

No, this wasn't good. It could be difficult for him to reinsert the distance he had always kept between him and his mistresses, but as he hailed a cab at the end of their night, he determined to do just that. If it required a valiant effort, so be it.

CHAPTER EIGHT

Shane

S HANE PULLED TO a screeching halt at the emergency room entrance of the nearest hospital. He had barely turned off the engine before he was jumping from the car and rushing to the passenger door. Two paramedics hurried out as he was lifting Lia into his arms.

"She was at a party. I think they may have drugged her!"

"Lay her down on this gurney. We'll get her in immediately."

"Sir, come with me and fill out some paperwork, please."

"Like hell! I'm going with her," Shane told the nurse trying to stop him. It would take a lot more than a hundred-pound woman to keep him from staying as near to Lia as possible.

"Are you a relative, sir?"

It took Shane a few moments to figure out what the woman was asking him. Meanwhile, Lia was being led further away from him into a private room, where a doctor went in after her and began his examine.

"I'm a friend of the family," he finally answered as he again tried to get past the growing number of medical members blocking his path.

"We can't allow non-family members into the room," the woman insisted while a guard appeared at her right-hand side.

"I'm the one who brought her here!"

"We still can't break hospital policies, Sir. I'm sorry. If you can just fill out this paperwork and let us know what is wrong with her, we can get her treated." The woman remained calm, which escalated Shane's anger even further. She was keeping him from Lia.

Finally, he jerked the clipboard she was holding out to him from her hand and started filling in Lia's information. He knew it by heart. The next couple of minutes seemed to be the longest in Shane's life as he waited to hear what was wrong with Lia. He hoped he hadn't arrived too late.

When the doctor stepped through the doorway, he pulled one of the nurses aside before coming over to Shane. It was a good thing he hadn't delayed any further, because Shane was ready to start throwing punches.

"Hi, Mr. Grayson. I understand you brought Ms. Palazzo in?"

"Yes. Now I need to be with her," Shane insisted as he tried to push through.

"I understand, sir. I'm very concerned about her right now. Do you know how we can get ahold of her family members?"

"They're all out of town at the moment," he answered with frustration as he pushed his hair back and paced the floor in front of him. "Do you know what's wrong with her? I believe she was drugged."

"We won't know what drugs are in her system until we get the labs back. I'll put a rush on the work order so we can begin treatment immediately, but it's important to know how long she has been unconscious. Do you know?"

"About half an hour. I got her here as quickly as possible. Tell me she'll be all right," Shane demanded, grabbing the doctor's arm.

"We'll do all we can for her," was the doctor's only response as he pulled his arm away. It wasn't the answer Shane was hoping for. As Shane waited out in the hall for lab results, the time trickled by. If something were to happen to her, he couldn't imagine what it would do to him, or her family.

When he'd first met her so many years ago, she'd been nothing but a pesky little sister to his best friend. As the years had passed and she'd become a woman, he'd found himself drawn to her — the way she lived life so fully.

Dammit. Lia was too young, had too much to give to the world, and to think of her so frail in the bed was messing with his emotions. OK, so his feelings for her were strong, but he couldn't act on them — hell, he wasn't the settling-down kind of guy anyway. He had to treat her like nothing but a little sister. Too bad he was feeling less and less brotherly...

In the late morning, Lia suffered a grand mal seizure; Shane heard the doctors as they rushed in, and his heart stopped momentarily. Granted, such seizures could be one-time things with no major effects, but there was no way to count on that. So it was past time that he called her family. He should have done it the second he and Lia had arrived at the hospital. He'd been hoping it would turn out to be nothing more than a hangover. It appeared he was wrong.

Rafe picked up on the second ring.

"You need to come home now. It's Lia. We're at the hospital and she had a seizure."

"What? What happened?" Rafe demanded.

"She called me about three this morning. Apparently your little sister decided to attend a rave for the first time, and not only that, but she went alone. The doctors don't know exactly what is in her system, but she passed out on the way to the hospital, and she just suffered a seizure."

"Why in the hell didn't you call me immediately?" Rafe shouted into the phone.

"I didn't think it was that bad, Rafe. You were out of town, so she called me. I got her here as quickly as I could, but I'm scared, brother. Just get here."

"Have you notified my parents yet?"

"No. You were the first one I called. If you can call your dad and Rachel, I'd appreciate it. I just don't want to explain this over and over again."

"Yes, I'll call them on the ride to the jet. We're leaving now — and, Shane — thanks for being there for her."

Rafe had managed to calm his voice as he thanked Shane and hung up the phone. Shane felt that some of the weight had been lifted from his shoulders. He could handle a crisis, but he needed his friend here. If something happened to Lia, he couldn't go through it alone.

As the hours passed and the stress continued taking its toll on Shane's sleep-deprived body, he stood and paced the hallway, never getting too far from Lia's room. He knew caffeine would help, but he didn't want to leave for even the ten minutes it would take to obtain a cup. What if it was at that moment she awoke and nobody she knew was nearby?

Once Rafe arrived, Shane could catch a power nap, the two of them taking turns watching and waiting. She would wake; there was no other acceptable alternative.

"Mr. Grayson, can I speak to you out here?"

Shane turned to find the admitting doctor standing in the doorway, and from the expression on his face, it appeared he wasn't the bearer of good news.

"Of course."

With reluctance, Shane rose on stiff legs. He didn't really want to hear whatever the doctor was about to tell him, but he had little choice.

"Mr. Grayson, the officers need to speak to you, please."

Shane turned to find two uniformed policemen standing a few feet from the doctor. What in the hell was going on now? He had neither the time nor the patience to keep repeating the same story over and over again. He didn't know what Lia had done before he'd arrived. There was nothing else he could tell them that he hadn't already.

"I'm sorry, but it won't do you any good to keep questioning me. I wasn't there until after she'd taken whatever it was that has made her so ill. You're wasting your time and mine, and I'm at the end of my tolerance level for appeasing people."

Shane turned to walk back into the room when he felt a tight grip on his arm from behind. He spun around and swung without thinking about it. When his fist connected with one of the officer's faces, he knew he was in for a very long day.

"That's it, Mr. Grayson. You're under arrest for assaulting an officer, and for suspected assault against Ms. Palazzo."

Shane struggled to process what the officer had just said as the two men yanked his hands behind his back and cuffed him, but from high stress and lack of sleep, he couldn't wrap his brain around it. It didn't make any sense. Did they actually think he was the one who'd drugged Lia? Were they truly that idiotic?

"Are you kidding me right now? She's like my little sister. I suggest you undo these cuffs before I get my attorney on the phone and have you brought under charges of false arrest."

Shane was personal friends with the district attorney and their police chief, and he was fairly sure he could have the officers not only reprimanded but suspended if he felt like pushing it.

"We'll take our chances, Mr. Grayson," one officer answered in a level voice, not even slightly intimidated. "We have some questions for you that we'll ask down at the station. It's a serious crime to hit an officer, and an even more serious crime to take advantage of a young woman," the other officer said with unconcealed disgust.

Shane had to have a smidgen of respect for the man. Although the cop had the wrong guy right now, at least he was trying to do right by Lia. If Shane's stress level hadn't been at an all-time high, he'd probably have gotten a kick out of getting arrested.

With Lia lying helplessly in bed, however, he wasn't up for a trip to the police station.

"Call your chief and tell him who you have in handcuffs. I think you'll be releasing me pretty damn fast and apologizing," Shane said as he glared at the two men.

They glanced somewhat nervously at each other before he saw their eyes harden. *Damn!* It looked as if he was going for a ride in the back of one of their disgusting squad cars. He just hoped like hell he didn't end up sitting in some drunk's puke.

"You have the right to remain silent. Anything you say can and will be used against you in a court of law. You have a right to an attorney. If you cannot afford an attorney, one will be appointed for you. Do you understand these rights, Mr. Grayson?"

"Oh, I understand them a hell of a lot more than you. I'm done fighting with you about this. When we get to the station, your asses are going to be chewed from here to New York!"

Neither man said anything more as they led him outside. Shane could continue screaming at the cops, but it would only delay their ride, and he'd rather get to the station, where he could speak to Bill, their chief.

As they unceremoniously pushed him into the back of the car, where he gagged on the smell of sweat and various other body odors, he thought again how he and Rafe both would have had a good laugh over this if it had been during any other time than when Lia was so vulnerable.

As the car moved through traffic, Shane laid his head against the back of the cheap vinyl seat and counted to one hundred. When he still hadn't calmed down, he started over.

By the time they reached the station, he was more furious than ever.

"I want my phone call," he demanded as they led him inside.

"You'll get it when we say so," one of the officers snapped as he pushed him toward the cell block.

"Are you really this incompetent? Let me speak to your chief of police right this minute."

"We'll get right on that," the other guy said with a smirk before shoving Shane inside a cell and shutting the door. The two men walked away, and Shane watched their retreat with an incredulous look on his face. He didn't know what to think as he sank down on the cold bench and waited.

He was going to be there for a while.

CHAPTER NINE

"WHAT'S WRONG, RAFE?"

"We have to go now. That was Shane. Something happened to Lia," he said as he rose from the table.

"What's going on? Is she going to be OK?" Ari asked as she jogged to keep up with him.

"Shane sounded worried. I don't know. I have to call my parents."

Ari kept silent as the car was brought around, and the two of them climbed in the back seat. Rafe immediately called his pilot and had him prepare the jet. The next call was to his parents, who said they'd return to California immediately.

As they boarded the jet, Ari realized they'd left everything at the hotel. She didn't want to bring it up, but what if there was something he needed?

"Rafe, we didn't grab our belongings," she mentioned gently. The ashen look on his face as he turned toward her shocked Ari. She'd never seen him appear so helpless before. How could a man who so obviously loved his sister care so little about the other females in his life? She didn't understand him and probably never would.

"I'll have Mario arrange for them to be sent to us. I need to get back now." Rafe's answer was barely above a whisper.

As the jet lifted, Ari sat back, wishing there were something more she could do. Being unsure of what role she was supposed to play made it difficult to know how to act.

When the attendant came and gave them each a drink, Ari decided she needed to treat Rafe like any other person in her life who was going through a hard moment.

She stood up from her seat and walked cautiously to him. Hearing her approach, he peered up at her warily, as if afraid she would take full advantage of his vulnerability. Great. Knowing he felt this way about her, Ari felt a sting in her eyes as tears attempted to form.

Nevertheless, without hesitating further, Ari sat down in his lap and curled up against his chest, wrapping her slender arms around his neck in a warm embrace. She might be crossing the line of what he deemed acceptable, but he surely needed emotional support right then, whether he wanted to admit to it or not.

For a moment, his arms remained stiff and flat against his chair, then slowly he brought them up and flattened his palms on her back as he pulled her closer and leaned his head against her shoulder. For a few seconds, at least, he was allowing her to comfort him. She didn't know who was receiving more from the small gesture — was he or was she?

"She'll be OK, Rafe. Lia is a strong girl. I don't understand what happened, but there are some people in this world that are simply too wonderful to leave the rest of us behind. Both of your sisters have shown tremendous kindness to me when they didn't have to. People like that have to be OK because otherwise nothing makes sense."

"I wish that were how the world worked, Ari, but murderers take lives, sometimes without ever having to suffer a single consequence — babies die for no reason in their sleep — and good people do die. I refuse to give up on my sister, but I will feel a lot better once we get there."

Ari didn't know how to respond to his statement. Yes, he was right, but if they always dwelt on the bad, they would miss it when the good happened. Life was full of enough misery that to focus on only that would bring a saint down.

Because she didn't know what to say to make it right, she did the only thing she could do — and that was silently comfort him. Neither of them spoke further as the jet moved in what seemed like slow motion across the United States.

*****

"I need to see my sister, Lia Palazzo."

"One moment, sir," the nurse said as she looked at her computer.

"Rafe!" He barely had time to turn around before his other sister was barreling into him.

"Do you know anything yet, Rachel? Is Shane with Lia? Have you spoken to Mom and Dad yet?" He fired off questions, not giving his little sister time to answer.

"Lia's fine, Rafe. She woke up about an hour ago," she answered with a watery smile. It took a couple of seconds for her words to process in his brain, but once they did, he squeezed her tight. Relief flooded through him.

"Take me to her," he demanded as he pushed her back slightly so he could see her face.

"Of course. The only reason I'm out here now is that I've been waiting for you to arrive." She turned toward Ari and moved over to give her a powerful hug of appreciation for taking care of her big brother on their return flight. "Thank you for calling the second you landed."

"I'm so glad to hear she's awake. Is everything going to be fine?"

"Yes. Some piece of scum drugged her at the party, but the doctor figured out what it was and he's successfully treating her now. If I weren't so worried about her, I'd beat her to a pulp for scaring me like this," Rachel said as she steered them down the hall to Lia's room.

"I'm glad it's getting better now. I can wait out here while you spend time together," Ari offered. Before Rafe could object, his sister stepped in.

"No way are you waiting outside. Lia needs all the friends and family she can have right now, especially since Shane got arrested and totally ditched her to wake up with no one around."

Rafe stopped in his tracks as he looked down at the mischievous smile on Rachel's face.

"After I've seen Lia, you need to explain that to me in detail — not in front of her, though."

For a brief moment, he didn't think she was going to answer him, but then she shrugged and started speaking. "Apparently, a couple of officers came to talk to Shane about what happened to Lia. He was in a mood and took a swing at one of them, so they handcuffed him and hauled him off."

Rafe waited for her to keep speaking, but she just turned and started moving toward Lia's room again. He watched her back in stunned disbelief as she pulled away from him, before he got his feet to move and caught up to her within a few long strides.

"Do you care to elaborate? I'm really in no mood for games, Rachel!"

"I know you're worried right now, so I won't snap at you for using that tone with me, but that's all I know, so you'll just have to ask Lia. Not that she knows that much as all of this happened while she was knocked out cold."

"How can you act so cavalier about our sister being harmed?" he snapped as they reached Lia's room.

"Believe me, I wasn't acting cavalier a couple hours ago, but Lia's awake — dealing with a headache and extreme exhaustion, but otherwise fine. Now, I just want to hurt her all over again for being so stupid. She knows better than to go to some party in the middle of nowhere — especially without me."

Rafe gave up for the moment. Both of his sisters needed to do some major growing up. Rachel just wasn't taking this disaster as seriously as she should. He'd protected both of them so much their entire lives that they had no clue about the dangers in the real world. It looked as if he needed to educate both of them, extensively.

Rafe and Rachel entered Lia's room, and her eyes brimmed with tears as the three of them moved to her bed.

"I'm so sorry you had to rush home, Rafe. I'm getting better now. I promise," she assured him in a weak voice as she slowly held up her arms to receive his loving hug. He pulled her gently against his chest and held her head there, just as he'd been doing since she was a toddler. She cried softly against his neck.

"It's OK, Lia. When you're stronger, I'll give you a lecture, but right now, I'm just happy to see that you're alive and well. I couldn't handle it if anything ever happened to you," he said as he relished being able to hold her again, knowing there had been others in similar situations who had not been so fortunate.

"I screwed up. I won't ever do something so foolish again. There's no need to lecture me at all," she promised with a sob.

Rafe had his doubts. He was sure she'd soon forget about her foolishness, and be right back to being self-destructive. There were times he wished he lived in a century where he could just lock both her and Rachel up. That way he could ensure their safety. But if he tried to tell *them* that, he'd be toast.

"Now that I know you're going to be all right, you need to tell me what's going on with Shane."

Lia pulled back and a slow smile appeared on her face, diminishing a bit more of his concern.

"Well, I wasn't awake, but the doctor told me he was being uncooperative and got his butt hauled to jail. I think we need to make him sit there a while longer." The heavy breathing at the end of her statement testified that she was nowhere near full strength yet, but at least she was well enough to smile in delight at Shane's being arrested.

"I thought you and Rachel liked Shane." Rafe was confused by both of his sisters' obvious glee at his best friend being thrown in jail.

"He's been a bit of a pain lately. Sitting in a stinky jail cell serves him right," she answered before leaning her head back and looking menacingly at him.

Rafe's suspicions grew as he watched the mixed emotions roll across Lia's face. It was time for him and Shane to have a good long chat.

CHAPTER TEN

"**Y**OU LOOK GOOD behind bars. I hope you haven't found yourself a girlfriend already."

Fury surged through Shane as he looked at the sardonic face of his best friend. How in the hell could Rafe stand there smiling while Lia was lying helpless in a hospital bed several miles down the road Maybe his best friend really was as cold as people said.

"Get me the hell out of here, now! These idiot cops who wouldn't know their asses from their faces wouldn't let me make a phone call or speak to Bill. If they aren't suspended for at least a month, I'm going to—"

"Calm down, buddy. I spoke to Bill as soon as I found out the situation. The two arresting offers are transfers from LA, where things are done a bit differently. I don't think they're going to have seats left when the chief is done with them. If I have this nice officer here open the doors, are you going to behave?"

"How in the hell can you crack jokes while Lia is injured, unconscious, and maybe worse? I thought you were a better guy than that, Rafe," Shane thundered, his voice almost catching before he shoved the emotions down. He didn't need Rafe seeing how hard he was falling for Lia.

"You do know me, Shane. Do you honestly think I'd make any kind of joke if Lia weren't OK?"

It took several seconds for Rafe's words to sink in, but when they did, Shane's eyes widened in surprise before he plopped back down on the hard bench in his cell. Of course Rafe wouldn't be cracking jokes. He'd be freaking out just as much as Shane was. Lia must have pulled through while he'd been gone.

"She's OK," Shane said, needing to hear his words out loud.

"Yes. The drugs are out of her system and the seizure was just a side effect from whatever those animals gave her. She's demanding food and eating up all the attention she's getting. I will say that she's been quite irritated that you left, even if it was in handcuffs," Rafe said with a laugh.

"I can't wait until the day we're on opposite sides here, Rafe, and believe me, you *will* end up behind bars at least once in your life," Shane retaliated.

"Keep dreaming, my friend. Before we open up this cell door, I thought we'd have a little chat," Rafe told him as he grabbed a chair and sat down as if he were planning on getting comfortable.

"What are you talking about, Rafe? I want out of here now! These morons have broken about every civil right I have. Don't tell me you're condoning that."

"Of course not. However, I do have a few questions for you, and as it seems you tend to run off when you don't like what's being asked of you, I think this is a perfect time for me to get answers."

Shane was going to punch him — just once — give Rafe a big black eye. His friend deserved it for making him sit in the piss-reeking cage one second longer than he needed to be there. Shane also knew Rafe better than just about anyone, and furious as he felt, he knew he wasn't leaving until Rafe got whatever it was he wanted to say off his chest.

"Get this over with, Rafe. I've had a rough night and an even worse day. I won't hesitate to turn your pretty face black and blue if you don't get me out of here soon."

"I'll get right to the point then. Why is it that you're the first person my sister wants when she wakes up and finds out she's been drugged, nearly raped, and is stuck in a hospital room?" Though Rafe's voice was quiet, Shane clearly heard the suspicion in his tone.

Shane wouldn't lie to his best friend, but he certainly didn't want to tell him the fantasies he'd been having about Lia. He'd rather be just about anywhere else than sitting behind bars with Rafe's accusing eyes staring him down.

"Honestly, I don't know, Rafe. You know Lia has always had a crush on me, but I've managed to detour her for years. But she's really stepped up her game this past year. I'm not going to lie to you — I have some feelings for her, too. Wait! Before you come unglued, I'm working on that. I know nothing can happen," Shane said, holding up his hands in defense.

Rafe glared at him for several moments, before his shoulders sagged, making him look almost defeated.

"I know how persuasive Lia can be. Just make sure you keep your hands off her — got it?"

"I have to say, it really ticks me off that you feel you need to tell me that. I'm not some horny teenager who has nothing better to do than chase innocent females and try to get into their pants. I think that's far more up your alley," Shane snapped back.

Rafe grinned, and Shane knew the crisis was averted, at least for now. After a minute of silence, his friend turned back to him with a wicked gleam in his eyes.

"All right, then. Enough of this. Let's get back to your current predicament. As I asked earlier, are you going to behave if I have this nice officer let you out?"

"I swear that if you don't get me out of this room in the next ten seconds, I will kick your ass up and down these *halls of justice*," Shane thundered.

Laughing at the dripping sarcasm, Rafe nodded at the officer, who was looking between the two men as if they were both nuts. He wasn't going to say a word to the two friends, though, as it was obvious his chief was livid over the way Shane had been messed with.

With quiet efficiency, the small man opened the door and Shane strode out, throwing a glare toward Rafe before he headed down the hall and toward the stairs. He wanted to go as far from this jail as he possibly could.

He needed to see Lia, but there was no way he was going to her hospital room smelling like somebody's tossed cookies.

"Take me to your place. It's closer. I need a quick shower and then I want to get back to the hospital."

"I guess I can do that, considering I was able to get a few good shots in at your expense," Rafe replied.

"I swear, Rafe, if you had any real idea what my last twenty-four hours have been like, you would be a lot less vocal right now," Shane warned him.

Of course, Rafe never had been afraid of a threat. Shane decided he'd better shut up before the two of them ended in a fistfight. He wasn't afraid of Rafe, either — not even a little. But he just didn't want any more delays before he saw Lia.

"All kidding aside, Lia really is doing well. You saved her life. Hell, I owe you everything."

Shane turned in shock to see the sudden serious expression on Rafe's face. "There was never any question that I'd help her, Rafe. It's Lia."

"I don't have a lot of faith in many people, but you're one of the good guys, Shane. Thank you." Rafe patted Shane's back in a half hug before he led him to his car.

As they rode in silence to Rafe's house, Shane felt even worse. Here was his best friend telling him how much he appreciated what he'd done — and Shane had spent many nights with fantasies starring Lia in very unsisterly roles. He couldn't get into a relationship with Lia. It was just too complicated.

CHAPTER ELEVEN

"IT FEELS AS if every inch of my body has been worked over with a jackhammer. I need some much stronger drugs than whatever it is they're giving me."

"Do you want me to find the doctor, Lia? I don't handle situations like this very well," Ari admitted, her face turning pale as she stepped into the bathroom for a damp washcloth to offer cool relief to Lia's forehead.

Ari returned by her bedside and Lia groaned as she applied the cloth to her heated skin. Ari could hardly believe that something so horrible had happened to such a sweet girl.

Being there with Lia brought up her own tequila-drenched night at a club and that disgusting waiter, Chandler, who'd slipped her a date-rape drug. Ari refused to dwell on it, but it was hard to suppress the memories with Lia lying before her in a hospital bed.

Considering how ashen Lia's complexion was, whatever she'd been given was a lot worse than what Ari had been drugged with. Ari decided that she should share some of the story for Lia's sake.

"I've been through this if you want to talk about it. I know that no two situations are the same, but if it hadn't been for your brother, I don't even want to imagine what would have happened to me."

Lia's eyes filled with surprise and a flash of relief. She felt such shame and embarrassment about the incident and was feeling so miserable physically — the saying *misery loves company* seemed to make sense all of a sudden.

"I know I should be more frightened, or even face what happened with more seriousness, but Shane got there, and to tell you the truth I can't remember much of it. I was having a great time one minute, and then the next, my head felt all foggy. I knew enough to know someone had slipped me something, so I made a beeline for my car and called Shane. The rest of the night is really fuzzy..." Lia trailed off.

"Well, I'm here for you if you need a friend. With these macho men in your life, you may think that you have to be stronger than you really feel, but it's OK to admit it when you're scared," Ari said as she took Lia's hand.

"You are a great person, Ari. I'm so glad to have met you. My family means the world to me, but they've always been so over-the-top protective that sometimes I do stupid things just to rebel against it all. I'm not saying they are wrong; I just want them to accept the fact that I'm no longer a little girl. I love being a woman, and I'd love it even more if Shane would notice I'm all grown up. I'm sure you think I'm acting immature, but if you had put up with this the way I have for so many years, you'd have gone a little crazy, too," Lia admitted with a deep sigh.

"I have to admit I covet your life a little. My father was a drunk who ran off before I was old enough to even remember his face. I probably shouldn't even touch alcohol, but sometimes it's nice to just take a step back from reality. I was always the good girl, partly to make up for the fact that my mom gave so much for me, and partly because I'm highly competitive — even with myself — and there are times I find myself breaking free, too, trying to experience all the things I missed. I'd give anything to have a big, loving family. You may feel smothered, but you truly are one of the lucky ones."

"I'm so sorry about your dad, Ari. Ugh. That's terrible. I can't imagine what it must have been like to grow up without a dad — but your mom must really be something because you turned out so well. I do know how fortunate I am to have been raised in my family... I just wish I could have my big, loving family *and* a few hot nights with Shane, as well," she said with a wicked smile.

"Lia!" Ari gasped as she looked toward the door.

"Oh, please don't start lecturing. It's not as if you haven't had some steamy nights of your own — speaking of which, how are things going with my brother dearest?"

Ari ignored the question, wanting to get away from this topic as quickly as she could. She went to the sink and cooled Lia's washcloth again before stepping back to the bed. Lia suddenly groaned as if she were in severe pain.

"What can I do? Is there anything I can get you?"

"Some ice water would help," Lia moaned.

Ari failed to see the piercing brightness and the twinkle in Lia's eyes.

"Here you go," Ari said while handing over the water. "When do the doctors think you can return home?"

"You have to talk to me about anything other than this hospital or my ailments. I don't know when I get to leave, and keeping my mind off all this stuff is the only thing that will make me feel better," Lia pouted.

Ari paused for a minute as she tried to switch gears. "I got to spend a day in Central Park —"

"Noooooo!" Lia whined pitifully, "I've seen Central Park a thousand times. Tell me about you and Rafe. Are you guys all hot and heavy? Does he rock your world?"

"Lia! I can't believe you. Not even an entire day has passed since you were brutally attacked, and all you care about is my sex life. Priorities!" Ari scolded.

"This *is* a priority. A serious one. You weren't there when Sharron ripped his heart out, then stomped on it a few times for good measure. Rafe was different then — kinder. I know he's a bit of a pig now, but I still see my big brother underneath it all. He's inside — just waiting for someone to free him. You don't know me that well, but since you've stepped into his life, I've seen him emerging — returning to the person I always idolized."

Ari mentally shook her head. Rafe didn't care about her; he just wanted her as his mistress, a sexual and occasionally social convenience. He'd told her so repeatedly. Lia was just seeing what she so wanted to see.

The really annoying part of it all was that Ari could see moments where Rafe *was* kind and good. She could see a part of him that he desperately tried to keep hidden, but once in a while it would leak out. What if Lia was right? What if he did want to be loved, but he was just afraid of trusting someone?

If Ari opened herself up to this impenetrable man, and then he got bored with her and walked away, she'd be the one who was crushed. It would be *her* heart that was broken. Could she go through that? And what if she was too afraid to trust him, and he turned out to be the one she was meant for? She closed her eyes for an instant. *We need a distraction; I don't want to deal with this now. Please, God...* She was too confused to think about Rafe.

"Now that you're obviously feeling better I can give you the scolding you deserve, Lia. I can't believe you went to the middle of nowhere with a bunch of strangers and didn't call me!"

Ari grinned as a guilty expression washed over Lia's face when her sister breezed into the room.

"I'm sorry, Rachel. I just wanted to try something new. It wasn't a big deal until some idiot decided it would be fun to give me a spiked drink."

"That's crap and you know it. I'm just grateful Shane got there in time. So much worse could have happened to you. Someone drugged you and then you nearly got raped. Do you understand how dangerous a situation you were in? You could have been killed. You don't go to places like that — ever — especially not alone."

"Would you have come with me, Miss Innocent?"

"I wouldn't have liked it, but I would not have let you go alone," Rachel insisted.

"I think what Rachel is trying to say is that she's very happy you're OK, and in the future she wants to be with you when you are feeling…adventurous. I don't know what it was like for you guys to grow up in a home with siblings, but I grew up an only child and it was *really* lonely. You may drive each other crazy at times, but the bottom line is that you love each other and that's something you should always appreciate and respect."

Ari wasn't sure if the girls were going to turn their anger on her, go back to fighting with each other, or make peace. Before she could get an answer, Rafe walked in with Shane.

"I couldn't have said it better myself, Ari. Thank you." The wind was taken out of Ari's sails when Rafe walked right up to her and tugged her into his arms, giving her a long, scorching kiss in front of his family. He wasn't leaving any doubt to his sisters and Shane that he and Ari were a couple.

When Rafe drew back, Ari wobbled a bit on her feet before she managed to pull herself together. The man just *really* knew how to *kiss*.

"As for you, Lia, if you so much as hint at doing something so foolish again, I'll personally lock you up and throw away the key. You could have gotten yourself killed."

"I'll help him do it," Shane said as the two men flanked Lia's bed.

"You're both Neanderthals — and I couldn't love you more. Thank you for caring about me, and trust me, I will *never* do anything so dumb again. I've learned my lesson," Lia said with a thoroughly innocent expression.

Ari had a feeling the girl was only just getting started. From the adoring looks on both Rafe's and Shane's faces, it looked as if the men were buying into her heartfelt apology — hook, line and sinker.

"Now that it seems everything is under control, I'm going to go visit my mother," Ari said as she backed away from Rafe toward the door. She wished her voice sounded a little less breathless.

"I'll come with you."

"No! I mean, that's OK; you stay and visit with your sister. I'll meet you back here, Rafe. Thanks for the offer, though." Ari bolted out the door and down the hall.

The last thing she wanted was for her mother to see her with Rafe. Not only couldn't she seem to sort out her tumbling emotions toward the man, but she in no way wanted her mom to know what she'd done.

Ari's mother, Sandra, would get to leave the hospital in two more days, and because of Rafe, she'd be returning to her home, never the wiser that Ari had sold it. Rafe had hired men to move her mother's furniture and other possessions back into the house, and Ari would just explain that any missing items had been sold for medical costs. It was a small price to pay for her mother's health.

She stopped by the bathroom to freshen up and make sure none of the inner turmoil coursing through her was displayed on her face. Her mom had been through more than enough and didn't need to see Ari looking as if she were about to fall apart.

When Ari finally considered herself ready, she went to the elevators and traveled up to the sixth floor, where her mother's room was located.

As she stepped inside and saw her mother looking so much healthier and sitting up in bed, much of her stress evaporated. Her wonderful mom would be back to normal soon, even working in her beloved floral shop!

The creations her mother made were unique and beautiful, and customers came from near and far to snap them up. On top of her talent, she made each person among her clientele feel as if they were her top priority.

Sandra ran herself ragged, but she was happy, and Ari would do anything to ensure that she stayed that way, even if it cost her some of her own happiness. Her mom had sacrificed so much for her — it was now Ari's turn to return the favor.

"I thought you weren't going to be back until tomorrow, sweetie." The sound of her mom's voice prodded her into action and she moved forward.

"Mr. Palazzo's sister had an accident and we had to come back early," Ari said as she went her mother's bed and leaned down to give her a hug.

"Is she all right?"

"Yes. She's fine. Her family is there with her now, so I wanted to come see you. It's only been a few days, but I missed you. I bet you can't wait to get out of here. It has seemed like forever."

"It's felt like an eternity. I just want my own bed again," Sandra said as she reached for her cup of water. "How was New York?"

"It was amazing. We were there only a few days and didn't get much work done, but I was able to spend an afternoon in Central Park! I also got to ice-skate at Rockefeller Center.

I'm terrible at it, but I'd do it all over again. I hope to go back someday and explore more."

"We'll have to go together. I've never been to the East Coast. We'll make it a nice little vacation and stop in to see Niagara Falls, too."

"That sounds like a date, Mom. We'll want to do it in the summer because I've heard those falls get pretty cold."

"Do you like your new job, Ari? Are you going to be able to finish school while doing it?"

When Ari was in New York, she had told her mother only that she'd received a promotion in the company she'd been hired at originally and was now working directly for Rafe. She hadn't known what else to tell her. Sandra absolutely didn't need to know the whole truth.

"I love the job, not that I really know what I'm doing yet. I think it will be a good experience. I'm going to try to get back to school soon, Mom. I promise. I *will* finish that degree so you can be proud when I accept my diploma at the department of history ceremony."

"Ari, don't you know that I'm proud of you no matter what you do in life? I just want this so badly because you worked your tail end off and deserve to finish. It's a shame to stop now when you're so very close. I'd never forgive myself if you didn't graduate because of me."

"Mom, the accident was my fault, so none of this is because of you!" Ari insisted.

"We can go back and forth all day long about whose fault it is, but the bottom line is that I won't be happy until you have that diploma in your hand. You gave up a lot of your childhood so you could earn scholarships to go to school, and now it's time for you to shine."

"I am shining, Mom. You know, most college kids dream of getting a job for a company as prestigious as the Palazzo Corporation. They are high up there on the food chain. I see that look in your eyes, so you don't have to say it. I won't settle.

I promise you, I'll be there no more than six months, and then, even if I have to pimp myself out for college tuition, I'll get back in the classroom."

Ari winced at how close to home her statement was. She might not be selling her body for tuition money, but she was for her mother's security. The worst part was that she was developing feelings for her captor.

"Ari! Don't even joke about such a thing," Sandra exclaimed. "But you know," she went on in a deceptively even tone, "you need to tell me more about your boss — this Mr. Rafe Palazzo, who was so kind to me."

Ari squirmed beneath her mother's intense gaze. She'd managed to avoid the subject many times over, but her mom was an observant woman. Ari would have to be darned convincing to persuade Sandra there was nothing going on with her "boss."

"He's a great man who has decided to give a college dropout a chance. There's really nothing much I can tell you — he's a pretty closed book," Ari hedged.

"It seems to me that he's more than your boss."

"That's ridiculous, Mom. Mr. Palazzo is just one of those men who really stand out in a crowd. He's...helpful," Ari concluded lamely.

"You honestly expect me to believe there's nothing going on between the two of you?"

"No, absolutely nothing!"

"Now, Ari, I think your mother is a smarter woman than that."

Ari turned around to find Rafe leaning against the doorjamb as if he didn't have a care in the world. She sent an urgent look his way, pleading with him to stick with her story. When he answered with a wink, she didn't know what to expect.

"Excuse me, Rafe. Did you want to add something?" Sandra asked as she looked back and forth at the two of them.

"It's a pleasure to see you looking so much healthier, Sandra," Rafe replied as he sauntered into the room and reached down to pick up Sandra's hand and lift it to his mouth for a kiss.

In amazement, Ari watched her mother practically swoon. The man just had a way with women — both young and old. He could probably stop a riot with nothing but a smile and flirtatious wink.

She was becoming increasingly grumpy the longer he was around. The ease with which he wrapped her mother around his little finger exasperated and disturbed Ari.

"Are you going to tell me the truth?" Sandra asked in a throaty whisper.

"I couldn't lie to you. I'm infatuated with your daughter," he answered before stepping over to a very stunned Ari and bending down to give her a feathery kiss. His lips touched hers for only a moment, but it was enough to make her a bit light-headed.

"I knew it. I could tell when you were bringing me back and forth to her room. No man does that much for an old lady unless he's getting something out of it," Sandra said as if she'd solved a great puzzle.

"Mom!" Ari was horrified at her mother's speculation.

"You are but a spring chicken, Sandra. With your grace and beauty, it was no hardship to wheel you around. If I were just a few years older, I'd be chasing you instead of your daughter."

Ari stood there with her mouth open as her mom actually blushed. Was she seriously buying into this crap? Ari's own heart was buying into it as well, to her utter disappointment. She had to get Rafe away from her mom.

"Don't we have to catch up on work, Mr. Palazzo?" she asked, hoping to give the situation a more professional turn in her mother's presence.

"There's no need to be so formal, Ari. The cat's out of the bag," Rafe replied as he slunk toward her. Ari retreated so quickly, she hit a wall.

"My mom's right here," she warned when he hemmed her in.

"Later," he whispered in her ear before running his hand lightly across her cheek. Ari was a nervous mess as he took her hand.

"It's been such a pleasure to see you again so soon, Sandra. We'll be by the day after tomorrow to see you home."

"Thank you, Rafe. Take good care of my little girl," Sandra said in her mother hen way.

"I most certainly will."

Ari wondered if he had his fingers crossed somewhere. If her mother knew some of the things Rafe wanted to do to her little girl, she'd probably fly out of the bed with a needle and stab him in the eye. Or maybe her mom would inflict serious injury lower down...

"I love you, Mom. I'll come by again tomorrow. Then you'll have only one more day to go until you're in your own bed again."

"Just knowing that will make time creep by. When you want the day to pass quickly, that's when the clock stands still. I love you, too. Now, get out of here; I'm sure you're exhausted after all that traveling."

"I may just sleep for twelve hours straight. See you soon." Ari reached down and hugged her mom before reluctantly turning and allowing Rafe to escort her from the room.

The two of them walked to the elevators in silence, and then stepped inside an empty car. Just her luck — no one else there to break up the tension.

As soon as the doors closed, Rafe backed her against the wall and took her lips in a far less gentle kiss. Just at the point her knees were shaking, he pulled back and reached into her hair to tug her head back.

"I should punish you for lying, figure out a sweet method of torture…"

"I didn't want my mom to know," she defended.

"I don't hide my relationships, Ari. The situation becomes too…complicated when that happens. I like to have my mistresses out in the open where there's nothing to speculate about."

Ari was shocked at how cavalier he was about the whole mess. Of course, he'd been in many of these relationships, so what was one more to him?

"I wish I could have the same careless attitude as you, but I can't. I didn't want my mother to know about us."

"I'm a very public man, Ari, and your face will end up in the papers. Unless your mother doesn't read, watch television, or gossip at the hairdresser's, she'll find out. As I said, I find it's much easier to stave off the media if I'm not hiding anything."

"Well, she didn't have to know so soon," Ari pouted. She had to win on at least one point.

"I find it's always best to rip off the bandage and get difficult situations over with. Considering we're going to be together for quite some time, it's best not to worry about whom we tell and what we tell them."

"First off, we're not going to be together for that long, and secondly, my personal life is no one's business but mine, so if I don't want to tell people, then that's my right."

"Just as it's my right to tell anyone I please. You're not going to win this one, Ari — you're not going to win much at all when you battle me. Haven't you figured that out yet?" he asked as he bent down and kissed the side of her neck.

She was once again in a place where she both lusted after and loathed him all at once. If this was how she felt the entire time she was with him, it would be a very long three months.

CHAPTER TWELVE

"I CAN'T BELIEVE YOU'RE leaving us!"

"I'm just moving to another building. I'll still be in the city," Ari assured Amber. Although she was saying the words, she knew the truth of the matter — that it would be difficult in the future for her to see her friends.

"You might as well be leaving for another country," Miley pouted as she hugged Ari.

"You're all being overly dramatic. I promise you I will somehow make time to see you all as often as possible." She didn't know how she was going to make that happen with Rafe's demanding schedule, but Amber, Miley and Shelly had been good to her and she didn't want to lose their friendship. It tore at her heart to even imagine that happening.

"If you're so sure, then let's go out this Friday," Amber said with narrowed eyes.

Ari cringed. Rafe had already made plans for Friday, and for pretty much every Friday and Saturday. She had just Sundays to herself.

"I am free on Sunday. Why don't we meet for lunch?"

"Sunday! That's no fun at all," Amber insisted.

"With this new job, Friday and Saturday nights are going to be hard to get away, but I am free on Sundays for sure."

"He can't work you six days a week, Ari!"

Ari wished that were true, but she'd known what she was doing when she caved in and accepted Rafe's offer. She couldn't even regret it after taking her mother home and watching the joy fill her face.

Sandra hadn't said a word about any of her missing things. She'd only praised Ari over how nice the house looked. Rafe had hired professional cleaners to scour it from top to bottom, so Ari couldn't even take credit for that.

"We sure will miss you here, Ari. I know you were with us just a few months, but you have been a real asset to our team," her boss said as he walked up to their small group with a plate piled high with cake and cookies.

The girls had gone out of their way to give her a beautiful bon voyage party. Ari had been fighting tears all day knowing she wouldn't walk into these offices anymore and see her friends. She had no idea what was in store for her the next day at the Palazzo building.

She hoped Rafe kept his word and found her an actual job to do, because she hadn't been bluffing when she'd told him she wouldn't accept payment to be his mistress. She needed real work, and she wanted to do her best at it — no matter what the position was. If nothing else, working for the Palazzo Corporation would boost her résumé.

"Thank you, Mr. Flander. I will truly miss working for you. You've been a wonderful boss." Ari felt her throat tightening and fell silent. She had made friends here and it was hard to let go.

Since she'd been so focused on her education her entire life, friendships hadn't come easily for her, and losing that sense of belonging was almost more than she could take. Yet self-pity wasn't acceptable. How could she regret any sacrifice she made for her mother?

"OK, we'll quit trying to guilt you. Sunday it is. Don't you dare try and weasel out on us," Miley said as she hugged Ari again.

"I am marking my calendar right now," Ari said. Knowing she got to spend time with her mother and her friends on her days off would make anything Rafe asked of her easier to endure. Her weeks would be exhausting, she was sure, but there would always be something good in store for her at the end.

"I've been dragging my feet for an hour, but I'd better go now. There's a car waiting for me downstairs," Ari admitted.

"Ooh la la. You have a driver?" Shelly teased.

"It's not like that. I think Mr. Palazzo was just helping out since my car gave up the ghost and I have to move this heavy box." Lying to her friends wasn't easy and Ari felt her cheeks heat. She hoped they didn't notice and call her on it.

Though Amber gave her a suspicious look, she kept her mouth closed, which Ari was grateful for. After another round of hugs, she lifted her box and started making her way to the exit. Amber followed behind. When they reached the elevator, her friend gripped her arm and stopped until Ari met her eyes.

"You know, if you get in a bind, you can call me. I know our friendship has been all about fun and new adventures, but you're one of the good ones, Ari, and I've been worried about you. If this Rafe Palazzo does anything you don't like, just call me and I'll be there for you."

Ari couldn't speak for a moment as she looked at Amber. How was she supposed to continue seeing this wonderful woman when she'd be lying to her all the time? It seemed wrong, but she couldn't tell her the truth. For one thing, Rafe had his stupid confidentiality clause. For another, she was ashamed at what she had been willing to do to give her mother back her home.

"I'm doing well, Amber. I promise you. This promotion is a great thing, and yes, you know, there's a bit more than meets the eye when it comes to my relationship with Rafe, but I will be OK. I swear I'll call you if I need you."

Amber looked at her hard for a few more seconds before giving her one final hug. "You do that." With that her friend turned around and went back to her desk.

As Ari stepped into the elevator and hit the lobby button for the last time, she fought back tears. Though she knew she'd try to maintain the friendship, it wouldn't be easy. She might eventually lose these women who'd been there for her during a very difficult time.

Walking slowly through the lobby and out the front door, Ari was surprised when she saw Rafe standing next to the car. What was he doing there?

"Are you OK?" he asked as he quickly walked to her and lifted the box from her arm. The genuine concern in his tone broke down the last of Ari's defenses, and a couple of tears streaked down her cheeks.

"What is it?" he asked as he handed the box to Mario and pulled her into his arms. What was she supposed to say to him? *I'm miserable because you're making me leave everyone I know behind*? She doubted that would go over well.

Rafe helped her into the backseat, then climbed in and quickly pulled her onto his lap as he gently brushed back her hair and allowed her to cry.

"Ari, talk to me."

"I liked my job. It just really sucks to have to leave it," she admitted. Rafe stiffened for a moment before his frame relaxed.

"You'll like your new position, too. I've put you in my charity department. You'll be picking organizations to give money to, and also going around to hand the money out and visit the projects we fund."

Though Ari didn't want to be intrigued, she was, and her tears stopped as curiosity overcame sadness. Lifting her head so she could see his face, she asked, "Did you make the position up for me?" She hoped not. She wanted to feel valuable.

"No. There are six people in that department, and we need about ten. I'm just very choosy whom I'll hire to work in our charitable arm. Some of the places we donate to have gone through very tough times and they need their liaisons to be kind and compassionate. As soon as you demanded a job from me, I knew you'd be perfect in that department."

The crooked smile on his face took any sting from his words. It was so much harder to hate him when he was kind. She hadn't been expecting to like her new job, but she couldn't deny that she wanted to know more. It could actually be fun.

"I don't know if that's a compliment or an insult," she said as she gave a small smile of her own.

"One thing I can guarantee you is that I enjoy your compassion. It's unusual, Ari. Why don't we have a nice dinner to celebrate your new job? I don't always fill the dictator slot that you have pigeonholed me into."

Ari didn't know what he was angling for now, but she didn't want to ruin his good mood. If she had to spend the next few months with him, wouldn't it be better for the two of them to get along? That wasn't going to happen all the time — they too easily butted heads — but for one night, she could enjoy herself guilt-free, couldn't she?

"That sounds nice. I'd like to hear more about my job," she conceded.

While Mario drove them to a small seafood restaurant, Rafe supplied more details about her new position, and she grew eager to start work. Maybe some of the changes in her life wouldn't be so bad, after all.

For a couple of hours, at least, Ari forgot that Rafe had essentially forced her into a relationship with him. She forgot she'd had to give up a job she liked. She even forgot that she didn't like him very much.

She had a good meal, found herself laughing a couple of times, and slowly the wall she'd put in place to protect herself, for the day she and Rafe parted ways, was beginning to tumble down.

CHAPTER THIRTEEN

ARI TOSSED HER purse on the stand by her door as she wearily made her way into her condominium. She hadn't seen Rafe for two days, which was unusual for him, and she was wondering what she was doing. One minute she cared about him, and then the next she couldn't get far enough away.

Confusion consumed her as the emotions escalated. She demanded time away from him, and then found herself missing him once he was gone, respecting her wishes. She couldn't even say he was the dictator she'd originally thought him to be as he'd backed down to her wishes many times over.

How was she supposed to last for three months with her emotions constantly in a jumble?

"Did you have a pleasant evening?"

Ari jumped at the sound of Rafe's voice. It was Sunday night, and he rarely made an appearance, respecting her time alone, but as her emotions remained on high alert, she didn't know what to feel about his being there.

"Yes. I met up with the girls and we went to dinner and then dancing."

Rafe's gaze narrowed at the mention of dancing. She couldn't blame him. Too often when she went out with Amber, Miley and Shelly, she tended to drink too much and then find herself in awkward situations — or worse.

"I drank club soda all night — don't look so irritated," she said with a smile.

"Good, I don't want you intoxicated for what I have planned. It's time for me to call in my favor."

"What favor?" she asked with confusion.

"The bet you lost in Central Park." Ari couldn't believe he'd actually bring that up. He'd cheated!

"What is that?" she asked with suspicion. There was an excited gleam in his eyes that had her on her toes. Some of the things he asked of her were just too much. He respected her decision when she said *no*, but she worried why he'd even *want* to do some of the sexual acts he was into.

"I've eased you into my life, Ari, but I'm very aware that you grow restless occasionally. I know the fear of the unknown eats away at you, so I want to show you that it's all far worse in your mind than in reality."

"What do you plan on doing?" she asked as she retreated a few steps as he stood up.

"Something you will highly enjoy."

"That's not an answer, Rafe. I want to know in detail what you're planning," she demanded as she retreated further. Rafe's eyes sparked to life as he followed her, his steps slow and steady, as if he had no worries.

"Do you trust me?"

"No."

He stopped as if she'd actually wounded him. Ari quit retreating as she looked at the hurt expression on his face. Did she trust him? He'd never done anything to harm her — had kept his word on everything he'd promised, and had made her feel pleasure beyond her wildest imagination.

So, taking all that into account, did she trust him? Yes, she actually did.

"That's a lie, Rafe. You've never hurt me. I'm just frightened," she admitted.

In a flash he was at her side, his hand coming up to stroke her cheek.

"I will never hurt you — that's my promise."

She wanted to contradict him. He might never physically hurt her, but what about her heart? He was surely going to shatter it, and the pain would be worse than from a broken bone. Yes, Rafe would hurt her — it was only a matter of time — but she was coming to accept that. He didn't know any other way and she'd been foolish enough to develop feelings for him. It was her fault her heart would tear when he walked out her door and never came back.

"I know you intend not to hurt me. What do you want me to do?"

The gleam entered his eyes again as he led her into her spare room. When he flicked on the light, she looked in confusion at what was before her. She closed her eyes, shook her head, looked again, trained her eyes all around the room, and even then she couldn't quite figure it out.

"Don't be worried. I plan on taking you further tonight than I've ever taken you before. When you release your body totally over to me, and trust me to make you fly, the pleasure will be endless," he whispered in her ear as his hand reached the bottom of her shirt and he began pulling it up.

Ari wanted to say no, turn around and walk out. Knowing she had the power to do just that allowed her the confidence to stand where she was as he lifted the shirt over her head. His hands came down and rested on her collarbone, his fingers softly rubbing the delicate skin.

A shudder ran through her as his hands roamed over her breasts, barely skimming their lace-covered surface. Her nipples hardened instantly, stretching toward him, eager for his touch.

He moved down the plane of her stomach, sending tiny goose bumps across the surface of her skin as he unbuttoned her jeans and slowly pulled down the zipper, all the while pressing his body up against her back so she could feel his obvious excitement.

Still moving in a leisurely fashion, his hands slipped inside her jeans and pulled them and her panties down. With his foot, he eased them off her before sliding his hands up her side and gently pushing her forward so he could reach the clasp of her bra. Within seconds she was stripped bare before him, and his hands roamed her body.

"Rafe…" she called, her knees beginning to grow weak.

"Shhh, just enjoy," he whispered as one hand came around and tightened on her stomach, pulling her flush against his clothed body. While that hand gripped her to him, the other wandered over her skin, skimming across her breasts and pinching her nipples, before his fingers moved down and slid across the top of her heat.

His lips began trailing a line of kisses along her shoulder, his teeth scraping her lightly as he marked her as his. She tried to turn, but he held her firmly as his erotic torment continued.

His legs pushed against her, forcing her to move forward toward the contraption before her. Fear crawled up her throat as she was faced with it again.

"Trust me," he encouraged her as he lifted her arm and slipped it into a fur lined leather strap, then attached it to a chain hanging from a large metal circle with two rings in it. The contraption reminded her of the ring around a world globe, but in this instance she was to be the globe.

She leaned against him as he trapped first one wrist and then the other. Before she could move, he dropped to the floor and encased her ankles in similar leather restraints, then clipped them to the circular bar, leaving her spread wide open while standing straight up inside a metal circle. She tugged against the restraints, but she was immobile, not able to move in the least.

He pushed against the metal, and it gently rocked, held tightly in place by a single steel chain dangling from the ceiling, making him able to move her in any direction while still keeping her locked inside. The back circle didn't move, bracing her body with a woven leather web, making him able to keep her secure while still giving him plenty of access to her backside.

"What are you going to do?" she groaned as he rose and his mouth made a path up the inside of her thigh before his lips captured the line of her womanly secrets.

"Everything" was his answer.

With a few skillful strokes of his tongue, she was panting, fear left far behind. He reached around her and gripped her backside, pulling her body closer to his mouth, where he devoured her in a never-ending kiss. She rose higher, lights beginning to spark behind her eyes as she tugged against her restraints.

"Please," she begged him as he inserted his fingers inside her and pumped in rhythm with his tongue. All of the sensations were too much, and she quickly spiraled out of control as her core shattered and she reached her peak of pleasure.

When she stopped gasping and finally opened her eyes, Rafe was gone. She looked around in panic, wondering what he was doing now. What felt like an eternity passed before she saw him walk through the door again, his body now bare of clothes. He was holding something in his hand, but the lights were too dim for her to make out what it was.

When he got closer she saw the paddle, and panic flew through her. He'd made her a promise. Everything he'd ever done had pushed her past what she thought her boundaries were, but he'd never hurt her — yet there he was with something meant to inflict pain.

Ari struggled against the restraints, true fear spiking inside her. She had to get out. It was time to leave. Maybe he truly was the monster she'd thought him to be in the beginning.

CHAPTER FOURTEEN

"I THOUGHT YOU PROMISED to never hurt me," she choked out as she struggled against the restraints.

Rafe suddenly stopped, his face blanching as a tear coursed down her face. She didn't know whether this meant he was going to stop, but she was so frightened, she continued pulling against the binds on her hands and legs.

"Stop," he commanded, his voice firm, but gentle. "I won't break the promise. I will push you, Ari, and show you pleasure. I will send your body spiraling relentlessly out of control. I will make you beg me for more. I won't hurt you."

She didn't reply, but looked directly at the paddle. He paused as his face became thoughtful.

"You make me do things I have never desired to do before. I find myself compromising for you in a way I'm not sure I like."

He walked to her and slid his hand up her arm, sending pleasure everywhere his featherlike touch landed. Then he was untying her right arm. She looked at him expectantly when that was all he released of her restraints.

"I'm going to let you do something I've never allowed another woman to do. This will be the only time you're allowed to do this."

Without further words he grabbed her hand and set the handle of the paddle in it. Her eyes widened as she looked from the toy to his face. She didn't know what he wanted.

"Feel the fur against the leather. You will see how soft it is. If you rub it against your skin, it is soothing, feels like a gentle massage. When I do paddle it against the flesh of your butt, there is no pain, just a slight pressure that will heighten your pleasure. It will leave a slight pink glow to your skin, turning me on immensely, but whatever it does to me will be ten times more intense for you. My pleasure comes when I know you are at the height of yours. Seeing your body shake and watching you let go sends my senses spinning out of control."

Ari's breathing deepened as his words seduced her. She was beginning to think she wanted him to go ahead and experiment with her body. It would be worth it to feel such pleasure as he always so masterfully gave.

"Strike my stomach with the paddle. You will see that I don't flinch, that it's not hurting me. You will see the mark it leaves. You may hit me as many times as you like so you can understand the toy. However, this is a one-time offer. I won't allow you to do it after this night. *I* am the one who wants to bring *you* to the apex of your passion."

A strange excitement surged through Ari. Power. He was giving her power. It was an unbelievable rush. She didn't hesitate as her free arm rose and she sliced the paddle through the air.

As the soft fur made contact with Rafe's hard flesh, a crisp sound filled the air, and just the barest of shade of pink marked his stomach.

She lifted her arm again and hit his hip, then his other side. Ten strokes later and there was a soft pink coloring his skin, but no angry welts or marks.

Ari was breathing heavily as she lowered her arm and then met his eyes. He simply returned her look, not saying anything on trying to grab the weapon back.

She didn't want to admit her curiosity, but seeing that he didn't flinch, seeing his expression stay the same made her want to know what it felt like. Fear still lurked just beneath the surface, but curiosity was quickly taking its place.

"If I don't like it, will you stop?"

"Have I ever betrayed your trust with anything I've done to you? Have I ever left you in pain? I wouldn't do it if there were the slightest chance of hurting you. But, to alleviate your fears, if you ask me to quit, I will," he said as he held out his hand.

With just a moment of hesitation, she handed him back his paddle, and relief flashed in his expression before he gripped her hand and once again secured her.

Rafe circled around her body, leaving her field of vision only to return on the other side of her again. He did this several times, building up her anticipation, making her want him to get it over with. The waiting was agony.

Finally, he went behind her and she felt the soft fur rub against her neck. He swept the paddle across her back, then traced the curve of her butt, before rubbing it back up her spine again.

A moment later, he removed it from her skin, and then she felt contact on one buttock. She flinched at the unexpected hit, but then realized he was right. There was no pain, just a slight pressure against her skin. He rubbed the place he'd hit with the palm of his hand before she felt the paddle return to her skin on the other cheek.

Several times, she felt the fur strike her backside, followed by Rafe's hands rubbing along her skin. Each hit jolted her body, making her core shake and grow wet.

"Your skin has just the barest hint of a pink glow and I can see the shine on your core where you are readying yourself for me to plunge deep inside you." He rubbed the paddle against the outside of her swollen folds, and she shuddered, the contact bringing her close to shattering again.

"You like that, Ari. Tell me how much you like it," he whispered in her ear as he pressed himself against her backside, while he rubbed the paddle against her heat.

"It feels unlike anything I could ever imagine. I...I don't know how to...to explain what it is, but the pressure as it presses against me seems to make everything better. You are right, there's no pain...only pleasure. Please take me — I need to be filled by you," she begged as he lifted the paddle and brought it down against her core, making her cry out as she neared orgasm.

"Not yet, Ari. You've already been pleasured once. You'll have to wait a while to reach your second peak," he said as he swatted her folds again.

He might not think she was ready, but one more gentle hit against her pulsing core and she would be flying over the edge. She kept her mouth shut, hoping he would give her what she needed. A chuckle in her ear let her know he was on to her silence.

"I can read your body, Ari. I know when you're close. I know what makes you scream — and I know how to make you fly. Your pretense that you aren't about to go over doesn't deceive me. I know exactly what you are doing."

He dropped the paddle and came to stand before her, where she gazed upon his perfection. His muscular chest led to his narrow waist and incredible hips, and in due course to his magnificent erection, standing there so proud. She wanted to reach out and pull him into her hand, and delight in his sweet flavor on her lips.

He grabbed a couple of straps she hadn't noticed, and attached them to the metal circle, then placed one behind her back and one in front of her stomach, securing them tightly around her midsection. Then he gripped the edge of the circle and it began to move. The entire circular contraption began turning sideways, making her again panic as she fought against the motion.

"You're secure. You won't fall," he promised. She quickly forgot her fear as he moved forward, his erection perfectly aligned with her mouth. Yes, she wanted to feel his velvet skin on her tongue, needed to make him cry out in pleasure.

Soon his thick staff was resting on her lips. She opened for him and slipped her tongue out to taste his pleasure. He moved forward and slipped further inside her mouth and she greedily sucked on him, taking him as far as she could before he pulled back.

His hand came down to grip her head, holding her in place as he slowly moved his hips back and forth, his arousal disappearing in her mouth, then emerging wet with her saliva.

"Yes, Ari, this feels so good," he groaned as his movements picked up speed, the head of his shaft grazing the back of her mouth and touching the top of her throat. She wanted to take him all the way inside, but he was too large; she just couldn't do it. She wished her hands were free so she could grip him tightly in her hand while she sucked him inside.

Rafe pulled out with a groan and she enjoyed the sight of his pleasure dripping from the tip of his hardness. She loved that she made this strong man weak.

He turned her back so she was upright, then crushed her body to his as he devoured her mouth, plunging his tongue deep inside while his fingers found their way down to her butt and gripped her tightly, pressing his wet shaft against her opening. She tried to move against him, but the restraints held her in place. She wanted him to take her — she was tired of foreplay; she needed him filling her up, now.

She was dizzy at the thought of him on her tongue, those glistening drops that forecast his release.

Rafe pulled back from her, then pushed the circle she was trapped in, causing her body to lie back, and exposing her heated core to him.

When she was angled just right, he plunged inside, making her scream with pleasure as he pulled out and plunged back in. She couldn't see him entering her, could only feel as the walls of her swollen flesh gripped him tight, tried to prevent him from pulling out.

Rafe moved his hand down, his thumb circling her swollen pink bud as he picked up speed and thrust quickly in and out. Ari let go, let her worries and fears fade away and focused on nothing but the rapture of Rafe taking control of her.

Pressure built as he masterfully stroked her flesh, building her so high, she thought she might never come down. His groans filled the air as he reached higher and higher, climbing the wave with her so they could both tumble down together.

When Ari did shatter, Rafe was right there with her, following her over the edge in a seemingly unending wave. Her body gripped him, pulsing over and over as her cries mingled with his groans of ecstasy.

When the passion play finally came to a close, Ari had nothing left. If it hadn't been for the restraints keeping her up, she'd have collapsed to the floor. Being with Rafe drained her, but in a wonderful way, in a way she feared she'd never experience with another man.

How could she possibly feel anything as magical as what she felt in his arms? Barely conscious, Ari hardly noticed Rafe freeing her from his contraption. She rested her head against his shoulder as he carried her to her bed.

When he laid her against the cool sheets, she whimpered, not ready to let him go. Her last thought was shock and pleasure as he climbed in next to her and tugged her into his arms. She knew she'd wake alone, but she was with him for now.

CHAPTER FIFTEEN

ARI CLIMBED OUT of bed and winced. Her body felt as if it had been repeatedly run over during rush-hour traffic. Thump-thump, thump-thump… She'd never imagined that someone could have such an insatiable appetite for sex. If she had to continue the nighttime marathons, she'd have to start doing some intense workouts to get her strength up.

"Rafe?"

Ari waited, and when there wasn't an answer, she let out the breath she'd been holding. It wasn't that the sex wasn't great — it was out of this world. But it was just too much. How did people do it so many times in a single week?

She'd been Rafe's mistress for three weeks with only four days off during that time, and two of them only because he'd had to take a trip without her. He'd tried to get her to give up her other precious days, and she'd emphatically refused, saying that she needed them for rejuvenation. He'd made up for it the morning after each one.

Walking slowly into the kitchen, she smiled when she found a full pot of coffee and a note.

We have a business function tonight. I've hired a personal stylist for you who will be at the condo at ten. You have the day off. My driver will pick you up at noon to escort you to the salon.

Rafe

Ari really didn't feel like having a bunch of strangers plucking at her hair and body, especially after her last salon visit. It hadn't been pleasant. They'd waxed her in places a person should never be waxed, offending her innate modesty. And her visit with the doctor last week had been almost as bad. Rafe had insisted because he didn't want an unexpected pregnancy to throw a wrench into their relationship.

Their relationship. That was a joke. So far, she'd managed to get a job she actually liked, doing charitable work. Though she knew he was simply humoring her, she chose to work as hard as possible and therefore take pride in what she was doing. The reality was that she was being told what to do night and day and had enacted so many scenes from the *Kama Sutra* that she didn't remember what the missionary position was anymore.

The thing that really confused her was that she wasn't miserable. Rafe wasn't treating her badly — quite the opposite, in fact. He was distant most of the time, but not unkind.

Glancing at the clock, she was relieved to see it was only eight. She had two hours until she was bombarded. That was plenty of time to soak her sore muscles in a nice hot bath.

Grabbing a thriller novel off the shelf, Ari walked to the bathroom and turned on the tap. No way she wanted to read anything having to do with love or romance — she wasn't sure she even believed in the mythical emotion anymore.

Ari remembered her mother warning her that sex wasn't love's equal, and telling her that she had to be careful because too many people equated the two. Ari could now see how that could happen.

When she was in the throes of passion in Rafe's arms, she had strong feelings toward him. When he left her lying in the bed all alone afterward, she felt an overwhelming emptiness and couldn't prevent the abundant tears from soaking her pillow. How was she supposed to keep her heart uninvolved when the man was there each and every day?

Sinking deep down into the water, Ari closed her eyes and inhaled the subtle scent of mango oil. The water jets soon soothed her legs and lower back. And after lying back for fifteen minutes and relishing doing absolutely nothing, she started to feel human again, so she took a sip of her tea and decided to lose herself in her newest read.

An hour later, Ari realized the time and put down Stephen King's *Under the Dome*, though she did so with great reluctance. What sort of barrier could have possibly sealed off the townspeople in the story? She would much rather soak in the tub all day and read make-believe than attend some stuffy function with a bunch of uppity strangers.

Since her puppet master had commanded her to dance on his strings, it looked as though she didn't have a choice. What if she stood him up? The thought brought a smile to her face. She knew she could tell him to kiss off, in so many words, but he'd honored his end of the bargain, and it felt wrong to not give a full effort on her end.

Working for the charitable side of his company, reading donation requests and sending replies, was very engrossing. Some of the letters coming in had brought her to tears.

What had completely surprised her were the thank-you letters that frequently arrived. Not only did Rafe donate millions of dollars to worthy causes, but he also made personal appearances. She'd stolen one of the pictures an elementary school class had sent.

Rafe was surrounded by six-year-olds and he was wearing a T-shirt they'd obviously made him with their handprints all over it. The letter thanked him profusely for the donation enabling them to go on field trips that year.

Letter after letter came pouring in, full of gratitude for everything from computers for senior centers to money for programs cut for lack of funds. Rafe had a generous heart. Why he guarded it when it came to women she didn't understand.

So what if his ex had cheated on him? That was an old song that many had danced to. Most marriages ended either because of infidelity or financial problems. Divorcés and divorcées didn't normally turn into coldhearted monsters.

What Ari was learning about Rafe, though, was that he was far from a monster — he just wanted women to think of him that way. What it would be like, she wondered, to peel back a few of his hardened layers?

Was she bold enough to do just that? She honestly didn't know if she was. Maybe he would behave abhorrently one too many times, and she wouldn't care enough to find out what lay beneath. She could certainly imagine that scenario a lot more easily than one in which he had a change of heart.

With a grudging sigh, Ari climbed from the tub and was just finishing up flinging on clothes when the doorbell rang. It looked as if it was time to play dress-up.

The next two hours whirled away as Ari tried on dozens of dresses. Finally, the woman seemed satisfied and freed Ari from that ordeal. Which of the outfits would she be wearing? She honestly didn't know, and at that point she couldn't have cared less. The salon beckoned almost as a reprieve from all that zipping and buttoning and tying.

Ari knew from her high school and college days that a lot of women loved getting dressed up and being pampered — if you could call it that — but she'd never been that girl. She'd been far more interested in studying than in the latest Paris fashions. It all just seemed so trivial.

Granted, Ari did get off on finding that flawless pair of jeans — a pair that slid on and fit her as if they had been made just for her body. She had one pair in her closet that she loved. Those were from the days before she made such an attempt at hiding her curves. When she slipped them over her hips and they molded to her behind, she felt sexy and sleek. Yes, she'd take a pair of jeans over silk any day. Ari smiled at that thought.

Since she was able to bring her thriller with her to the salon, having her hair tugged, ironed and twisted in all directions didn't bother her. She became lost in the story again and was able to tune out the constant droning of the many people gossiping all around her. Before she knew it, this second ordeal was over, too.

By the time she got home, put on the gold satin dress that had been laid out for her, and then turned to look in the mirror, Ari was shocked. Wow! She wasn't in the least bit vain, but she just about took her own breath away. Slowly, she approached the mirror and looked at herself from head to toe.

Her hair was partly up, so it was away from her face, but the rest was left cascading down her back in soft curls. Just how did she feel about the dress? She had no words. It molded to her curves like a second skin and dipped dangerously low in front and to nearly indecent levels in back. One more inch and she'd be showing parts of her behind not meant for public consumption.

The makeup artist had transformed her features, making her appear almost exotic with dark eyes and rose-colored lips. With her mysterious look, her tumbling locks, and the golden gown, she felt like a princess from another era. Now all she needed was a knight to come riding in to rescue her from her lofty tower.

As she twirled in front of the mirror, assessing the effect of four-inch heels, she felt invincible. Being a *little* vain wasn't so bad, she decided with a laugh. Maybe the day, and night, wouldn't be a terrible loss, after all.

With a new bounce in her step, Ari made her way to the elevator and rode down with a smile that refused to leave her lips. Rafe was running late at work, so he would meet her at the business bash. She was anticipating his reaction; her grueling beauty boot camp had earned her at least a little head turning.

"You look stunning, Ms. Harlow."

"Thank you, Mario. I was dreading the entire 'day of beauty,' but wearing this gown has changed my opinion of being pampered,'" she responded with a giggle.

"The gown is gorgeous, indeed, but you're the one who makes it shine."

"You are about to sweep me off my feet," she said, taking his hand as he helped her into the back of the car.

"I don't think my wife would be too happy to hear that," he joked as he shut the door, then made his way to the driver's side of the car.

"I didn't know you were married, Mario. Your wife must be a lucky woman."

"I think she'd agree with you on some days, and disagree on others." Ari loved how comfortable Mario made her feel. He was a kind man, even if he refused to call her by her first name. She had argued with him too many times over the matter already; why resume the fight this beautiful evening?

They chatted for a few more moments, and then Ari rested while he chauffeured her across the city. She wondered what Rafe would think of her look. But she hated that she cared.

CHAPTER SIXTEEN

RAFE GLANCED AT his watch for the twelfth time in the past hour. It was ridiculous. He didn't care if he was late to a function he hadn't been interested in attending in the first place, so why was he continually checking the time?

His life had stopped making sense. Sheesh. He couldn't even make it through a simple business meeting without having Ari repeatedly pop into his head. And now he was rushing through town in the back of a limo to meet her at an event that promised nothing but boredom.

He was losing control and the frightening part was that he didn't much care half the time. When he was in her presence, he felt alive — as if he could do anything. No matter how much he tried to pull back from her, a secret smile on her face was all it took to make him fall to his knees.

The situation was absurd and he knew that, but still he couldn't stop himself from glancing at his watch, yet again.

"How much longer until we arrive?"

"We'll be there in five minutes, Mr. Palazzo."

Rafe found himself wanting to snap at the driver to pick it up, but he forced himself to sit back and take a drink. If he didn't want to pin Ari to a wall the second he saw her, he'd need a hell of a lot more bourbon before the night was over.

Never had his sexual appetite been so endless. He wanted her night after night — no breaks in between except for those miserable Sundays she reserved as her own. She might not have realized it, but he was holding himself back. He could see that her body was sore, though she wasn't complaining. She was still argumentative, and about the worst submissive he could imagine, but she made him — happy.

When they arrived, Rafe didn't wait for the driver to come around and open his door. He stepped from the vehicle the second it stopped and found himself rushing inside the exclusive country club.

The function was to celebrate a new collaboration between his company and a foreign electronics manufacturer. The merger would create tens of thousands of jobs and billions of dollars in revenue for both countries.

Rafe should be joining in the celebration, seeking out his new business partners, not searching the crowd for a small, dark-haired minx who had his insides turned upside down.

Snatching up a couple of glasses of champagne from a passing waiter, Rafe made his way through the crowd, intent on finding Ari. He'd get her alone for five minutes, and then he'd be back to himself and could handle his investors.

When he turned a corner and heard the sound of Ari's laughter, his apprehension faded. Then he saw her. For a stunned moment, Rafe stood motionless, gripping the champagne flutes almost too tightly as her beauty stole the air from his lungs.

Ari was facing him, sheathed in a gold creation that flattered her every feminine curve. He drank in her alabaster complexion, touched with just enough makeup to bring out the fire of her eyes and the natural plumpness of her lips.

When she threw back her head and laughed, his stomach tightened at the sight of her enticing cleavage, showcased by the exquisite cut of the gown. But when the man she was speaking to raised his arm and caressed her shoulder, rage quickly crowded out lust.

Ari was his — and some man had just made the very foolish mistake of touching her.

Rafe moved swiftly through the parting crowd, ignoring the few people unwise enough to try to speak to him. Ari didn't notice his approach until he was grabbing her arm and pulling her away.

"Rafe! That was rude. I was speaking to someone," she scolded.

"You were done," he snapped as he dragged her across the room, intent on getting her away before his anger escalated.

"What is your problem?" she asked as she stumbled along beside him, his pace making it hard for her to keep up in her heels.

Before Rafe could answer, he got a glimpse of the back of her dress while prodding her to go through a doorway before he did. The amount of skin she was exposing for all the men to see jacked up his anger to a new level.

Needless to say, his stylist was fired.

"What is going on? Why are you acting this way?" she asked as he led her down the terrace steps and out to the back lawn. He spotted a secluded path and hurried her down it. When he found a small alcove with a bench, he pulled her inside and crushed her against his chest.

"You are mine! Don't ever forget it," he growled before his lips crashed down on hers. The kiss was all about possession and need, about untamed hunger. He wanted to brand her, make sure she never looked at another man again.

Even though Rafe knew jealousy was egging him on, he couldn't seem to stop. His hand gripped her hips as he pushed against her — pressing his solid manhood against her body.

He backed up and sat on the bench, pulling Ari forward so she was standing between his thighs. The anger still gripping him fused with an overwhelming passion that pulsed straight through his erection. Rafe leaned down and gripped the hem of her dress, sliding it over her seductive hips, his frustration mounting at the semidarkness and his inability to drink in her full beauty.

"Straddle my lap," he ordered as he drew her forward. Ari stumbled before he caught her and assisted her onto his muscular thighs.

The feel of her straddling him was indescribable. His hands traced the curve of her back as he lost himself in the taste of her neck.

"No one should see you in this dress except me," he growled.

"It's just a dress, Rafe," she panted.

Surprise made him lift his head. He needed to look into her eyes, but he could just barely see the outline of her features through the dim moonlight.

"You're right, Ari. It is just a dress — but with you in it, the material comes to life, showcases your curves, and makes every man in the room think of taking you home and ravishing you until the morning light breaks the dawn. That right belongs only to me."

Ari shuddered in his arms as she leaned toward him, and he couldn't resist taking her mouth as he moved his hands to shift his clothes. He didn't want foreplay — he wanted to sink deep inside her. He hoped she was ready because he felt on the verge of exploding.

"Take me, Rafe. If I'm yours, then show me," she demanded as her hands gripped his shoulders.

Relief coursed through him as he finally freed himself from his pants. Moving his hands back to her hips, he ripped her panties free and then pressed himself against her aching core, with her wet heat summoning him to enter.

"Mine," he growled as he gripped her hips and thrust deep inside her, their bodies now fused into one.

Ari took over as she clutched his shoulders and began moving up and down his shaft, her hips swinging forward, torturing him with pleasure. She wasn't in a hurry, taking her time as she groaned with each seductive movement.

"Faster," he urged.

Ari stilled as she bent down to kiss his neck, making a slow journey to his ear where she licked the outer lobe. "Don't you know the voyage is what it's all about, Rafe? Listen. Can you hear the music?"

Her husky words confused him until she started gyrating her hips and rising and falling to the beat of the slow song that drifted out from the clubhouse and trickled down to them.

"Yes, Ari. You can't imagine what you're doing to me right now," he groaned as his head bent forward and he ran his tongue down her cleavage.

Her moans encouraged him to go on and he shifted the delicate fabric with his teeth, not caring if her dress ripped in the process. With a shrug of her shoulder, the small strap fell down her arm and the material moved, exposing her naked breasts to his mouth.

Normally, Rafe didn't like having sex in the dark. He wanted to watch his partner plunge over the edge of pleasure. With his sight out of commission, however, he needed his other senses to take over. Pricking up his ears and making his mouth explode with *flavors*, he was able to focus so much more on the sound of her moans and the taste of her skin.

With a tug of his jaw, her dress slipped further and he immediately sucked in the delicious peak of her breast and nipped at her greedily.

As the music picked up rhythm, so did Ari's synchronization. She began moving faster, pushing down on him with

MELODY ANNE

each beat of the bass, making him lose his breath as he neared completion.

Lifting his hand, he pushed down her other strap and shoved her dress down so both breasts were exposed for his pleasure. He alternated between the toothsome mounds, teasing her peaks and making her cry out.

She was his — and he could do whatever he wanted with her.

What he wanted was to pleasure her.

"I want to hear you scream my name," he whispered before taking her lips, thrusting his tongue inside her mouth and committing her texture to his mind.

It still wasn't enough — he could never get enough.

"Now, Ari. Your heat is gripping me — I can't hold out anymore," he said as his hands held tightly to her backside.

"Yes...now...Rafe...I'm ready," she agreed, her halting words ending on a groan.

Stars exploded as she sank fully on him, his manhood deep inside her quivering flesh, their groans now mingling together.

Tremors continued racing through his body long after the last of his release. What she did to him was criminal. In that instant, he knew he couldn't let her go — not ever.

Rafe held her tight as their bodies relaxed against each other, her moist heat holding him safely inside her. Even telling himself they needed to get up, needed to move, he couldn't force his body to respond.

He didn't want to let her go — didn't want to put the distance between them that he always insisted on after sex. He wanted to hold her in his arms and fall asleep so they could wake in the morning and start all over again.

Rafe didn't know what was happening to him — but the longer he was around this woman, the more he didn't care.

He felt Ari slump against him and a smile flitted across his lips. Though the night was quickly cooling and their bodies

116

were still fused together, she was so comfortable with him, she had fallen asleep in his arms.

He hated to disturb her, but he had no choice.

"Ari, we need to go out front and get the car. I'm ready to take you home."

"Mmm" was her only response.

With great reluctance, Rafe lifted her from his body, feeling an unaccustomed emptiness as he pulled out of her. She grumbled as she half awoke, but didn't put up further protest.

Rafe straightened their clothing, then led her through a trail to the front of the clubhouse. It took less than a minute for his driver to arrive and for Rafe to step inside the back of the limo. He pulled Ari onto his lap and held her while she fell back to sleep, her head resting on his shoulder.

As he leaned his head back, he didn't know what he was going to do. He was in way over his head with his mistress — his feelings for her were becoming too much of a burden for him to want to deal with.

CHAPTER SEVENTEEN
Shane

SHANE LOOKED AROUND his favorite club and felt nothing but boredom. He needed to get back down to South America, but he had too much going on here to leave right now. The fact that Lia was still in the U.S. wasn't helping him deal with his vow of keeping their relationship platonic.

After she'd been released from the hospital, it had taken all his restraint not to check on her in person, but he didn't trust himself enough to go to her place.

Her parents had come and gone again and Rachel was in and out. If he showed up at her home and she was all alone, he could hardly be held responsible for his actions. For him to be thirty years old and out of control over one woman —that just didn't compute.

"Hey, gorgeous, you haven't been here for a while."

Shane turned up his megawatt smile without a thought. Flirting, to him, was as natural as breathing — he didn't even think about it.

"Hi, Gwen. I've been working a lot lately, sad to say. Don't tell me *you're* here all alone."

"My date turned out to be a total snooze fest. But the night just got a whole lot better since I spotted you. How long am I going to stand here looking beyond fabulous before you buy me a drink?" she asked with an exaggerated pout.

Shane held up his hand and the waiter practically tripped over himself to get to Shane's table. Tipping insane amounts of money, Shane had found, was a very rational tactic.

"My lady friend will have a Manhattan, and I'll have a re-fill."

The man scurried away toward the bar while Gwen sat down, pressing her panting chest against Shane's arm. On some other night he might have been happy to take her home and relieve the ache that was a constant in his life now. But since his kiss with Lia, he just couldn't seem to psych himself up for one of his normal one-night stands. At this rate, he might never have sex again… That thought jolted him into turning to face Gwen, who was practically in his lap.

"I've missed you, Shane. Since sharing your bed, I haven't been properly satisfied — not even once," she said as she traced his chest with one of her long red fingernails. She didn't stop when she reached his pants, and he found himself grabbing her hand before she grabbed hold of him.

"You're not holding anything back tonight, are you, Gwen?"

"I'm extremely aroused, doll; just looking at you always gets my motor humming. Why play coy? You're the best lover I've had in ages and I want a repeat."

Shane heard a gasp and looked up to see his waiter sweating and shaking as he placed their drinks on the table. The poor kid was barely of drinking age, and right now his eyes were directed at Gwen's overflowing cleavage. Shane couldn't blame the kid. She certainly wasn't trying to hide them.

"I've always appreciated your honesty, Gwen, but it's not going to happen tonight," he warned her as he picked up his drink.

"Never say never," she purred, not in the least put off as she lifted her own drink.

While Gwen rubbed up against him, Shane's eyes traveled over the dance floor. Maybe he was just getting too old to play the games he'd once enjoyed so much, over and over and over. Whatever. But he couldn't find even a spark of interest in his old flame.

Gwen continued rubbing against him and just as something like annoyance was starting to set in, Shane's eyes connected with Lia's. He'd almost passed her by in the throng of people on the dance floor, but then his gaze zeroed in and he suddenly felt some excitement in an otherwise dull evening, some emotion to rouse him from his apathy — unfortunately, that emotion was anger.

When did she get there, and what in the hell was she wearing?

Shane's eyes narrowed as they traveled across her skin-tight black dress. If the skirt had been any shorter, the entire club would have seen what color panties she was wearing. Her brother would have killed her if he'd known what she was doing.

She was currently pressed up against some jerk who had his hands all over her. Shane was trying to decide whether to pound the guy in the face, or simply to throw Lia over his shoulder and drag her home kicking and screaming, when he was jostled, his drink spilling from his glass.

"Hey, handsome. Boy, am I glad to see you here. Lia dragged me out tonight and then she hooked up with some hot banker and now I'm just a third wheel."

"Honey, you're a third wheel here, too," Gwen snarled.

"Nice to see you, Rachel," Shane replied.

"Oh, I'm *so* sorry. Am I interrupting something? It's just that I didn't want to be all by myself in this club, where the only thing thicker than the smoke is the sex hormones oozing through the air," Rachel said with big, innocent eyes and a pouty lip.

Shane had to hide the smile fighting to break free. Rachel was one hell of a good actress. She had *innocent schoolgirl* down to a science and she also had a way of bringing him out of his lousy moods. She was just so full of life, with an infectious exuberance about her. He wondered how he could see Lia and Rachel in such different lights.

"Of course you're never interrupting. What would you like to drink?"

"Thanks. I'm parched. I'll take a martini and a plate of hot wings. Lia promised me some good food before she decided to let her hormones lead her to the nearest dance floor, and I'm starving — not that I'll eat well *here*."

Shane's eyes were drawn back to Lia. She was no longer looking at him, but instead rubbing up against a different guy, who looked quite pleased with the situation. Shane's fists clenched in his lap.

"What is your sister doing out? Hasn't she learned her lesson yet?" He couldn't believe Lia had put herself at risk again after landing in the hospital. Was she really that foolish? Maybe he'd misjudged her.

"You know Lia — if you tell her to go right, she'll turn left. She told me that since you're an idiot, she's on the hunt for someone who appreciates that she's a woman. You're not jealous, are you?" Rachel taunted him as she batted her eyes.

Rachel was getting under his skin — not that he'd let her know that. She was also wrong. Lia and he had skirted around a *minor* attraction, but they both knew it wasn't going to lead to anything. Lia was just being a spoiled brat who needed a good spanking. Of course, in this kind of club, that would just be considered foreplay.

"Not at all, Rachel. Lia's a grown woman who's free to do whatever she likes with whomever she pleases," Shane answered through clenched teeth. "For the millionth time, there is nothing going on between the two of us."

"Now that we've got that out of the way, maybe you will remember *I'm* still sitting here. I want to dance, Shane," Gwen demanded.

"Sorry, Gwen. Rachel's like my kid sister. If I leave her here alone, her brother will have my hide," Shane answered, giving her his most apologetic grin.

"Fine, but you could have had one amazing night," she snapped as she scooted out of the booth and stomped off.

"I hope I didn't ruin your plans," Rachel said, her tongue tucked in her cheek.

"Yeah, I bet you are, kid."

"I'm not a kid. In case you haven't noticed, I have real boobs and all, now."

Shane wanted to block that image from his head forever. He snarled at her as he raised his hand for the waiter and ordered more drinks and a few plates of appetizers.

"So, your big sister hasn't gotten the partying out of her system yet?"

"No. But I do have to say, with Mom and Dad on vacation, we're having a blast. We have the house all to ourselves. You know, we're thinking of having a party later on tonight. Want to join us?"

"Why don't you just have some food and get your sister to go home — alone?"

"That will never happen. She's going through a midlife crisis or something."

"She's only twenty-six, Rachel. That's a bit young to have a midlife crisis," he replied with frustration. He was sure he felt gray hairs sprouting.

"You can take that up with her. I'm just tagging along to make sure she doesn't get drugged and attacked again and maybe end up on some stranger's bathroom floor."

"Neither of you would have to worry about that if you didn't go to places like this."

"You're here," she pointed out.

"I'm a lot wiser than the two of you."

"Whatever, Shane. You can either join us or get out of the way," she said stubbornly, crossing her arms in defiance.

Shane suspected it was going to be a very long night. While he sat with Rachel and ate lousy food, his eyes kept straying to Lia. On her fourth dance with the sleazy guy, Shane had had enough.

"I'm getting your sister. It's time to go home," he said, getting up and starting toward the dance floor.

"I don't think she'll like that," Rachel called out after him before her laughter was swallowed up by the music.

Shane prowled forward, parting the crowd to reach Lia. When she was in sight, her dance partner snaked his hand low and squeezed her ass.

"I'm cutting in," Shane said, elbowing the fellow away.

"Find your own date. This one's mine," the man growled and grabbed Lia's arm.

"I'll give you to the count of one before I rearrange your face," Shane threatened, needing to smash something and hoping the guy didn't back down. *Make my day...*

"Sorry, John, the dance is over," Lia told him as she reached for Shane.

"You teasing bitch," the guy spat before turning and getting lost in the crowd. Shane took a step to go after him before Lia grabbed ahold of his hand.

"Are you going to chase after a drunk guy or are you going to dance with me?"

Lia's words spoken close to his ear stopped him. He turned back to face her and she molded her body to his. As her curves aligned to his body, he clenched his teeth, his hands automatically wrapping around her to pull her in tight. It was as if he were powerless over himself when it came to her.

"I thought you were never going to ask me to dance," she said, wiggling her hips against his. Shane instantly hardened, and took a moment to thank whoever had invented the six-inch heels she was sporting.

"You realize you're nothing but trouble, don't you?"

"That's what all the boys say," she answered with a giggle as her breasts rubbed against his chest, and his throbbing body tightened even more.

"Why are you doing this, Lia?"

She looked at him thoughtfully for a few seconds before her eyes dilated. "If I can't have you, then I'm not going to sit at home crying. I'm an attractive, young, wealthy woman whom most men would find a catch. The crap thing is that I'm not attracted to anyone but you, or so it seems. I think you ruined me when I was a teenager, but I'm still searching. I figure one of these guys will turn out to be prince charming eventually."

The sadness in her tone frightened him. She was smiling, as if what she was saying were nothing more than a joke, but he could hear the truth beneath her teasing words. Maybe he should give a relationship with her a try. Hmm...

Shane shook his head. He didn't do relationships. He did one-night stands. It was less complicated. No one got hurt. If he ever hurt Lia, dammit, it would be like ripping a piece of his heart out. He would destroy everything — betray his best friend and lose the entire family. A hot night of sex wasn't worth all that — no matter how tempted he was.

"Don't you think it's time to head home, Lia?"

"I thought you'd never ask." She grabbed his head and pulled him to her as she connected their mouths.

Shane's mind went blank as her teeth bit his bottom lip and her tongue slipped inside. With a sigh of defeat, he grabbed her backside and pulled her tightly against his erection, all thoughts of dancing forgotten. Her hands wound behind his head and her fingers tangled in his hair and he wanted nothing more than to find somewhere to lay her down so he could worship every inch of her body.

Lia's scent invaded his senses, and the noise from the club faded away as blood rushed through his veins. He'd been attracted to many, many women, but none of them had brought him to the brink of passion so quickly. She could consume him in seconds.

A couple bumped into them, bringing Shane back to the present, making him realize he was all over Lia in the middle of a crowded dance floor.

"You're deadly, woman," he said as he pulled back and grabbed her hand. She giggled as he placed her in front of him while leading her to his table. He had to hide his condition until he got himself back under control.

Rachel looked up expectantly at the two of them. Shane raised his hand, then handed several hundreds to the waiter, making the poor guy almost pass out. Then, grabbing Rachel's arm, he led the two women from the club.

His driver picked them up in minutes, and the three climbed into the back of his car; he was thankful that the two sisters had been smart enough to take a taxi to the club.

"This has turned out to be a great evening," Lia purred as she snuggled up close against his side.

"For *you*. I'm not exactly painting the town red," Rachel grumbled.

There was no way Shane would grope Lia with Rachel sitting on his other side. He was more than a little uncomfortable on the fifteen-minute ride to their house as Lia rubbed against him and he had to fight against looking down and gazing at her extraordinary legs. That insanely short dress was sorely testing him.

When they arrived at the Palazzo family house, Shane told his driver to park while he escorted them inside. He knew he shouldn't follow them, but he had to make sure they'd get inside safely. It was the gentlemanly thing to do, after all.

"Let me show you my room, Shane," Lia said as she took his hand and led him up the stairs.

Say no right now. And whatever you do, buddy, don't think about sex. That's just not an option. But somehow he found himself following her. Had she cast some sort of spell over him? Though he knew entering her room was the wrong move to make, he was doing it anyway.

When they reached her door, Lia's face turned a little green and her eyes widened. Shane knew what that meant. He looked around and spotted the door on the other side of her room. Praying it was her bathroom and not a closet, he hoisted her into his arms and rushed forward. They made it just in time for her to empty out her stomach.

Shane held back her hair while she finished, then sat her on the lid of the toilet as he got her a cup of cool water to rinse out her mouth and wet a washcloth to wipe her face.

"How can you keep doing this to yourself, Lia? You have a great life and yet you're putting yourself in these ridiculous situations. Wasn't getting drugged last week bad enough? Now you're working on getting alcohol poisoning."

"I need to lie down" was her only reply. He helped her brush her teeth, then lifted her in his arms and carried her to the very inviting king-sized bed in the center of her room.

How much restraint was one guy supposed to have? He'd damn well better get a medal after all of this because he was pushing his control to the very edge and somehow not diving over. His lower regions would never be the same again – not as long as he continued to deny himself.

Within seconds of lying down, Lia passed out cold. Shane ran his finger down her soft cheek, then bent and pressed a gentle kiss against her lips. As he pulled back, he was confronted with the awful truth: this was beyond a simple crush — and he was in deep trouble.

For about two seconds, Shane considered getting her into her pajamas, then realized how horrific a thought that was. She was drunk and passed out and he was thinking of stripping her. No, it was time he took off. Rachel would look out for Lia and call him if they needed anything. He just had to get out of the house before he wasn't able to.

Shane left the room to find a sleepy Rachel, who agreed to change Lia's clothes and stay with her for the night. With an unbelievable ache in his chest, Shane left the house wondering what the hell he was going to do next.

CHAPTER EIGHTEEN

"COME ON, ARI. You know you want to do this. It will be so much fun!"

Ari looked at Rafe's sisters and couldn't hide her smile. The girls were incredibly convincing when they wanted something, but she got only one day off from Rafe and there was no way she could sneak away for several without him throwing a fit.

Just the thought ticked her off. Rafe didn't own her, contrary to his opinion of the matter. If she wanted to spend a weekend away with friends, and she did consider Lia and Rachel friends, then she could darn well do it. He'd just have to deal with her decision.

"I don't know. It's pretty expensive..." she hedged, riding the fence on whether to join them.

"Oh, pish. It isn't expensive at all. The food is cheap, the liquor even cheaper, and you don't have to worry about airfare or the room. Just say *yes*. You know you want to," Lia insisted.

"What are you girls up to?"

Ari looked up guiltily as Rafe stepped into her office.

"Not that it concerns you, but we want to take our friend on a little weekend trip," Rachel quickly piped up. Ari's temper flared when Rafe narrowed his eyes. At the closed look on his face, her decision was made. He wasn't going to run her life completely. He had enough control as it was.

"Ari is busy this weekend," he said with finality.

"You can't work her seven days a week, Rafe," Lia pouted.

"We have plans."

"Oh, really? What plans?" Rachel countered.

"That's none of your business."

"I want to go with them."

Rafe turned incredulous eyes on Ari and she felt a deep level of satisfaction. Let him think about that. She was sticking with their agreement, but if she wanted a weekend off once in a while, he'd have to deal with it. Heck, if he didn't like her plans, he could always replace her.

The thought of him doing just that caused a small lump to form in her throat. Vivid images took over her brain, images of him with another woman on his arm, and of the two of them in private, doing heaven knew what —oh, but she knew what, and it killed her.

"Where are you girls planning to go?" he asked, now wearing his poker face. Oh, yes, he was a master at hiding his emotions. At the moment he looked as if he didn't have a care in the world. Ari hated it when he acted that way.

"Vegas!" Rachel announced, and began to sing "*Viva, viva…*"

Rafe's expression darkened and a shudder passed through Ari.

"Why do you want to go to Vegas?"

"Do you seriously need to ask that? Um, let me see, hot guys, cheap drinks, exotic shows. Do I need to continue?"

"You've been on a mission to cause as much trouble as possible lately, Lia. I think a trip to Vegas is a train wreck waiting to happen," Rafe scolded.

"Well, it's a good thing I'm over twenty-one then, isn't it? I can go wherever I want to."

Rafe and Lia glared at each other for several tense moments before Rafe shrugged. Before Ari could get too excited over his apparent acquiescence, he spoke again.

"Fine. If you insist on going, I can't stop you. I'll just have to escort you there. I have business I can take care of in the city."

"We weren't inviting you," Rachel spoke up, her eyes rounding in near panic.

"Tough. I'll call Shane. We have a new hotel going in and we can check on its progress."

At the mention of Shane's name, Lia perked right up and Ari knew she was done for. Her weekend with the girls had just turned into a family affair. She didn't know whether to be excited or…OK, she'd say it to herself! — *pissed off*. At the fuming look in Rafe's eyes, excitement was starting to win out.

"If you insist, I guess you can tag along. There are rules, though," Lia warned.

At her words, Rafe's lips quirked, and he lifted an eyebrow and waited. Ari knew he was thinking, *This ought to be good.*

"This is a girl trip, which means we get time alone. You don't get to trail us everywhere we go, and you *don't* get to rain on our parade for having a good time. That means no bodyguards tagging along, and no telling us we aren't allowed out of the room unless you're by our side."

"And if I don't agree to your rules?"

"Then we'll sneak Ari out of here right now and disappear to some unknown location where you'll never be able to find us," Rachel piped up with a confident smile.

Rafe couldn't help himself — he burst out laughing. Ari's jaw dropped at the sound. The man was handsome when he was brooding, but with a smile on his face and laughter pouring from him, he was breathtaking.

His eyes caught hers; his laughter died and his pupils dilated. Ari knew that look well, and she expected to be feeling *very* satisfied not too long after Rafe's sisters left the room.

"I'll agree to let you go to a show on your own, but you have to keep your cell phones with you in case something happens. You also have to use my driver. I'm not agreeing to your…request for no bodyguards until I assess the situation."

"Fine. We'll agree to that…for now. We'll discuss the bodyguard issue later," Lia conceded.

"Good. Now, get out. Ari and I have a lot of work to do."

"I'll just bet you do," Rachel snickered as she grabbed her sister's arm and led her from the room.

Ari swallowed as Rafe steadily walked to the door and casually turned the lock. The sound of it latching seemed like a loud boom to her sensitive ears — her heart picked up speed.

As he turned around with a predator's gleam in his eyes, she stood on trembling legs and automatically began backing away. She didn't understand why, because she wanted him to take her. Her body was more than ready.

"You know, Ari, when this all started I was very generous in giving you one day a week to yourself."

He spoke as he advanced on her slowly but steadily, as if he had all the time in the world. And he did. Ari stopped in the middle of the room, refusing to retreat any further.

"I've decided I'll take whatever time I want for myself," she answered him bravely.

"That doesn't work for me. You see, we have an agreement — and the deal we've made doesn't have provisions to change the rules halfway through the game."

"You don't own me, Rafe. I've played along with you, but I'm still my own person and I can do whatever makes me happy. If I want to take a weeklong vacation, then I will do just that!"

A gleam entered his eyes as if he was hearing exactly what he wanted. Excitement coursed through Ari. She should be furious with him, but their little dance was stirring feelings inside her that rivaled a volcanic explosion.

The closer his steps brought him to her, the stronger her cravings grew.

"I don't think so. It just might be time for you to be reminded of our agreement."

"You can't make me stay," she called, though she didn't want to leave. She *should* want to run screaming, but she was rooted to the spot.

"You're right. I would never force you to do anything. I *will* certainly persuade you — I *will* demand obedience, but the bottom line is that you can walk out the door at any time."

Ari looked into his eyes as she tried to figure out what he was doing now. Was he releasing her from her duty — calling her debt *paid in full*? Did she want it to be over or would she be devastated? Confusion coursed through her.

"You don't want to go. I think you're very satisfied, but you don't want to admit to that. You think that admitting to liking our arrangement makes you a bad person. There's no shame in feeling excitement over what others find taboo. Leave the rest of the world out of this. It's just you and me — right here — right now."

"I don't know what you want!" she said in frustration.

"I want to remind you of who I am — I want to leave no doubt in your mind that I'm the one in charge. I *choose* to give you choices, but I can take them away when I'm unhappy."

"Do you want me to leave?"

He stopped with a genuine expression of puzzlement. His brow furrowed as if he needed to think about her statement.

She held her breath as she awaited his response. This could be it. Maybe he was offering her freedom.

Ari's heart sunk with the realization. She didn't want to be free of him — not yet. She would, she convinced herself, just not at this moment.

"You have a decision to make, Ari. You can stay and take your punishment, or you're free to walk out that door — all debts settled."

Ari couldn't turn her gaze away from Rafe's intense stare. He was offering her an out. It had only been a month since they'd made their deal. She'd agreed to three months. She expected to hate every minute of it, but she'd never felt more alive. *Was he unhappy with her performance?*

If she stayed, though, she'd be shifting the power to him. He'd know he owned her — know he could do whatever he wanted.

Ripping her gaze from his, she looked toward the door. It was right there — all she had to do was walk through it and she could have her life back. Her mother was fine, back at work and oblivious to the difficulties her daughter had suffered in the past year. Ari's life could return to normal.

She opened her mouth to speak but couldn't get words to surface. Rafe didn't move as he waited for her decision. When several uncomfortable moments had passed, Ari finally gazed into his eyes. When she saw a flicker of emotion cross his face, she knew she wasn't leaving.

"I agreed to three months. I don't go back on my word," she said. There was no way she would admit to staying for any other reason. For a split second she thought she observed relief in his expression, but she had to be wrong. Rafe didn't really care if she stayed or went — did he?

In the blink of an eye he crossed the room and walked her backward until he had her pinned to the desk.

"This is your choice, Ari. You had better be sure," he commanded, his mouth an inch from her own, his scent surrounding her, stirring her appetite.

"I'll stay, but I won't ever be what you want. I'll never submit to you, Rafe."

Staying strong was the only way she could justify her decision. If ever the day came that she gave herself fully over to him, she feared it would be too much — that she'd never be the same again.

"Ah, it will be my mission to change your mind — and, Ari — I'll fully enjoy the challenge," he said with a smile before his mouth crashed down on hers.

Ari grabbed his shoulders and held on. She could pretend this wasn't what she wanted, but what would be the point. She was hungry and it had nothing to do with food.

Rafe punished her mouth, kissing her fervently until she could no longer breathe. His hands moved down her body, molding her curves and tugging her tight against him. She squirmed to get closer, gasping as she felt his hardness press against her belly.

Desire pooled in her core, waiting for him to enter her slick folds. It was always so good. He hadn't touched her in two days and she was about to explode in his arms. He'd turned her into an insatiable animal, and she didn't care.

Rafe pulled away and she whimpered. *No!* She needed him to finish what he'd started. She could later berate herself for wanting him so much, but right now, she needed him inside her, needed to feel the conjunction of their bodies.

Without a word, he turned her around and hiked her skirt just enough for her cheeky *Victoria's Secret* panties to show. Oh, *yes*, they hadn't done it on a desk yet. Oh, the places he'd taken her – the kitchen table, in front of the giant fireplace, against the front door – but not yet bent over her desk. Anticipation built as he slid her panties down her legs and bent her across her desk.

His hand pushed against her back before sliding down the curve of her bottom and into the V of her legs. He pushed against her thighs, spreading them wide, then slid two fingers deep inside her heat.

"Rafe!" she called, her desire so intense it was almost painful. She wanted him buried deep inside her.

His fingers pulled out and then nothing touched her but the warm air drifting through the room. She squirmed beneath him, but he held her tightly against the desk as he stood behind her, so close, but not nearly close enough.

"Now," she demanded as she twisted beneath him.

Suddenly he pushed inside her, his hard staff plunging deeper than he'd gone before. He stopped when she was completely full, and then bent forward, his breath brushing across her neck.

"Tell me I'm in charge, Ari," he whispered, as his body moved backward before he thrust inside her again.

"No."

"Tell me," he demanded as he plunged in and out.

"No." She was so close, almost delirious from the building pressure.

Rafe pushed in and out of her several more times, his hips slapping against the softness of her backside as he gripped her hips tightly.

She was reaching the edge when he slammed against her, taking her breath away, and then his body began to shake as he groaned low in his throat. A few more strokes and he stopped. Ari pushed against him. She was on the edge, needing just a little more of a push to reach her goal.

He pulled from her and turned her in his arms. Satisfaction filled his features as he pulled her tightly against him.

"I like your defiance, Ari, but now you get to suffer the rest of the day. When you submit and follow my rules — I'll reward you with more pleasure than you can image."

Ari gasped in frustration. Her eyes narrowed as she looked into his confident eyes. He was so sure she'd cave — that he held all the power. She could go into the bathroom and take matters into her own hands, but then he'd have a victory.

Her victory would come by showing him that it didn't matter. She pulled back and pushed her skirt down before holding out her hand.

"Do you want something?" he asked innocently.

"My panties, please?"

"No — I think I'll hold onto them. You can think about what you're missing out on as the air caresses your womanhood all day."

Rafe turned and walked to her door, unlocking it before turning around. "If you want me to relieve the ache, all you have to do is come to me, sit on my desk, and ask." His gaze held hers for several tense seconds as he smiled in victory.

Ari glared at him, feeling ready to scream as he walked through the door and left her standing there, nearly shaking in her frustration. If she wanted him to own her pride, she could go to him, but this was a game — one that she was determined to win.

With as much dignity as she could carry, Ari patted down her hair, then followed him, making a beeline for the women's bathroom, where she could clean herself up. As she wiped away the evidence of their quick joining, her body shuddered.

It would be so easy to ease her ache, but he'd know and then he'd win. With a growl of frustration she washed her hands and walked back to her office. Not having her panties on intensified the throbbing. It was going to be a long afternoon.

As she sat at her desk, a smile appeared. Either she could sit there and pout, or she could plot revenge. He might think he held the power, but it was time she started turning things around. Yes, he was in possession of her panties, but that meant that he knew she was naked beneath her skirt. She would see who cried uncle first.

With that thought, Ari got back to work, feeling a lot better about the way things would go over the next day — week — even month.

CHAPTER NINETEEN

" **A**RI, REPORT TO my office immediately."

Well, that was rude. Hesitating for a moment so she wouldn't snap, Ari took a calming breath before hitting the reply button on her speaker.

"Do I need to bring anything?"

"Yes. Your laptop. My secretary became ill and had to leave for the day, and I have an important meeting in fifteen minutes. I need you to take notes."

"I'll be right there, Mr. Palazzo." It seemed only fitting to use his last name when he was acting the way he was.

"Ari…" Her name came out on an exasperated breath. She chose not to reply.

Sitting for a few moments, Ari glared at her phone. First, he had the gall to take her in his office without offering her any satisfaction, then he took her panties with him, and now he was demanding she take notes for him. Take, take, take. Who did he think he was?

She thought briefly about ignoring his summons and staying right where she was. But after her initial impulse to defy him had simmered down, Ari smiled. He was giving her a great opportunity for retaliation.

They both knew she had nothing on beneath her skirt. Maybe it was time for her to remind him of that fact, which would be especially fun in a room full of people where he could do nothing about her taunts.

With a determined set to her shoulders, Ari stood, grabbing her laptop. She stopped by the bathroom, applying shiny red lipstick and unbuttoning her top button. With a gleam in her eyes, she made her way to Rafe's office.

Since his door was open, she sauntered in, wondering what her next move should be. She'd never been a seductress before and didn't know where to start.

"The meeting is in the formal conference room. Follow me."

He didn't even bother glancing up as he delivered another curt order. This must be something important — even better!

Ari trailed behind Rafe down the hallway and they entered a large room with a massive table surrounded by twenty chairs. She hadn't been there before and had to admit that the décor impressed her.

Elegant snacks and beverages sat atop the table, and the chairs, though suitably businesslike, looked plush and comfortable This room was clearly designed to welcome superstar investors and clients.

A smidgen of fear slithered down her spine at the thought of playing games with him in such an environment. When she was just about to talk herself out of antagonizing him, she stiffened her shoulders and reminded herself that he always managed to get the upper hand. It was time he lost a bout.

"Sit in the chair on the end next to mine. Type up everything we speak about; there's no need for you to contribute. I've been working with these men for two years now on a deal that is invaluable to the Palazzo Corporation."

"I understand," she said through gritted teeth.

Rafe took his seat, and Ari slowly moved toward her chair. Just before sitting down, she stumbled, making sure she fell against him. Rafe caught her with quick reflexes, leaving her face inches from his own.

Pressing her body in more tightly against his, and breathing against his neck, she remained there for a few seconds longer than necessary before trailing her hand along his thigh and whispering in his ear. "I'm so sorry about that, Rafe. What a klutz I'm being."

His short intake of breath gave her a measure of satisfaction. Using his thigh to help herself back up, she made sure he had ample opportunity to see her cleavage, then she stood up and went to her chair.

She could have called him on being a Neanderthal and not holding her chair out for her, but they were working — this wasn't a date.

"Try to be more careful," he finally said, his normally tight control just the tiniest bit unraveled.

"Oh, I will," she purred at him as she leaned forward with her elbow on the table, squeezing her arms together. When his eyes shot down to her chest, she fought back the smile wanting to burst forth as she leaned back while rubbing her painted fingernail against her thigh, raising her skirt, reminding him she was pantyless. His sharp intake of air was a well-earned reward.

"Mr. Palazzo, your visitors have arrived."

The two of them looked up to see one of his employees standing in the doorway with a clipboard.

"Send them in. We're ready," Rafe responded, instantly back to businessman mode. Ari would just have to shake him right back out of that.

Rafe stood as several men walked into the room. Ari was unsure whether she should stand or not, so she did the safe thing and rose from her seat. When the final visitor walked in, her mouth dropped open for an instant.

The man had to be several inches over six feet tall, and his olive skin and sparkling near-black eyes fit his masculine features perfectly. The bold red sash over the front of his dark suit made the man stand out even more.

Ari had no doubt he was the one in charge. His eyes scanned the room and honed in on hers, his lips turning up in a smile as he moved forward.

"Prince Adriane, I hope your travels went well," Rafe said as he offered his hand.

"Yes, I have had quite the pleasant journey. Thank you, Rafe. Now, who is this divine creature?"

Both men turned to stare at Ari, and she had to fight not to melt to the ground. With Rafe's intense purple eyes gazing at her, and *Prince* Adriane's dynamic black ones doing the same, she was rooted to the spot.

Holy hell, the two of them could start a war with a single word as long as they stood side by side. She felt as if she should pull out her camera and start snapping pictures for a magazine spread.

"My secretary became ill, so Arianna is filling in for her today," Rafe finally answered. Ari barely managed to hide her irritation at his words. Yet that was exactly what she was doing. She didn't expect him say, *This is my mistress, whom I screwed in her office a few minutes ago.* She thought maybe he might have been a bit warmer with the introduction, though — to let the men know she wasn't available.

Ari nearly laughed aloud at that thought. This was a freaking prince, for goodness sake, and certainly wouldn't be asking her out on a date. His men hadn't even bothered looking at her, so she was pretty safe with them. Man, she needed to pull herself together.

Prince Adriane stepped forward, walking with sure movements until he was standing right before her. He reached out and grasped her fingers, raising her hand slowly to his lips as he bent forward and kissed her just above the knuckles.

"Such a beauty may call me Ian," he practically purred.

Ari couldn't help a slight swoon at his velvet-smooth voice. She'd never met a man so suave. She was sure he had an entire harem willing and ready to do anything he asked.

"It's a pleasure to meet you, Ian," she finally gasped, wanting to smack herself for the breathy sound of her voice.

"Now that introductions have been made, let us start the meeting."

Ari was yanked out of her trance by the deadly steel behind Rafe's voice. He sounded angry, though she couldn't figure out why. Yes, she'd sounded a bit awed, but surely she wasn't acting abundantly ridiculous.

"Yes, sir," she muttered as she pulled her hand back and waited for Rafe and the prince to take their seats. She didn't want to commit a faux paus by sitting first.

"Please sit, Arianna. My men wouldn't dare be so rude as to have a seat before a beautiful lady has first become comfortable."

This man was good — really good. Ari was back to feeling as if she were melting.

"Yes, please have a seat, Ari," Rafe quietly growled.

Ari's head whipped around to look into his tumultuous eyes. He was undoubtedly ticked off. Maybe now wasn't the time to pursue a mission of revenge, with Rafe so dangerously moody.

Ari sat down, then watched in amazement as Rafe and Prince Adriane took their seats. Only then did the rest of the men sit, as well.

Twenty minutes into the meeting, Ari's fascination with the prince had dimmed. Yes, he was still just as stunning, and yes, his voice could melt butter, but her eyes were drawn to only one man in the room — Rafe.

The prince continually looked her way, but soon Ari was able to tune out the flirtatious looks and smooth voice, and simply do her job of taking notes of the meeting.

If she put everything else aside, what they were planning was quite amazing. If it worked, thousands of jobs would be created and better conditions brought to both the prince's country and some impoverished areas in the U.S.

As she continued taking notes, she learned more about Rafe. She knew he had a good heart beneath the hard exterior he showed to the world, but listening to the excitement enter his voice as he spoke of a multibillion-dollar merger was still eye-opening. She had a feeling he would do so much good during his lifetime — control issues aside.

Without her realizing it, several hours passed. She could have sat there all night listening to his and the prince's plans.

"Rafe, I think we have a deal. I look forward to getting this started. We'll meet in January to break ground." Prince Adriane stood up and stretched his arms. He had removed his jacket earlier, and the sight of his muscles flexing beneath the white silk of his shirt proved a real treat. Ari might not want the prince, but that didn't mean she was immune to his aura. She was human, after all.

"I have to admit, this is the first project I've been truly excited over in some time," Rafe said. "I look forward to spending time in your beautiful country. I hope you feel the same about your time here in the States."

"Yes, I am going to take some time off in a couple of months to observe the better areas here where I would like to see our business grow. I haven't had time in a while to relax, but with your people so kind and helpful, I always find myself quite happy after a vacation here."

"We'll have to get together when you return."

"I will give you a call." He then turned to Ari. "It was a rare treat to meet you, my lady. I look forward to seeing you again." With those words, he kissed her hand once more, before walking from the room.

Ari was glad she wasn't expected to come up with a reply, because she had no clue what to say.

It was a minute after the door shut that she realized she was still staring at it. She also realized she was standing alone in the room with a very riled-up Rafe.

"It appears you were quite fond of the prince," he snapped.

"I was being polite. Did I do something to upset you?"

"I don't share my mistresses, Ari," he reminded her. As if she didn't know that already! She wanted to call him on his idiocy, but thought better of it.

"I'm not interested in the prince, but considering he was the first royal person I've ever met, I was a bit starstruck. I'm so sorry if I'm not as sophisticated as you." Ari had to suddenly fight tears. He was making her feel like a fool.

He might have been used to mixing in high circles, but she wasn't. She'd read about princes in books and magazines, had watched movies on Lifetime TV about princes marrying poor maidens, but she'd never thought she'd meet a real live prince. *Of course* she was a bit flustered.

Even if she had imagined meeting a royal, she never would have expected him to call her beautiful and kiss her hand. Rafe could stick his crappy attitude where the sun didn't shine. She wasn't going to allow him to make her feel bad when she should be floating on a cloud.

She turned to storm from the room when Rafe grabbed her arm and whipped her back around to face him. He studied her face for several long seconds, then his features relaxed and he softened his grip, pulling her tightly against his chest.

"I apologize. I'm not prone to jealousy, but you tend to bring out the worst in me. You did nothing wrong." He bent

145

down and gently caressed her lips in a tender kiss. Ari's anger evaporated as she leaned into him.

How she could go from humiliated to seduced in a couple of seconds, she would never know, but Rafe had a way of doing that to her. As she swayed in his arms, she knew the difference between being starstruck and being swept off her feet.

The prince had certainly made her swoon a bit, but Rafe... Well, Rafe made her feel as if the ground were coming up to swallow her whole. He did things to her she couldn't come close to describing.

"It's late; I'll order dinner in," he said as he draped his arm around her shoulder and led her from the room.

For one moment, Ari allowed herself to lean into him. It had been a roller-coaster ride of a day and she could afford to let down her defenses for a brief moment. How badly could it really hurt her in the end?

A lot more than she was prepared to deal with.

CHAPTER TWENTY

"I WANT YOU TO know that my friend Amber is furious with me. She can't believe I'm leaving for a fun-filled weekend while she's stuck at home with a sick child."

"That's what happens when you get all happy, fall in love and start producing the next generation. You miss out on all the fun," Lia said with a laugh.

"Do you not want kids?"

"I want an entire houseful of the little monsters, but not for a few more years. I'm still too selfish to dedicate my life to a brood of children, but someday I want them crawling all over me. I know that sounds strange, but the thought of being all alone later on in life isn't appealing. I want noise during the holidays, and messy fingerprints on the cupboards. I want the whole white-picket-fence thing," Lia answered.

"I can see it now," Ari joked. "A Palazzo in a megamansion surrounded by a white picket fence." Still, she sat back and thought about Lia's words. She'd never really thought very deeply about a family. She'd always just assumed she'd have one someday. That's what people did — they grew up, got married and had kids.

What if she didn't want them? What if she never got beyond being self-absorbed and then ended up an old lady with twenty cats? As she and Rafe's sisters pulled up to the airport, doubts flooded her. She was way too young to be stressing over such a thing, so she needed to push it from her mind and focus on today only.

"OK, enough of this talk, you two. We're about to board a beautiful jet, and set off to fabulous Las Vegas. I want the weekend to be about hot guys stripping and all-I-can-drink-margaritas," Rachel demanded.

Her words pulled Ari from her disturbing thoughts — that was until they approached Rafe's jet. Ari's nerves jumped as they neared the steps. The last time she'd entered Rafe's jet from this location, she'd been given an ultimatum. Approaching the beautiful aircraft now brought the turmoil she'd felt that dark day to the forefront of her mind.

"What took you ladies so long? Do you always need to make an entrance?"

"You know we do because we're fabulous," Rachel quipped as she ran up the steps.

Ari turned to face Rafe and her stomach clenched. Only two days ago, she'd had the choice to leave him, yet here she was, about to board his jet again. After his intense lovemaking in her office, and then the even more intense board meeting with the prince, he'd been called away and she hadn't seen him since.

"I can see you're fighting yourself again, Ari. Sometimes it's much better to just go with the moment and not overthink everything," he said as his arms wrapped around her and he leaned down to gently kiss her lips.

It was these moments when he was so human, so caring, that confused her most. Mr. Hyde she could handle, Dr. Jekyll, not so much.

"I'm just looking forward to Vegas," she said in a falsely high voice.

"Good. I think you'll enjoy the trip if my sisters don't get you into too much trouble."

"I happen to be very fond of your sisters," she replied honestly.

"That's how they get you. They suck you in and then you become one of them," he warned with a wiggle of his brows.

"I'm standing right here," Lia said as she smacked his wrist. "Come on, Ari. Ignore my worthless brother." Lia grabbed her arm and pulled her up the stairs.

Knowing Rafe was right behind her, most likely staring at her rear end, made Ari put a little more wiggle in her hips. He'd left her hurting; now with an audience, he couldn't do anything, so she decided finally to repay the favor. Prince Adriane had thrown her off her game, but she was making a grand comeback.

They all boarded, but Shane was running late, so Rafe told them to settle in and have a drink and snack. Ari chatted with Lia and Rachel for a while, then turned her head and noticed Rafe sitting in one of the corner chairs, working on his computer.

Slowly, she stood and walked toward him. His eyes lifted and he watched her with suspicion. She stopped and bent down so only he could hear her.

"I had a dream about you last night."

His eyes widened as he waited for her to continue.

"I think it's the best sex I've ever experienced. I was a little sad to wake up and find out it wasn't real." Rafe's eyes narrowed as he reached for her. She backed up just out of his reach before she leaned in again. "By the way, I'm not wearing any panties — or a bra."

With that she turned and walked back to his sisters. The air exploding from his lungs was sufficient enough to put her in an incredibly good mood. She only hoped he ached the entire flight to Vegas.

After another ten minutes passed, Ari could still feel Rafe's gaze burning a hole through her. She finally looked up and met his desire filled-eyes. Though she was melting from the inside out, she winked at him as she lifted her glass and licked the rim.

As his eyes narrowed, she grabbed an ice cube from the drink and ran it along her neck, the cold liquid dripping down her shirt. "It's really warm in here, don't you think?" she asked him.

"Why don't I take you in the back? I can crank up the air conditioner so you don't overheat," he responded as he rose to his feet. Ari had no intention of caving in to him — the point was to make him suffer. Slowly, she walked to him, rubbing against his chest.

"I don't think so. You left me high and…wet the other day; now it's your turn," she said with a smile as she quickly backed away.

"You're not going anywhere, Ari," he growled, stepping forward. Dancing backward quickly, Ari found safety in between Rachel and Lia. Rafe didn't look as if he were going to let his sisters stop his advance. The thought of the way he might retaliate made her stomach tremble.

"I'm here! The party can officially start."

Ari jumped at the sound of Shane's voice as he walked inside the aircraft. The distraction of his arrival was better than a bucket of cold water. Rafe stopped in his tracks, and everyone turned toward the newcomer.

Ari bent down and grabbed another ice cube to run along her neck just to drive the nail in a bit harder with Rafe, and when he turned back in her direction, she could swear there was steam coming from his ears.

Looking down at his pants, she noticed a definite bulge. This was one round she was winning.

"Thanks, love," Shane said as he grabbed Rachel's drink; she snarled at him.

"Nice of you to join us," Rafe commented dryly after quickly pulling himself together.

"Duty called. Sorry," Shane replied, though he didn't look the least bit apologetic.

Rafe let the captain know they were ready, and soon the door was shut and the jet was rolling toward the runway. Vegas was only a short flight away, and Ari couldn't contain her excitement as the jet began its ascent.

"What was so important that you had to keep all of us waiting?" Lia asked.

"I don't want to bore you with business. We're on our way to Sin City. It's time to have some fun."

"Do you even know what fun is, Shane? Last time I checked, you were the babysitter, trying to kill all the fun of an otherwise perfect night."

"You're just pouty, Lia, because I've now had to save you at two separate occasions in which you keeled over at my feet," Shane replied with a wink.

"Do you want me to kneel at your feet in undying, heartfelt gratitude, you pretentious pig?"

Before Shane could make a response, Rafe cut in.

"Lia, what has gotten into you?"

"Chill, big brother. I was just kidding. If anybody needs to have a little fun while we're in Vegas, it's you."

"I'd appreciate it if you didn't harass Shane," he warned.

"Last time I checked, Shane was a big boy. I think he can defend himself. Do you need your bestie to defend your honor, Shane?"

"I know exactly how to handle you, Lia."

"Oh, really, and how's that?"

"Never has a little girl needed to be bent over a knee and spanked as much as you do."

Lia's mouth hung open as fire burned from her eyes. "I'm not a little girl, Shane!"

"Quit acting like one, then."

Ari watched Lia cross her arms and sit back. Now both men were irritated, and Ari had to chuckle to herself that these confident businessmen were allowing women to get under their skin. If only their board members could see them now.

Amid all the tension, Ari decided to take full advantage. Rafe looked up and their gazes connected. Slowly, she crossed one leg over the other, causing her already short skirt to ride up almost indecently high on her toned thighs.

With a painted fingernail, she rubbed the edge of her skin where the fabric of her skirt rested, then slipped her index finger inside and pulled the material another inch higher. Rafe gaze was glued to the movement of her hand, making her feel triumphant and feminine.

Bringing her hand up, she toyed with the V of her blouse, then waited for him to look her in the eyes again. Batting her eyelashes at him, she pasted on a wide-eyed, innocent expression, suggesting she had no idea why he was squirming in his seat.

Sending a glare her way, Rafe quickly stood, and Ari wondered whether she might have just lost the round — was he going to come over and carry her off? Not that it would have been much of a loss — unless he left her aching.

"Let's go to the back and discuss business," Rafe finally said, and he and Shane walked from the main sitting area.

Ari was shocked until she realized she'd gotten to him so much, he'd had to run away. It was a powerful feeling.

As soon as the men were gone, Rachel leaned in.

"Good job, Lia. Way to get them out of here."

Ari was glad they hadn't seemed to notice her seductive little ploys. Or maybe they just weren't saying anything.

"I got the tickets for Thunder from Down Under, and we'll be in the VIP section. Mmm, I hope we get to do some touching."

"Rachel!" Ari said with shock as she looked toward the back of the jet, praying Rafe couldn't overhear.

"Don't be a prude, Ari. This is a girls' trip. Now I know Rafe will put his foot down if he knows where we're really going, so we're telling him we're going to the La Rêve performance and then dinner. He'll probably figure it out when I post pictures of me groping the hot guys, but by then it will be too late for him to stop us," Lia said with a big smile.

Ari gulped at the thought of Rafe's reaction when he saw pictures of that kind. After the way he'd acted over Prince Adriane, she was going to make sure her hands weren't anywhere near any strippers' body parts.

"He doesn't own you, Ari. Besides, a little jealousy is a good thing. It reminds your man not to take you for granted. Don't let him walk on you — and don't forget that you're a stunning, sexy catch. Make him chase you."

"I'm not worried, Lia. It's just that your brother can be… well, I guess, intense," Ari finished lamely.

"That just means better sex." Rachel sent her a wink before she got up and headed to the bathroom.

The men returned a few minutes later, and the women's discussion was put on hold as the jet began to make its descent into Vegas. As Ari looked out the window and saw the bright lights of the Vegas Strip appear, excitement bubbled through her veins.

Whether she paid for it later or not, she was going to have one heck of a fun weekend. As they made their way down the stairs, Rafe reached for her as she hit the bottom step.

"Are you having fun with your games, Ari?"

"I don't know what you're talking about," she countered.

"You never do lie well," he reminded her.

"Obviously, I won that round," she said, feeling not only satisfied, but victorious as well.

"Did you really win, Ari? Yes, you made me hard, but I bet right now, you are soaking wet, and aching for me to slam inside you. Plus, I still have your panties," he countered with a smirk as he shifted his hand in his pocket implying they were in there. Ari looked around at the others in their party, hoping he didn't have them, and *really* hoping that if he did, he wouldn't pull them out. Her victory had been very short-lived.

Grrr, the man was driving her insane. Just once, she needed to win. Was that asking too much? With an angry scowl, she stomped off, refusing to give him the pleasure of seeing her grab for the trophy panties.

The sound of Rafe's laughter followed her as she made her way to the waiting limo. Let him laugh now — she would figure out a way to bring him to his knees sooner or later. The victory would be oh so much sweeter because she'd been waiting so long.

CHAPTER TWENTY-ONE

STEPPING THROUGH THE double doors onto the marble floors of the foyer, Ari was stunned. Such elegance! Such extravagance! She walked through the Venetian Suite to its tall living room windows to look upon the Las Vegas Strip twinkling far below.

"What a beautiful room," she gasped as she looked around. The penthouse featured virtually everything a person could imagine. Two stunning marbled bathrooms with deep jetted tubs and separate all-glass showers, a spacious bedroom with an enticing king-size bed, a living room with a glowing fireplace, and a dining area with a table that had seating for their entire party, plus a few extras.

"Yes, I always enjoy my stays here. The hotel and casino that we're developing will have much of the same. I build only the best," Rafe said as he took off his jacket.

"Ari, you have thirty minutes to dress. We're heading out soon," said Rachel, while appearing through a doorway with a big smile on her face.

"Where is your room?"

"Right next door; the rooms connect. I'll be right back," she called as she flew past and went through a doorway that Ari hadn't even noticed.

The suite was bigger than most people's homes. Ari was afraid of getting used to a life of such luxury.

"You have a moment to enjoy a glass of champagne and strawberries, don't you?" Rafe asked as he approached holding a bubbling flute out to her.

With an appreciative smile, Ari accepted the glass and took a sip. She really didn't like champagne, but she didn't want to spoil the moment by seeming ungrateful. Walking to the table, she picked up one of the juicy red berries and took a bite, the sweet fruit squirting into her mouth. When she took her next sip of the champagne, its taste had greatly improved.

Maybe that was the trick with the awful stuff. She managed to finish her glass in between bites of berry.

"Thank you," she said to Rafe before gathering some clothes and walking into her large bathroom. No, it wasn't quite as nice as Rafe's — what did she expect? — but, with the marble tile and counters, she wasn't hurting.

Although Rachel had put her on a time crunch, Ari couldn't resist taking a quick shower. Her toiletries were already laid out, after all, and it didn't take her long to wash, dry and dress.

She felt a bit like a princess as she sat on the comfortable bench and applied her makeup in front of the vanity mirror. This was something she'd love to have in her own home some-day — a place she could pamper herself in the most comfort-able way possible.

But a glance in the cheval mirror made Ari cringe. Lia had insisted that she wear the outfit, but Rafe would have a fit when he saw it. Was Lia trying to infuriate her brother or did the girl just like really short, tight dresses? Either way, Ari didn't know what was worse — arguing with Lia, or fighting with Rafe.

As she gathered up her courage to open the bathroom doors, she gave herself a pep talk. Tonight was supposed to be all about fun — something she hadn't had enough of lately.

*****

"Are you sure you ladies wouldn't like to have us along for protection?"

"If we wanted bodyguards, we'd hire some of the sexy men advertising themselves on all these nice billboards, Shane."

"Ouch! That wounds me deeply, Lia."

"I think you're just pretending to be worried about us, but deep down, even a man as manly-man such as yourself, is dying to see La Rêve. I'm sure we'll be safe among the other ten thousand people out walking on this stretch of Las Vegas Boulevard," Rachel mocked.

"I'm not dissing your dancing show, but I'll take the Ultimate Fighting Championship fight card that's on this weekend any day over a chick concert, even if it is at a nice venue."

"Oh, you macho, macho man. How could we have been so wrong about you?" Lia said as the door opened.

Rafe was trying hard to tune out the bantering between his little sisters and Shane while he waited for Ari to appear. He wished that the three of them would leave so he could show Ari what happened to little teases. Her act on the jet deserved to be…rewarded.

He couldn't even pretend he hadn't liked it. He'd been ready to throw her on his bed and sink deep inside her, but he wanted more than that. Her growing confidence was like fuel to a fire. He wanted to take her so hard, she wouldn't be able to sit down for a week.

"Are you kidding me?"

Everyone in the room had stopped talking and turned in his direction before Rafe realized he'd spoken the words out loud. At what must have been a furious expression on his face,

Ari had the nerve to smirk at him before sending a wink his way and then swaying her hips as she walked up to Lia and Rachel.

"Is there a problem, Rafe?" the minx asked innocently.

Hell yes, there was a problem. Her dress was indecently short and hugging her in all his favorite places, and with her hair tied back in an elegant knot, the smooth lines of her neck screamed its own come-on to half of the world. Rafe knew that every single — and married — man who came within twenty feet of her would be picturing himself in the most X-rated positions known to man — and those images were for him alone.

"Don't you think you're dressed a bit inappropriately for a nice show?"

As his sisters gasped in outrage and disbelief, Rafe knew he'd said the wrong thing. He'd never win this battle. Even if Ari gave in and decided to cover herself up, his sisters would drag her from the room first. Rafe *really* hated it when women banded together. They were more impenetrable that way than the freaking Great Wall of China.

"On that note, we'll be leaving now, you egotistical a-hole," Rachel said as she took Ari's arm and pulled her from the room.

Rafe thought about chasing after her, but then he saw Shane's face and sent a withering look his way before walking to the wet bar and pouring himself a double shot.

"You know, you were the object of their fury first," Rafe reminded him. Shane's laughter spilled out and Rafe had to admit the humor of the situation.

"Damn, Rafe. With you around, I look like a superhero. I think we need to start double-dating again like we did back in the day. You play bad cop, because you've got the role down pat. I'll swoop in and save the poor damsels."

"And how does that help me?"

Oh, I was just thinking of myself, but I guess there are *some* women out there who like assholes."

If Rafe hadn't known his friend so well, he might have been tempted to slug him, but even though Shane was wearing a deadpan expression as he spoke, the twinkle in his eyes gave him away.

"I need to get out of this room," Shane said. "Let's go play cards."

"I've never understood your desire to gamble, Shane. You sit there playing a game in which the outcome doesn't affect you in the least. Who cares if you win twenty thousand? You have more money than you'll ever need in this lifetime, and the next."

"Rafe, why are you always so serious? The point is to sit at a table with other people, let loose, drink a lot, and, most importantly, watch the entertainment."

"You expect me to go to the Pussycat Lounge again?"

"Come on, Rafe. You have to admit, the dealers are a whole lot easier to look at than at most places," Shane answered with a laugh.

"I'd rather work."

"Tough. You dragged me to Vegas and we have nothing to do until tomorrow. Tonight we get drunk, eye the ladies and lose a bunch of money."

Rafe thought about refusing, but it had been a while since he'd enjoyed himself like that. Besides, he knew Shane wouldn't let up, so he might as well go and at least enjoy a good cigar. He could be doing worse things than spending an evening with his best friend.

*****

"You girls have no idea how much Rafe is going to flip out if he finds out we've done this."

"Loosen up, Ari. The man doesn't own you, and believe me, you're going to want to see this show."

"I'm not protesting *too* much," Ari said with a big grin as they walked in the front doors of the Excalibur Casino. Ari wouldn't admit it, but she was beyond excited. Before meeting her three girlfriends at work, she'd never gone out on the town.

Now that she'd had a taste of the weekend social scene, she had to admit that she'd really missed out over the years. She would certainly avoid clubs with spiked drinks, but watching a good male strip show while hanging with friends seemed to be something all women should do at least once.

Ari loved Amber, Shelly and Miley, but she'd also grown quite fond of Lia and Rachel. When she and Rafe ultimately broke up, Ari was afraid that friendship would be lost. She'd tried to not get close to the girls, but they made that impossible.

"I really don't want to put a negative note on the evening, but what happens when Rafe and I are no longer…friends?"

The two girls stopped and twisted around to face her, for once wearing serious expressions. Lia turned first with Rachel right behind as if choreographed, and both girls threw their arms around Ari, making her eyes fill with tears as the sisters held on tight.

"I hate to admit this, but Rafe has gone through a *lot* of women. We're not stupid. We know about his so-called rules. We hate that about him — despise how he is with his women. However, before you came along, there wasn't one of his girl-friends whom we wanted to know. We were relieved when he grew bored and off those bimbos went. They tolerated us and vice versa," Rachel started. Ari gulped down the knot in her throat.

"That being said, you're different, Ari. I honestly wouldn't say this to you if I didn't believe it. Rafe cares about you. I've never seen him act the way he does with you with any other woman — not even with his ex-wife. He may have thought he was in love with her, and he may think his heart was broken, but that's not really it. He was humiliated, disillusioned — but not heartbroken," Lia added.

"Rafe is healing with you, even if he doesn't realize it. Please, give it a shot — open your heart and search inside the man; ignore the hard exterior he has created for himself. Look at how good he is to us, and all the wonderful things he does for his community and the world. Give him a reason to trust again, and I know he'll earn it," Rachel finished.

Ari couldn't help the tears that slipped from her eyes. These beautiful women were amazing. They really loved their brother, and they seemed to care about her, too. Could she listen to them and give Rafe a real chance? He'd warned her not to fall in love with him — told her he absolutely didn't want that. How could she take such a risk?

"I don't know if I can do it," she finally answered.

"Well, to answer your question, Ari — you are our friend now. No matter what happens with Rafe, we won't allow you not to be a part of our lives," Rachel promised.

"Thank you." Ari knew they meant it — knew they intended to keep that promise. She also knew it would be impossible. How could she stay friends with them when she and Rafe were through? They were bound to mention their brother, and Ari wouldn't want to hear how wonderful his life was without her. It would be too painful.

"OK, enough emotional drama for the night. We came to get blitzed and watch a show, so let's go," Lia insisted as she pulled out tissues and handed them over.

The three women stopped in the bathroom to freshen up, and then went to find the theater.

CHAPTER TWENTY-TWO

THE LOBBY CRACKLED with excitement as a throng of women stood in line for the *Thunder from Down Under* performance. Ari couldn't keep from smiling as groups of females sporting bachelorette party banners called out to each other.

Rachel, Lia and Ari were next to the bar, and of course, Lia insisted on going in.

"I hate lines; let's have a drink." She tugged at Rachel's and Ari's hands as she stepped into the open space and marched up to the front cashier.

Before they could order anything, the bartender jumped on top of the counter right in front of them with a bottle in his hand.

"Are you ladies having a good time?"

A chorus of cheers echoed though the bar and out into the line of people waiting to get into the theater.

"Who here is going to see the boys from Down Under?" the bartender asked with a wolf whistle. Again the crowd roared. It seemed to Ari that Lia and Rachel were the loudest of all. Not wanting to be the dud of the party, she opened her mouth and cheered with the rest of them, which earned her a big smile and wink from the man on the counter.

"I have a problem, ladies. I need to empty this bottle and I just don't have any clean shot glasses. Can you help me out?" All the women yelled assent. "Who wants a shot?" Lia was the first one in front of him as she held her head back and waited for him to poor curaçao into her mouth.

Bending down, he tipped the bottle when it was lined up with her bottom lip, making the women scream again as the blue liquid cascaded down her throat. The excitement was catching, and when Lia pushed Ari to go next, she didn't hesitate to throw her head back as she waited for the man to give her the shot.

Ari almost gagged, but she managed to swallow the bitter liqueur, then waited for Rachel to take her turn. Each time another woman took a shot, the crowd grew louder. Ari was laughing as she turned and made eye contact with a stunning man sporting a dark suit and tie.

"Are you here for the show?" he asked with a laugh.

"Of course. You?"

"No. I'll pass on watching men strip, but how about I buy you and your friends a round of drinks?"

"I wouldn't pass that up," Ari replied, feeling the tiniest bit of guilt over flirting with the stranger. It *was* a girls' night out, though, and a bit of harmless flirting wasn't wrong, was it?

"Is that a cigar?" Rachel asked, making Ari scoot aside as she pushed up against the man; he didn't seem unhappy in the least at having the petite Rachel practically in his lap.

He held the large brown cigar out, offering it to her, and to Ari's surprise Rachel grabbed ahold of it and took a deep puff.

"That's such a disgusting habit, Rachel," Lia said with a laugh as Rachel blew a puff of smoke from her mouth.

"I only do it when I'm drinking. The smell reminds me of grandpa and it's so much fun to hold the sweet smelling tobacco," Rachel said as she took another puff before handing it back.

"Sitting here with you three beautiful ladies would make it almost worth it to watch a male stripper show," the stranger said as his eyes drank Rachel in.

"Sorry, bud, only girls tonight. You can give Rachel a business card, though — then, *if* you're lucky, she might call you back," Lia said as she downed her second shot, vodka-based Sex on the Beach.

"Phillip Monsoon," he introduced himself as he pulled a card from his wallet.

"And what brings you to Las Vegas, Phillip?" Lia asked.

"If you call me, you'll find out," he answered with a laugh. "It looks like they're starting to let you ladies in. Would you like one more round before I lose your company?"

"How could we say no to that?" Rachel answered as she grabbed his cigar again and took a big puff.

"Tequila shots," Lia called, and the dozen women at the bar all yelled their approval of her drink as the bartender pulled out enough glasses for them all, then flipped the bottle in the air before filling them in one long line.

To Ari's surprise, Philip didn't seem put out at all that Lia had turned his offer of three drinks into a dozen. The same sparkle remained in his eyes as he watched Rachel. It looked as if he was a little smitten.

The women all licked their wrists, poured salt, took their shot, then sucked on limes. Rachel sent Phillip a wink before they rushed to the door and entered the theater. As soon as they walked inside, all thoughts of Phillip were forgotten, at least by Ari.

Lia led them to the front of the room, right in front of the stage, and sat Ari front and center. The big screen showing a photo shoot of the performers had the ladies screaming. When the spotlight hit a shot of their naked behinds, the crowd went wild.

Several minutes later, a gorgeous man wearing a button-up shirt, a tie and some worn-out jeans jumped onto the stage and welcomed them, asking whether they were having a good time. The crowd went wild again. His sexy Australian accent had Ari melting as her stomach twisted into knots in anticipation, and slight fear, of what was to come.

"You're all just a bunch of horny women, aren't you?" he called out. The women noisily agreed, not feeling the least bit ashamed. They'd come to see sexy dancers strut their stuff, and they wanted the show to begin.

Ari had never been to anything like this before, and as smoke filled the stage and the screen started to lift, her heart thumped and thudded.

Seven men entered the stage, wearing suits and dancing with synchronized steps. Ari was surprised to find herself calling out as they swung their hips in time to the music. Somewhere in the middle of the song, their shirts came open and their rock-hard pecs and washboard abs made her salivate.

At the end of the number, they turned around and their pants descended, exposing their bare backsides. The crowd let out such a loud roar that it drowned out the sensual beat of the bass. And even in that steamy room, Ari could feel her cheeks flame. Wow. Rafe would throttle her if he knew, but who cared?

Soon the men were leaping off the stage and moving down the aisles of the intimate room, then jumping on tables and bending down to kiss a number of the fired-up women. Ari figured she was safe from their attention as long as she didn't make eye contact. Rafe would be ticked off enough if he discovered that she'd come to the show. Any kissing might make him explode.

During another number, one of the guys pulled a woman up onstage, put her in a chair and gave her the lap dance of her dreams. The woman blushed scarlet, in nice color contrast with the mouthful of pearly white teeth revealed by her huge smile. When the dancer jumped up and pushed his crotch close to her face, Ari was the one who went scarlet. The men certainly seemed to enjoy their job.

As the show was nearing its end, Ari's tipsiness overtook her, and when six of the men danced out onstage again, she clapped and hollered with the rest of the crowd. One of the men jumped down and suddenly grabbed her hand.

She looked up at his smiling mouth like a deer caught in headlights. She couldn't go up there! It was all good fun, and they were movie-star gorgeous. But they still paled in comparison with Rafe. Why bother to rub up against any of them when she had an amazing lover waiting for her return?

Then again, how much longer would he be waiting for her? One day, a week, maybe a month. Rafe wasn't known for keeping his mistresses longer than a few months at a time. She'd do well to remember that.

"Don't you dare try to get out of this," Lia yelled out with laughter in her voice as she gave Ari a push.

Ari had no choice but to follow the hunk onstage. He sat her down on a long bench, then ran back to join his buddies in a dance number. Ari didn't know whether she was supposed to look at him or the crowd, so she looked down as she waited for the tune to end. From what she'd already witnessed, she had little hope of escaping with anything less than maximum embarrassment.

The man sauntered back over seductively and stood directly in front of her, pressing his body against hers, then grabbed her hands and placed them around his back, with her fingers spread out on his buttocks. As the audience yelled out instructions, Ari got into the spirit of the thing and squeezed, and the dancer winked at her with his dark brown eyes.

When he went back over to the other guys, they gyrated slowly, accentuating their prized possessions, before two of them stalked toward her and rubbed up against her. Even through all the din, Ari could hear Lia shouting up at her to *grab his ass.* Ari thought it wiser, after her one lapse, to keep her hands to herself.

Soon, only one man remained before her. He stripped down to his boxer briefs and swayed around her several times before laying her down and lying right on top of her! She was sure that if the power suddenly blacked out, the heat from her face would be enough to light up the entire room — heck, the entire hotel.

After swiveling his hips provocatively above her for a few seconds, he finally sat her up, and then helped her stand as he grabbed her in a big hug, lifting her off her feet.

"Thanks for being a good sport, love," he said, his accent causing her insides to turn to jelly. He assisted her off the stage, and then finished his performance.

Ari was still glowing when the show finished. The dancers set up for pictures as soon as they were all presented by name. Lia, of course, insisted on having a few photographs taken.

The three of them stood in line, then each sat on a dancer's lap, and received a kiss on the cheek as the picture was snapped. Ari seemed to be walking on clouds as she and the rest of the audience departed. How fun to hang with two amazing women and receive so much attention from serious sex gods. So what if they were doing a show, the same thing they did night after night? She still felt beautiful and desirable. Yes, Rafe made her feel gorgeous when he was worshipping her body, but afterward, he just left.

To have a man want her so much that he couldn't possibly sleep in another room would be amazing. To have him want her in bed *and* out of it? Priceless. Rafe couldn't possibly ever give her that — he'd told her so.

If only she didn't have Lia and Rachel's voices in her head telling her a different story. She needed another drink.

"I can't believe they pulled you up onstage. I'm so jealous right now," Rachel said as they made their way downstairs toward the casino.

"This totally stays between us. You have to burn that picture," Ari responded with a laugh.

"There's no way I'm ever turning loose of this night. Are you kidding me? That was the most fun I can ever remember having. Those guys were so freaking hot."

"Mmm, can we take them home, pretty please?"

"Rachel, I'm sure if you bat your eyes at them, they'll be begging you to go home with them."

"Now that sounds like a plan. I could do all sorts of kinky things with that group."

"You two are terrible. Seriously, you have to promise me that Rafe will never find that picture," Ari insisted. Silently she added, *At least until our relationship is over.*

"There's nothing like having a little blackmail on a friend," Lia replied as she pulled out the photo and laughed.

"OK, the night's still young. Let's go downtown and lose some money," Rachel insisted.

"Yes. Ari's buzz is wearing off. We need to get her a liquor fix — stat."

Ari gave up fighting the two women. She'd learned that when they were determined to do something, it was best just to go with the flow and see where the adventure led, because otherwise she wouldn't put it past them to drag her off kicking and screaming — probably in handcuffs. In her semi-sloshed state, that thought gave her the giggles.

Linking arms with the girls, she smiled as they went off to whatever Lia had planned for them next.

CHAPTER TWENTY-THREE

"**N**INETEEN!"

"Yea! Great job, Ari," Rachel called as she leaped in the air, then turned to high-five several of the men surrounding them.

"You are good luck, baby!" one of the guys said as he picked Ari up and spun her in a circle. Ari laughed when he set her down, and she wobbled unsteadily on her feet.

Ari was losing complete track of time, but winning everything else as they moved through the casinos on Freemont Street. The girls were dragging her from table to table to enjoy her amazing run of luck, and a group of guys having a bachelor party was following the three around.

"Come on, Ari. Give Stephen a kiss for good luck. The poor sucker is getting married tomorrow, so he needs all the luck he can get," one of his friends shouted.

In the heat of the excitement, Ari leaned forward and kissed a blushing Stephen on the cheek as Rachel took a picture. Stephen then picked Ari up and twirled her while Rachel continued snapping shots.

Because of the sheer number of margaritas Ari had consumed, she saw nothing wrong with Rachel's documenting their night on the town.

"OK, pick a number," the dealer called, and Ari set a bunch of chips on seven. All the men followed suit and the dealer spun the roulette wheel. The guys all started chanting *seven* over and over, and Ari, Rachel and Lia joined in as the wheel started to slow.

It clicked closer and closer, then stopped on seven. The crowd around them exploded in triumphant cheers.

"Lucky number seven it is," the dealer called as whoops and hollers and whistles of celebration filled the air again.

When Ari was finally back down on her feet, she swayed as the room began to fade out. It was long past time for them to retire, but she hated to call it a night. She knew Rafe was going to be furious with her and she didn't want to face that sort of music.

"Whoa there, Ari, you just about face-planted. As much fun as I'm having, I think we have to head back now," Rachel said, looking slightly bummed.

The crowd around them all protested, promising them everything from free drinks to jewelry if they stayed just another hour longer.

"Sorry, boys, but we have to go before her boyfriend comes looking. It's only a matter of time — and no one wants to be here if he finds her like this," Lia warned.

Ari was grateful that Lia and Rachel were stronger than she was, because they managed to get her out of the casino and to the front doors, where they hailed a cab in what seemed like seconds. Her head was spinning.

"Do you know how mad my brother is going to be?" Rachel asked with a drunken giggle.

"Yes. Lucky for you both that I'm the one he's going to take it out on. Lucky for me that I'm drunk enough I don't care all that much. Did you know he is phenomenal in bed?"

"Ooh, that's way too much information, Ari. Please, please promise me to never say anything so horrific again," Lia begged.

"I can't promise, but I'll try," Ari conceded as she laughed with them.

"Where to, ladies?" asked the cab driver with such boredom in his voice and an attitude that screamed so clearly *I hate this job!* that Ari got the giggles. Sin City cab drivers doubtless saw it all.

"The Venetian, please," Rachel said before sitting back.

"I'm so glad you remembered that, because I completely forgot what hotel we were staying in," Ari admitted.

"We stay there all the time. The rooms are great and the shopping even better."

"Don't you ever get bored with shopping? I mean, you both are so dang rich that you can shop every day if you want. At some point it would have to lose its appeal."

"Ari, that's almost sacrilegious. How could anyone ever grow bored of shopping? New fashions come out almost daily," Rachel gasped in a mock-serious tone.

"My mother didn't want us to be brats, so we had a pretty normal life growing up. Now, as adults, we do tend to shop a bit too much," Lia admitted. "We have to make up for our deprived childhood!"

"I was never into the whole shopping thing before, but now, with Rafe demanding I wear all these dresses and fancy shoes, I have to do it all the time. It's taken a while, but I admit I've kind of grown to enjoy losing myself in this lifestyle. It's not the worst thing I've ever done before."

"That's more like it!" Rachel exclaimed.

They arrived at the hotel and the three of them stumbled in through the front doors. Ari had taken about five steps when she hit a wall of angry flesh. She didn't even want to look up into the fire she was sure was in Rafe's eyes.

Instead, she looked to the left where Shane was gripping both Lia and Rachel. His face had to be a mirror image of Rafe's. Rachel looked over at Ari and mouthed the words *hot, angry sex,* which sent Ari into another round of giggles.

Rafe had obviously been pacing the lobby for hours.

Shane and Rafe marched the three of them through the casino and straight to the elevators, where they rode to the top floor in suffocating silence. Maybe she *would* get hot, angry sex. She could certainly go for that.

"Are you going to take care of them?" Rafe practically growled at Shane.

"Gladly," Shane replied and he led Lia and Rachel into the adjoining suite.

Rafe dragged Ari into their own huge suite. "Did you have a good time?"

The tone of Rafe's deceptively calm voice alerted Ari that something sinister was up. If she hadn't been so drunk, she might have had a clue to what it was, but her brain refused to function correctly.

"Yes, we had a blast, thank you," she answered happily.

"At what point did you decide it would be wise to ditch the professional men I graciously hired to keep you safe? Obviously I need to find ones who are a lot more discreet if you were able to spot them so easily."

"Oh, we planned on that from the start. How can we have any fun with two incredible hulks following us all around? Discreet? Nahhhh. They were practically breathing down our necks, making it far too hard to socialize."

"The whole point of the bodyguards *is* to discourage people from getting too close and harming you," Rafe said tightly, fire leaping from his eyes.

"Well, we couldn't have any fun with them all up in people's faces. Chill, Rafe."

"Are you kidding me right now, Ari?" he thundered.

"No."

"That's it? Just *no*?"

"My head is spinning and I really need to lie down. Can you continue your lecture tomorrow, preferably after I've had at least two cups of coffee?"

With great reluctance, Ari glanced at Rafe and saw that the man was steaming mad. Fascinating. What had she and his sisters done, really? They'd seen a strip show, played some table games, and gotten back late — oh, and ditched the bodyguards. The point was, they had come back in one piece. She didn't see why he had to be so upset.

"You just don't get it, do you?"

"Get what, Rafe? Yes, I know — we have an agreement. You want to own me, blah, blah, blah. I was kinda hoping to have some great angry sex and then pass out."

Rafe's eyes bulged, as if she'd sprouted a third head. She smiled at him and sent a wink, making him growl while he walked over to the refrigerator and grabbed a bottle of cold water and a few pills.

"Drink it all up and take these or you'll be worthless to-morrow," he demanded as he held out his hand.

"I think that ship has sailed, Rafe. No matter what I do I'm going to be miserable," she muttered. When he didn't move, she finally took the bottle and horse pills from his hand. Choking the pills down, Ari then forced herself to finish off the bottle. It wasn't easy with him glaring at her the entire time.

"I really have to use the bathroom," she said as she stumbled to her feet, her knees nearly giving out.

"You're not a stupid teenager, Ari. Don't you think it's a little ridiculous to get so drunk that you can't even walk?" he snapped as he saved her from face-planting on the floor.

"You know what, Rafe? I'm not a teenager, and you're not my dad, so why don't you lay off the lecture?" she snapped back. Her temper was rising as some of her buzz began to fade. Her night of angry sex was fading further and further away, and that was putting her in an increasingly bad mood.

"Believe me, I know I'm not your father. That doesn't change the fact that I want to bend you over my knee right now and see how pink I can make your cheeks."

His words made her stumble to a stop. If he so much as *tried* to paddle her backside, she'd hit him where it hurt. Still, the thought of being bent over his knee didn't sound bad at all.

With a come-hither smile, she leaned into him and kissed his neck before she disappeared behind the bathroom door. Once inside, Ari got the bright idea of taking a shower.

The last thing she remembered doing was sitting down on the built-in bench and feeling the hot water cascade over her muscles, soothing away the aches now consuming her body. Rafe found her passed out a few minutes later, and he carried her off to bed.

*****

Rafe woke up with Ari in his arms. With surprise he noted the time. It was after ten! Not only had he stayed in bed later than he had in at least a decade, but he'd slept with Ari all night.

He'd lain down with her only to make sure she wasn't going to get sick and then pass out in her own vomit. He must have fallen asleep within minutes of her snuggling up against his chest.

Rafe allowed himself a moment to glide his fingers through her soft hair before he untangled her limbs from around him and slid from the bed. He wouldn't fault himself for a moment of weakness, but to continue lying there, especially after her behavior the night before, would be ridiculous.

He took a quick shower, ordered room service and sat down to read the paper while he waited for his coffee. Ari's phone buzzed on the table next to him, and he planned to ignore it until he noticed a man's name flash on the screen. Years of suspicion surfaced, and though he knew he shouldn't pick up her cell, he did so anyway.

Who in the hell was Stephen?

Without thinking twice about her privacy, Rafe opened the message; *Thanks for a great time last night. Hope you didn't get too busted. We had to call it a night after you left because you took all your luck with you, beautiful lady.*

What was this guy thanking her for? He began searching through Ari's phone to find out. At the images he pulled up, his mood went from stable to downright critical condition.

In Ari's drunken stupor last night, she'd requested angry sex — well, she was about to get some.

CHAPTER TWENTY-FOUR

ARI AWOKE TO feel her hands being pulled above her head and her shirt being yanked off. Before she had a chance to react, her pajama bottoms were gone and she was lying on the sheets naked with her hands immobilized in Rafe's strong grip.

The ire in his eyes should have frightened her, but instead, heat flooded straight to her core as she anticipated what was to come. She'd seen Rafe upset before, but the fire leaping from his gaze was hotter than lava. What had riled him up?

"Do you want to explain the pictures on your phone?"

In her half-asleep state, it took Ari's brain a few extra moments to figure out what he was asking. When comprehension dawned, a shiver of apprehension rolled down her spine as she recalled the pictures Rachel and Lia had taken.

She searched her memory, trying to figure out what they'd documented on film. She'd been having such a fun time, she hadn't worried much about it. What should have been on her mind now was what he'd been doing going through her phone. That was a clear invasion of privacy, and if the situation had been reversed, he'd have been furious. But now wasn't the time to bring that up.

"Just pictures of our girls' night out," she answered with a weak smile.

"Why in the hell were there pictures of men with their hands and mouths all over you?" he snapped.

"There weren't!"

"That's crap. I saw the pictures, Ari. Some man had you locked tight in his arms with his lips right on yours," he growled.

"We were winning. He just grabbed me. It wasn't anything. I didn't know the girls thought it a Kodak moment," she said, thinking she would repay both Lia and Rachel with a slow and torturous death.

"You are mine! Get that? No other man can touch you."

"I wasn't cheating!" she snapped, starting to get irritated by his interrogation. He'd done far worse things in his life than kiss a stranger while playing roulette. How dare he try to belittle her!

"That's not what it looked like. Do I need to remind you what it means to belong to me?"

Oh, yes! Ari wanted to shout, but she decided it might be wiser to let him get through his tantrum.

Ari attempted to wriggle away from him and find a more comfortable position than spread out before him while he fired off ridiculous accusations.

"You're not going anywhere," he informed her as he threw off his bathrobe, then lay over her. The heat from his skin nearly seared her as his hips settled between her thighs.

Even in his temper, he was highly aroused, his thick shaft poised at her quickly moistening entrance. She pushed up toward him, willing him to plunge inside. How could she be so angry with him and still desire him at the same time?

"You don't deserve rewards, but I can't keep from showing you who you belong to."

Rafe's head descended and he took her lips. His tongue demanded entrance, and she willingly opened to him, wanting to taste him deep inside her mouth. As his hands gripped her wrists tightly, and his mouth plundered hers, she fought to catch her breath.

Though with little seduction, she was melting beneath him, ready for his touch across her heated skin. In a matter of seconds he brought her body alive as only he could do.

Rafe groaned as he pushed his hips against hers, his considerable length rubbing along the line of her wet heat, but not entering. She wanted to demand he take her hard and fast, but she kept her thoughts to herself, too afraid he'd pull away as punishment. She hated it when he left her aching, resented the way he used it as an effective tool to prevent disobedience.

When Rafe's head moved from her mouth to her throat, she shuddered. He was so masterful with both his tongue and hands. She couldn't get enough of his sweet touch. Engulfing her breasts in his palms, he kneaded the soft flesh before squeezing her swollen nipples.

Ari reveled in the sight of his dark hair brushing her light skin. As he held his mouth back and ran his tongue along her nipple, she tried to move, tried to reach for him, but couldn't, for he had her trapped. Not being able to touch him was torture.

When his mouth finally captured her tight pink bud, her back arched into the air, her body straining against his as he devoured her skin. The nip of his teeth made fire spread through her core, intensifying her need to monumental proportions.

He moved his head and she groaned in protest, and then nearly panicked when he lifted his head before turning over onto his back. She would hate him if he left her unfulfilled again. How could a man bring a woman so much pleasure only to deny her the ultimate satisfaction?

When Rafe's arms stretched out and gripped her to him, her breasts flattening against his hard chest, she greedily sucked from his lips. Feeling a need to taste the salt of his skin on her tongue, Ari moved down his body, sliding open mouthed kisses along the firm ridges of his stomach, as she moved toward his straining erection.

But before she was able to reach his satin covered steel and pull his hardness into her mouth, he leaned forward and grabbed her by the hips, lifting her over him, and sat her body down on his chest. She was just a couple of feet too high up on his body. She tried to inch down, but he held tightly to her behind and began tugging her forward.

"I want to taste you," he cried as a guttural groan rumbled from his chest. Ari looked down in embarrassment as he positioned her spread legs over his face. Before she could protest, his tongue slipped out and moistened her heat, making her cry out. She forgot her discomfiture and leaned forward, gripping the headboard.

Rafe's fingers kneaded the flesh of her behind as his mouth devoured her heat, his tongue igniting sparks that shot through her limbs. Without conscious thought, she moved her hips in rhythm with his tongue, seeking more pleasure.

When he sucked her swollen pearl into his mouth and caressed the flesh with his lips, she shot over the edge, and continued to crash over and over again, her body shaking with the intensity of her release. He slowed his movements, drawing out her pleasure as she cried out, giving her much more than she'd expected considering his state of anger and agitation.

Before the last of her spasms ended, his strong arms lifted her up before he slid out from under her, leaving her gripping the headboard as her body continued to quiver. When he stood she thought he was done with her, but instead, he gripped her legs, twisting her body around so her back was flat against the mattress as he tugged her to the edge of the bed. His pulsing erection poised at her very wet entrance as he loomed above her.

"Don't ever kiss another man. Not in roulette," he demanded as he plunged forward. "Not in blackjack." He slammed hard inside her again. "Not in poker." He forced his entrance again as she tensed for his anger. "And certainly not for Any... Other...Entertainment." He bore into her with a momentum unlike anything before, emphasizing each word he spoke with his powerful thrusts — filling her to absolute capacity, rocking her entire body. He pushed her legs up high, exposing her core fully to him as he plunged in and out of her swollen flesh.

"I won't," she promised with a moan of painful pleasure.

"You are mine. I want to hear you say it!"

"I'm yours," she gasped, the pressure building higher within her.

"Say it again!" His movements were furious as he buried himself deep inside her again and again.

"I'm yours, Rafe — only yours," she cried and her body shattered, the orgasm even more intense than the first.

"I want your beauty all to myself," he called out as he shuddered, and his body collapsed on top of hers. She knew now how he felt — she felt as if she'd been ripped to shreds and was still searching for the pieces. Being with Rafe was like surviving a class five tornado. They would destroy either everyone and everything around them or each other — maybe both.

"I don't ever want to find out you've been out with another man — do you understand?"

"I already said it was a freak occurrence. I didn't mean for it to happen," she answered with exasperation. How many times was he going to bring this up? She just wanted to enjoy the afterglow of some incredible sex, not fight with him over a triviality.

"I'm a possessive man, Ari, and I'm used to controlling my world. You are not making my life easy. You break every rule I set, ignore my wishes and then flaunt your freedom in my face. With you, I do not feel in control, and I've had it. I want you to understand that this won't happen again — or there will be consequences."

Again, his overbearing attitude just rolled off Ari's back. Instead of shaking with fury, her body stirred to life, to her utter amazement after two incredibly electrifying orgasms.

As his body melded with hers, the message behind Rafe's words hit her. Between what his sisters had said and his bizarre behavior, her heart cracked open a bit. Maybe he had been wounded more deeply than she'd thought possible. He did a great job of presenting a cold, calculating face to the world, but in rare moments with her, his mask slipped.

Could it be that he did want love? Was he afraid of being hurt? Could she open up her heart and give him a chance, or would that only end up making her a fool?

All Ari knew was that, in this small moment of time, she was satisfied, mentally and physically. She ran her fingernails across the damp skin of his back, breathed in his spicy scent, and felt her heart beat strongly against his.

She didn't know how things would progress, but somewhere along the line she'd started to develop feelings for this man of steel. She'd started to let her guard down. He'd been a downright bully, but she couldn't help but get back to her old habit: dwelling on *what ifs*…

"If this is your idea of consequences, then maybe I should go look for another drunken bachelor party and have some more pics taken," she said with a relaxed laugh.

With a furious growl, Rafe pounced, his body pinning her to the bed, the fire blazing again in his eyes. She couldn't keep the smile from her face as he tried to sear her with his gaze. What brought her joy was the laughter behind the ire. He might have wanted to be angry, but he seemed to be enjoying their moment as much as she was. It appeared that Raffaello Palazzo had a sense of humor.

"You are nothing but trouble," he accused with a smiling glare.

"I never promised to be anything *but* trouble," she reminded him as she pushed her chest against him, loving the feel of his muscular chest rubbing against her peaked nipples.

"Let's shower," he said, surprising her. Before she could agree or refuse him, he was out of the bed and lifting her into his arms.

As the hot water cascaded over them, and her soapy hands massaged his rapidly recovering arousal, Ari couldn't remember ever being happier. If only this small moment would last forever.

CHAPTER TWENTY-FIVE

"**H**URRY UP, ARI. You are really dragging today."

"That's because you kept me up half the night, and then your brother woke me up way too early, Lia," she answered grumpily.

"It's two in the afternoon. You've had plenty of time to sleep. We're in Las freaking Vegas. You can recover once we get back home to our boring lives," Rachel said.

"I have to go back to work as soon as we're home. I won't get to recover even then," Ari replied, though they did have a point. When would she get to come back to Vegas again? She didn't see it happening anytime soon.

"We know your boss. We'll put in a good word for you so you have adequate time to rest," Lia assured her. If anyone could convince Rafe to give her a day off, it would be one of his sisters. They were the only two she could envision getting

187

their way with Rafe. Ari certainly didn't win rounds with him often — not once that she could recall.

"OK, let's go for coffee and then I promise to be in a better mood."

The three girls made their way across the casino and found a coffee shop; Ari guzzled down her first cup there, then ordered one to go before she let the girls drag her to who knew where next.

"Do you know what Rafe and Shane are up to today?" Lia asked.

"I don't have a clue," Ari answered. Rafe had been gone when she woke up. She assumed their fight was over, but she never knew with him. He ran hot and cold too often for her to be a good judge of his character.

"Why, Lia? Are you wanting to see Shane?"

"No! It's not that; I was just curious," she answered defensively.

"Oh, the heck with them. You promised me we'd get to go swimming. It's a hot day, and I can use the sun, so let's just relax. I'm sure Ari's all for that."

"Yes. That sounds perfect."

"Good, then its settled," Rachel said. "Let's run to the room and change and then get some sun. We can explore after dark."

"OK, the two of you win. I want you to know that I'm going against my will."

"Quit being such a sore loser, Lia. I'm sure you'll see your lover boy, Shane, again real soon."

Rachel took off running as Lia went to smack her. Ari hung back laughing at the sibling rivalry. The two were so charming and full of life.

It didn't take the three of them long to change into their swimsuits, and soon they were off to the pool. As they stepped outside, music could be heard drifting toward them. There were a few pools at the hotel, but as soon as Rachel found out which one had a live DJ, she tugged them in that direction.

"This looks like a scene from every spring break special I've ever seen," Ari grumbled as she looked around at the bikini-clad women dancing alongside the pool, with shirtless guys trying to decide which girl was catching their eye the most.

The pool was filled with nearly naked bodies playing a round of volleyball, and it looked as if there wasn't any available space anywhere. Ari had planned on a nap, but she didn't think she was likely to find a lounge chair in the massive crowd.

As if Rachel could read her thoughts, she turned and gave Ari a wink. "Don't worry, darling, I'll get us lounges." With that, she sauntered through the crowd, and Ari had no choice but to follow behind.

As she and Rachel went in search of a comfortable place to sit, Lia went to find them drinks. After her headache last night, Ari didn't want to taste another alcoholic drink again, but as the sun beamed down on her, she was willing to give up her ban on liquor just as long as it was icy cold.

"Right there," Rachel said with a Cheshire Cat grin. Ari followed her gaze to where three young guys were sitting on lounge chairs chatting.

With an exaggerated swing to her hips, Rachel approached them, gaining all three of their eyes as she walked right up without any lack of self-confidence blocking her goal.

"Hey, boys. How're you doing?" she asked as she gave each of them a direct look before trailing a manicured finger across her stomach. Ari had to hold in the laughter as their eyes took in her petite yet luscious figure.

"Great. How about you?" one of the guys finally responded after putting his tongue back inside his mouth.

"Oh, I'm OK. It's just so hot out here and my feet are killing me, but my two girlfriends and I just got here. It's too bad we might have to leave for the other pool, though," she said with an exaggerated pout.

At her words, the guys looked up and connected eyes with Lia before their heads whipped back to Rachel, and then bobbed between the two of them as if they couldn't figure out whom to keep their eyes on. Ari shifted uncomfortably on her feet as she tried to hide behind Rachel, but her friend turned around and grabbed her arm, yanking her forward before turning back to the guys.

"You don't have to go. We'd be glad to share our lounges with you," one of them said as he jumped up and placed his hand against Rachel's back to lead her to his spot.

"You don't have to do that...Wait, I haven't even gotten your name yet," Rachel said as she trailed her nail between his pecs.

"It...it's Lance," the guy stuttered. The poor kid couldn't have been older than twenty-one.

"Mmm, I like that name...Lance," she cooed. "What are you doing in Vegas?"

"It's my birthday weekend. These are my fraternity brothers, Alan and Dixon."

"Wow, all of you have such sexy names. I'm so glad to have run into you today. This heat is killing me..." she pointedly said as she looked over toward the bar.

"We'll get some drinks. What would you like?" Alan piped in.

"Ohh, such a tough choice. How about you surprise us? My sister should be back any minute now."

The three of them practically tripped over themselves as they made a rush to the bar, arguing about who got to buy the drinks.

"Have a seat, Ari," Rachel said as she lay back with a huge smile of satisfaction on her face.

Ari had to close her mouth before she guiltily dropped down into her stolen lounge. "I can't believe how good you were at that, Rachel. You had them willing to do anything you asked," she finally gasped.

"I was the baby of the family and learned quickly that guts and guile got me a lot further than crying or begging. It's helped me a lot in life."

"You're terrible, but this lounge does feel pretty nice."

"The best part is that there are countless females all over here, so after a few more beers, the frat boys will lose interest in us after I suddenly become boring. Then, they'll run off and play with girls their own age."

"Nice chairs, sis. How did you manage this?" Lia said as she came up and handed them each a tall glass with fruit floating in it.

"Your sister's unbelievable flirting ability," Ari replied as she took a sip and then sighed in pleasure at the sweet, cold taste.

"Yes, Rachel is better than anyone I know at getting what she wants from men. I don't know how she's still single."

"Because I don't want to settle down with just one guy. I want to flirt with them all and then leave them wanting."

The three of them laughed while they sipped on their drinks and soaked up the sun. Soon, the guys were back, and panting at their feet. Surprisingly, Ari found herself laughing at some of their stories. She did grow bored with them after a while, but that's when she laid her head back and tried to tune out the crowd and get some rest.

*****

"You have got to be kidding me!"

"What's wrong, Rafe?"

Rafe didn't even notice that Shane was looking around for a threat. Rafe's eyes were tuned in to Ari, who was clad only in a skimpy bikini while some guy was sitting on her lounge chair practically drooling over her. The thing that made it even worse was that the guy could barely be older than a kid. Was she that desperate for male attention?

He knew damn well that she'd been thinking of no other man but him as he'd made her scream out in ecstasy this morning.

"I need a beer."

"I can agree to that." Without questioning Rafe's outburst any further, Shane walked by his side as they made their way to the bar.

"Hey, sugar, what can I get for you?"

"We'll take two Coronas."

"Coming right up," she said with an exaggerated smile as her gaze took in Rafe's bare chest.

This he was used to — women flirting, checking him out. Ari was good at bruising his ego, and he shouldn't allow her to have that kind of power over him.

"Here you go."

Rafe turned his attention back to the blonde bartender as he pulled out a hundred and placed it on the counter. "Keep the change," he said while giving her his best smile.

Her eyes widened as she got caught in his stare and Rafe leaned forward closer than he needed to as he grabbed the drink. "Th...thanks," she finally replied. Gaining back her composure, she added "I'm off shift in ten minutes."

The hope in her eyes did nothing for him, but as he turned to see Ari kicking back with his sisters and the guys circling them like sharks, his fury rose again.

"I'll be right here," he said with a wink before Shane grabbed his arm and pulled him away from the counter.

"What are you doing, Rafe? Harmless flirting is one thing, but if you're considering messing around with this girl, that's an entirely different matter. Have you forgotten that you're here with Ari?"

"I haven't, but she sure as hell has forgotten she's here with me. Not that I give a damn. I can replace her in a heartbeat," Rafe growled.

Shane turned to see where Rafe's gaze had landed and then Shane tensed as he watched Lia lean forward, her hand resting on one of the guy's legs.

"I think we need to go see the girls," Shane said as he started parting the crowd on his way over. Rafe followed slowly behind as if he didn't have a care in the world.

"I wasn't expecting you girls here," Shane said as he glared at the young men. Rafe had to fight to keep his fists from clenching. As he glared at the man sitting too close to Ari, he took pleasure in seeing fright penetrate his eyes.

"We're just relaxing," Lia said as she glared at both of them. "Boys, this is my brother...and his friend," she added as an afterthought. Rafe noticed that she didn't tell Shane and him the *boys'* names.

"I talked my friend into covering the last few minutes of my shift. Want to take a swim?" Rafe watched Ari's eyes widen as the bartender pressed her large, barely clad breasts against his arm.

"That sounds like a great idea, sugar," he said as he placed his hand on her lower back and tugged her even closer. She purred with happiness as her hand came up and ran down his chest. He was sure she'd hurried out to him before he could catch the eye of another girl. Rafe knew that he was a great catch; he had no illusions that his attractions went deeper than good looks and ready cash.

"Excuse me, bitch. You can take your slutty paws off my brother. He's here with another girl," Lia said as she stood up and glared at the bartender. Heck, Rafe didn't even know the woman's name.

Claws came out as she glared right back and her body tensed against Rafe's.

"In case you didn't notice, he's got his hands around me, so whether he came with someone or not isn't the point. Obviously, he's leaving with me," she said before grabbing his head and pulling it down to hers.

Rafe didn't fight her when she pressed her lips to his and kissed him. His hand tightened on her waist as he pulled her close and kissed her back in front of everybody.

When he finally pulled away, the bartender sported a smug look on her face, which he could understand. But when he turned his head, guilt rose up as he saw the devastation on Ari's features. Maybe he'd taken this a bit too far.

"You know what? Go off with your tramp, Rafe. Ari is far too good for you," Rachel snarled as she took Ari's hand and started leading her away.

"Ari, stop!" Rafe released the bartender and stepped toward the girls. Three heads turned with blazing eyes and zinged him with a nasty look.

"I'd give them a bit of time to cool down, brother," Shane said with a slow whistle.

"Forget about her. I'm more than you need," the blonde said.

As Ari and his sisters left, Rafe pushed off the girl's clingy hands. "It's not going to happen. Leave me."

Her mouth dropped open before she raised one lip in a sneer, then stomped off to find her next wealthy victim. It seemed Rafe had pissed off just about everyone he could today. He didn't know how he was going to get out of this one.

"I'm sure glad I'm not you right now," Shane said with a laugh. "I'm going to text the girls and tell them how sorry I am that you're such an ass. I get to be the white knight once more."

"You're a prick, Shane," Rafe growled before downing his beer. He decided he'd probably do best to avoid all three of the girls for the rest of the night.

CHAPTER TWENTY-SIX

"HURRY UP, SHANE. I can't believe you guys complain about how long it takes us to get ready when you've been in the bathroom for an hour primping," Rachel called with irritation.

"It's called personal hygiene, Rachel. You might want to try it sometime, squirt. Besides, if you don't like how long I'm taking, you can always go back to your own room," he called back, not in the least offended by her taunting.

"I like your room better. It's bigger than ours, which is just wrong. Besides, I prefer the grunge look. As a matter of fact, I was thinking this whole toothpaste and shampoo thing is for wimps. I'm going to go au naturel," she mocked.

"Mmm, you'll fit right in with all the woodland creatures in the forest," he said as he walked by and ruffled her hair.

"Shane!" she cried out as she rushed into the bathroom to fix her carefully styled hair.

"You started it."

"Grow up!"

"Are you two at it again? I swear, it's like babysitting," Lia grumbled as she walked from the room looking like his wet dream incarnate.

As Lia stepped toward him, he couldn't take his eyes off her long hair tumbling down her back, and the way the stunning black stilettos accented her bare legs. Her dress molded to her breasts and then ran out over her hips, the shimmering material swirling around her legs like the thundering end of a waterfall.

Rachel's phone rang and she excused herself, but Shane was oblivious to her. When Lia finally looked up and their eyes met, he wanted to march her backward toward his room and make her his.

No matter how much he told himself that sleeping with her would be a mistake, the longer he was in her presence, the more he seemed to forget that fact. He needed to be buried inside her body while her fingernails scraped down his back, as she claimed him as her own with the same intensity.

The absolute need to have her was starting to short-circuit his brain.

"Sorry, guys, but you're officially on your own."

Shane turned to see Rachel taking off her silky blue shrug.

"What do you mean?" Shane asked, feeling a bit light-headed. There was no way he could spend the evening alone with Lia with the way she looked now. Each day around her zapped a little bit more of his will to resist.

"I have an important call I have to make," Rachel said as she breezed away and closed her door. Lia followed, but no matter how much she knocked, her little sister wouldn't open up.

Neither of them knew it was all a ruse — Rachel was giving them the night together alone.

"Well, Shane, it looks like it's just you and me," Lia said with a wink as she grabbed her shawl.

Shane felt pressure build in his gut as he watched her turn her well-defined yet feminine back to him. No matter which angle he faced, she was just as appealing. He beelined for the liquor cabinet and poured himself a double, downing it in one gulp. *Please give me strength*, he thought before walking to the door and opening it for her.

"Which show are we going to see?"

"I don't know. Your little sister is the one who purchased the tickets. She told me to hold onto them since they wouldn't fit in her purse, but I haven't had a chance to look yet," Shane replied as he grabbed the envelope from his pocket and walked by her side to the elevators.

"You were putting a lot of trust in her."

"She wouldn't stop pestering me until I caved in. I'd rather be playing a bit of blackjack than attending what I'm sure will be a girlie show."

"Oh, have some faith. Rachel has great taste."

It wasn't Rachel's taste in shows that had Shane on edge — it was his fear of not being able to keep his hands to himself. As Lia walked ahead of him, the sway of her hips caught his eye. She had just the right amount of curves for a man to grab hold of while he thrust deep inside her heat.

His imagination took over as he pictured peeling off her tight dress and revealing those beautiful curves to full view. So hypnotized was he by her walk that sweat broke out on his brow. And when she turned suddenly, it took a moment for him to lift his eyes to her face.

The knowing look she gave him didn't instill confidence. She wanted him — he had no doubt about that. The only doubt he had at this point was whether or not he should take what she was offering. His resistance could last only so long.

*****

As Shane and Lia were being escorted to their seats, excitement was building inside her. He'd been glancing her way repeatedly from the moment she'd stepped out of her bedroom, and the car ride had been filled with enough heat to melt the Arctic Circle. Maybe tonight would finally be their night.

"What in the hell is your sister planning?"

"I don't know what you mean." Lia replied as she surveyed the small theater.

"Well, for one thing, is that a stripper pole in front of me?"

"It looks like one, but it isn't as if I've ever been to a strip show, so how would I know?" she said, shrugging her shoulders.

She looked around her with growing anticipation. All she knew was that they would be watching a burlesque show. She and Rachel had gone to a couple of burlesque classes last year, and she'd had a blast. Never had she felt so sexy.

"I had assumed we'd be going to something more classy," he snarled.

"All I can tell you is that it's burlesque," Lia defended.

"There's a big freaking X in front of the *burlesque* word!" he snapped.

"Well, maybe it's just really sexy burlesque. Be quiet; people are starting to stare at us."

Shane threw a withering look her way, and everything became clear to her. Lia now knew beyond a doubt that he was fighting the urge to take her back to his room and finally take her. That's why he was so upset. But the sexy atmosphere — her clothes — being in Sin City — it all added up to her getting what she wanted.

The two of them sat back as they waited for the small theater to fill. The venue did surprise Lia a little; she had expected Rachel to pick one of the Cirque du Soleil shows. Still, Lia was relieved because the dark room was small and intimate, and Shane's leg was pressing against hers. The stage was in touching distance, and the waitress had just brought them each a nice large glass of wine.

She wanted to giggle when she realized she was hoping to get Shane drunk so she could take advantage of him. She wasn't usually so bold, but something about him brought out her hunting instincts — he was currently in her sights and she wasn't letting him escape.

"I think we should just go, Lia," he murmured as he turned to her and pulled at his collar.

"Quit being such a prude. If you were here with Rafe, you'd be drooling over the stripper pole, hoping and praying that some hot thing was about to come out onstage and get naked."

"I'm not with Rafe — I'm here with you."

"Is that really so bad, Shane? You know, I took a few burlesque classes not long ago. I will have to show my moves when we get back to the room." Lia's hand moved to his thigh and she ran her fingernail from his knee nearly to his groin.

Shane's hand snaked out and stopped her before she reached her prize, but by the way his eyes dilated Lia's confidence shot through the roof. Tonight was going to be their night — even if she had to drug the man. He was going to have to get over the fact that she was Rafe's little sister. She wasn't a kid now — she was all grown up, with very adult needs.

The lights dimmed and the music started as a giant projector screen dropped down in front of the red velvet curtains hiding the stage, and two sensual women sauntered through a burning X on the video they were playing.

Wearing only G-string panties, garter belts with fishnet stockings, and minuscule bras, they gazed out at the crowd through the large screen with take-me expressions on their faces. Oh, this was going to be so good…

As the video ended and the screen began rising, a sensual music started filling the room from the strategically placed speakers, the pulse of the music pumping through Lia, making her body hum in anticipation.

When the screen disappeared into the top of the stage, the curtains opened and the real show began — seven incredibly hot women in hats, suit jackets and tight pants strutted their feminine curves out onto the stage.

Lia's eyes were drawn to the performers' gorgeous bodies as their sultry movements carried them around the stage. Shane took a sudden interest in his shoes after loosening the top button of his shirt to help him breathe. The more uncomfortable Shane became, the greater Lia's enjoyment.

As the performance progressed, the dancers started shedding clothes, a pair of pants flying off the stage and landing in Shane's lap. The tiny thongs the women were wearing covered less of their bodies than Lia's most immodest swimsuit, but the way they moved was exquisite.

By the middle of the first song, the women reached up and unclasped their bikini tops, pulling them free and exposing their breasts. Shane's head immediately went down again as he squirmed in his chair.

Since the girls were now wearing *far* less clothing than when they'd started the song, Lia was worried Shane might have a heart attack. Being there with her was probably about as pleasant for him as sitting through a poetry read. If he could watch this show and still not take her afterward, the situation was hopeless.

Thank you, Rachel!

"They're just boobs. Half of the population has them," Lia taunted, and he lifted his head long enough to send her a quelling stare before he resumed looking at his feet. She put her hand back on his thigh and rubbed her fingers against the soft material of his pants.

When her hand brushed against something hard, pure joy possessed her. She was going to get the benefits of that impressive erection.

Lia tried to memorize some of the dancers' moves over the next thirty minutes. The women undulated across the stage, and the closer they approached to her and Shane, the more he tensed up. When the performers got to a scene involving a bed and lots of lots of hip movement, Lia was ready to jump into Shane's lap and show him some of her own choreography.

Halfway through the performance, in the middle of a dance featuring flight music and the girls in skimpy flight attendant costumes, one of the dancers moved directly in front of Shane and held out her hand. He glanced up, mortified.

"Go with her — don't make her look bad," Lia hissed, and Shane reluctantly stood and followed her up onstage, where she had a large lounge chair waiting for him. The dancers wiggled around him for a minute before wheeling him and the chair behind the giant screen.

When they brought the chair back out, Shane's buttoned shirt was hanging open and his face was grimly expressionless. His eyes connected with Lia's, and they were promising punishment.

She could hardly wait.

When the show ended, Shane grabbed Lia's hand, pulling her from the theater and straight to the front of the hotel, where he made a beeline for the open doors. Ignoring the people passing by, he dragged her out to the sidewalk and began to walk briskly toward their hotel.

"Aren't we taking the car back?"

"No. It's not far and I need fresh air." Shane said nothing else as they practically ran down the street, passing drunk and rowdy vacationers.

By the low growl in his voice, Lia knew things were about to get hot and heavy. Excitement mingled with apprehension. What if it weren't as great as she expected it to be? What if the two of them had zero chemistry when it — or rather they — got down to it?

She'd been picturing this moment for years, and now that it seemed to be arriving, nerves were overcoming her. Doubts and fear crept in as Shane and Lia neared their hotel. What if he were to just dump her off at her room?

If he didn't take her after she'd put herself out there so boldly, she was done. She'd gone with the man to a topless burlesque show, for goodness' sake. If that didn't get him in the mood, she sure as heck didn't know what would.

With insecurity now crowding in to help fog her mind, she began to imagine he was going to dump her off and then go find some floozy down in the casino. Anger swamped her other emotions as they entered the lobby of their hotel and he made a beeline for the elevators.

When they reached their floor and he made the long walk down the hallway, she was prepared for the fight. She'd demand he either step up and come in her room, or stay away from her for good.

"Listen, Shane —"

Lia was cut off as he inserted the key in his door, and used his body to shove her through. The next thing Lia knew, she was pressed up against the wall. Shane bent down and consumed her mouth.

Finally!

There would be no interruptions, no self-consciousness, and no regrets. This was her night to finally feel Shane's power as he took her right over the cliff of pure bliss.

"I shouldn't be doing this, but I can't resist you anymore," Shane gasped as he reached behind her and tugged down the zipper of her dress in one mighty pull. It took only seconds for the sleek material to pool at her feet, leaving her standing before him in nothing but her teal lace panties and high heels.

"You've been taunting me for too long."

"I want you, Shane. I'm not afraid to admit that. Now, shut up and take me," she demanded as she reached for his shirt. With no patience to work the buttons, she grabbed the material and yanked, satisfaction filling her as the buttons flew off, the fabric tore and his chest was laid bare before her.

Lia bent forward, running her tongue along his breastbone, tasting his salty skin and kissing every inch of him he allowed. She kissed her way to his pecs, biting down on his nipple, making him yell.

"Mmm, I can play rough, too," he said as his hand fisted in her hair and he pulled her head back, once again taking her mouth. His fingers wrapped around the dainty lace of her panties and tore them apart, the wisp of material dropping to the ground, leaving her nearly bare to him, only her high heels left.

With a quick movement, he lifted her in the air, using the wall to brace her as she wrapped her legs around his waist. Taking only a second, he grasped a condom out of his pocket before sliding his pants out of the way and sheathing himself.

"Thank you," she whispered when he moved his lips to her neck. She hadn't even considered protection in her state of arousal.

"It's been too long — I can't wait," he apologized as the head of his thick arousal pressed against her opening, demanding entrance.

"Then take me now!"

Shane needed no more encouragement. With a hard thrust of his hips, he buried himself inside her, making Lia cry out as he stretched the swollen walls of her core.

She'd had nothing to worry about. This was everything she'd dreamed of and so much more. Gripping her hips tightly in his hands, Shane thrust deep inside her, bringing her excruciating pleasure by slamming his hips against her.

Throwing her head back against the wall, he rocked against her before slowing so he could bend his head and attend to her swollen nipple. As he sucked the pink bud deeply into his mouth while rocking against her, her body tightened.

Lia felt the buildup of pressure, felt her orgasm nearing. Her hands tangled in his hair and she pulled him up to join his lips with hers as she enjoyed the friction of his dusting of chest hair against her sensitive breasts.

"Don't stop," she begged him as he picked up speed, groans emerging from low in his throat. Opening her eyes, Lia was elated and enthralled by the look of pure pleasure on Shane's face. He was so incredible — so gloriously beautiful.

With one more thrust, he drove Lia's thoughts away; she flew over the edge, her body convulsing around him, gripping his manhood tightly within the warmth of her core.

"Lia," he cried out, and his staff began pulsing as he achieved his release. Lia's legs trembled, and drowsiness overtook her.

Shane's grip on her hips loosened; he pulled out and set her on her feet, his body still pressed against hers as he held her securely against the wall. Fear suddenly crept into Lia's heart. What would happen next? Would he stay? She wouldn't, couldn't beg, but…

"That was ridiculously fast," Shane said as he began moving toward the bedroom with her cradled in his arms.

"It doesn't matter, because the result was explosive," Lia sleepily replied, her body completely relaxed now as he held her close. He hadn't just run away.

"Well, now that I've taken the edge off, let me show you what real pleasure is like," he promised as he laid her down.

"I can't…" she whimpered; he picked up her foot and kissed the sole, sending a shiver down her body.

"Oh yes, you can, Lia. You can come again and again and again…" With that, his lips traveled up her legs and he began showing her exactly what he meant.

"Shane…" she cried as his hands caressed her legs, his fingers skimming her skin, causing her flesh to tremble.

"I've pictured sinking into you a thousand different times. I've imagined the two of us entwined together in my bed… your bed…hell, on top of the Golden Gate Bridge. I love your soft curves, the way your hips flare and your waist narrows. I love the rise of your breasts, and the expressive look in your eyes. There isn't anything about you I don't idolize," he said as he kissed the small swell of her stomach, then ran his tongue up to her belly button and gently nipped the skin there.

"I feel the same way, Shane. I've wanted you for so long," she groaned.

Her breathing deepened as he lifted her arm and ran wet kisses from her palm to her shoulder, touching erogenous zones she'd never known she had. Never had a man worshipped her so fully, made her feel so womanly.

"I've fought against taking you — what a fool I've been. If I had known how good it would be, I would have burned in a glorious blaze with you that night we were at the hotel together."

"Yes..."

His hands ran through her hair while he turned her neck and sucked on the skin at the base of her throat. He was touching her everywhere, kissing every pulse point, building up her desire slowly and surely to the point of explosion.

Lia twisted around, desperate for her turn to taste Shane. He'd denied her the privilege earlier, and now she refused to heed his protests. Thrusting him onto his back, she trailed her fingers down his chest as she bent forward and tasted the hard muscles, then inched lower and lower.

Shane groaned when she reached his stomach, her fingers trailing across his hips as she licked the skin at his pelvis bones. He was so defined, with his six-pack abs and sharp hips. She squeezed the top of his buttocks as she moved even lower, the dim light allowing her to see his spectacular erection.

"You're so beautiful, Shane, so solid and thick. I've wanted to taste you on my tongue for as long as I can remember," she whispered, smiling as a shudder passed through him.

"Lia..." he groaned as her fingers encircled his thick flesh and ran up and down the length of him in slow, steady strokes, her thumb brushing across the head of his arousal.

"Please..." he begged, and she knew what he wanted.

Bending down she ran her tongue across the red skin of his moist head, tasting his preliminary drops of pleasure on her tongue before encircling him with her mouth and greedily sucking him as deeply inside as she could. As she tasted him, she grew hungrier, unable to get enough as her movements quickened and she pressed her head swiftly down and then up again.

His breathing quickened; his stomach quivered. She was making this big, strong man weak, and she couldn't get enough of him. Grasping him tightly in her fingers, she lubricated his staff with her tongue as she sucked him deep into her mouth.

"Enough…" he cried out and his hands gripped her head to stop her. As much as she wanted to keep tasting him, she wanted him buried deep inside her more. Obeying his command, she rose up and positioned her body over his, easily sliding onto his wet staff.

"Protection…" he groaned as she slid down him. With a groan, she pulled off and allowed him to sheath himself before she quickly surrounded his strength again.

Shane grabbed her by the back and pulled her forward, kissing her with raging hunger while she moved up and down his powerful staff. Her own body was on fire from the stunning sensual feast of their lovemaking.

As he grabbed her hips and started controlling their movements, she felt herself sliding out of control. It wasn't long before she was ready to explode again.

As Shane pushed up hard inside her, Lia splintered, colors spraying behind her closed eyelids. He gasped and groaned as he, too, found release for himself. With not an ounce of energy left inside of her, Lia collapsed against his damp chest, then practically purred as he rubbed up and down her spine with his comforting hands.

"Thank you for that, Lia. It was so much more than I could have ever imagined," he said as he kissed her temple.

Feeling completely indulged, Lia curled up against Shane and seemed to drift through time and space. It was more than she'd imagined as well. Now, they wouldn't have to fight these feelings. Now, they could be together all the time, maybe *for* all time.

With those thoughts, Lia let exhaustion carry her away. She fell into a blissful slumber, still connected with Shane through fairy-tale dreams of happily ever after.

CHAPTER TWENTY-SEVEN

"TIME TO WAKE up. We have a full day ahead of us."
Ari grumbled and rolled over as she tried to tune out
the sound of Rafe's voice. It had to be some ridiculous
hour of the morning, and she refused to get out of bed. Didn't
he have work to do?

"Rise and shine. Come on, Ari — you can do it." The obvious smile in his voice made her want to throttle him. She
wasn't a morning person on the best of days, but when she'd
had only a few hours of sleep, she was especially grumpy.

She'd received only a little sleep the night before last, and
then spent yesterday recovering from her adventure with
Rafe's sisters. As she thought about yesterday, Rafe's kiss with
the slutty girl at the pool came flooding back, and she pulled
the pillow over her head. She had no desire whatsoever even
to speak to him.

He hadn't come back to their room last night, so he'd most likely spent it with the blonde bimbo. Well, Ari didn't care. He could do whatever he wanted. It wasn't as if she liked him or anything, she thought angrily.

When the covers on the bottom of the bed moved, she seriously thought about kicking him as he exposed her feet. The room was a bit chilly and she just wanted a couple of hours of additional shut-eye; she certainly didn't want to think about him.

"If you leave me alone, I promise to not kill you."

"Ah, Ari, you can't stay mad at me forever. I have a lot planned today. I don't normally apologize, but I may have been out of line yesterday. I wasn't into that woman at all. I was just pissed off about you and the bachelor party."

Ari was shocked to hear him admit to jealousy. Was he telling her the truth? Could he truly have been acting out of some weird need for revenge, and not from lust for someone else? Did it matter? He was still slime.

"Come on. I promise if you let it go, I'll make it up to you. I have a full day and night planned." Ari felt herself starting to thaw, though she didn't want to. She kept silent as she tried to hold on to her grudge against him.

When she felt him sit on the bed and lift her foot onto his lap, she knew he wasn't giving up. Just when she was about to snap at him, he applied pressure to the ball of her foot and a groan emerged from her mouth instead of the snarling words hanging on the tip of her tongue.

His strong fingers massaged her foot, rubbing from the heels to her toes and back again. Thoughts of sleep evaporated as he soothed her sore ankles. As gorgeous as high heels made her legs, the pain at the end of the night rendered such shoes almost not worth wearing.

When Rafe set her foot down, she whimpered, not wanting him to stop his soothing ministrations. He chuckled, and she was tempted to throw her pillow at him until he picked up her other foot and gave it equal attention.

"OK, I forgive you. But only if you do that every single morning," she said as he kneaded her foot, and then moved up her calf.

"Ari, I have no problem touching you every minute of the day," he replied, making her heart skip a couple beats.

Several more minutes passed before she felt him rise from the bed. That had gone by far too quickly and she was now wide awake.

Still, if she rolled over, and put a pillow over her head, she might be able to fall back to sleep. She was more than willing to give it a try.

"Ah, ah, ah," Rafe said and ripped the blankets off her. Sitting up with a pout, Ari pushed tangled hair from her face.

"What's the hurry to get me out of bed? Don't you have meetings all day?" she grumbled.

"No. I canceled all of them. I told you that I have planned the whole day to make up for yesterday. It will be fun; you'll see."

The look on Rafe's face and the surprise of his words washed the last of Ari's cobwebs from her sleep-deprived brain. He looked…excited. She couldn't recall ever seeing him look quite so upbeat before.

"OK," she agreed without any further arguments. She wasn't going to miss an opportunity to spend a day with him when he was acting so pleasantly out of character. Maybe the Vegas sun had fried some of his brain. Whatever it was, she was going to enjoy every minute of it.

Ari jumped from the bed, and before she could take a step, he swatted her lightly on the butt, making her turn and glare at him.

"Get a move on, woman," he said as he walked from the room whistling.

Ari watched him leave with her mouth hanging open. Who the heck was this guy? And what had he done with her Rafe? She'd expected the rest of their trip to be awkward and miserable, but instead, Rafe was acting almost cheerful and carefree. She didn't know if she should be worried about the other side of the coin flipping over and jinxing her.

Confusion leading the way, Ari stepped into the bathroom and turned on the faucets. A hot shower, followed by a steaming cup of tea, and she'd be ready to face the day.

She hurried through the shower, then wrapped herself in the hotel's soft robe before she made her way to the small table by the large windows overlooking the Las Vegas Strip. In the early morning hours, she enjoyed sipping on her tea as she watched the city begin to wake up.

"What are the plans for today?" she asked him as the caffeine kicked in. She finished her first cup and poured a second before picking up a croissant and taking a bite.

"That is to remain a surprise," he answered as he browsed through the paper.

"I need a clue, at least, so I know what to wear," she replied. It was a good excuse to get some kind of answer.

"A pair of jeans and a T-shirt will be fine."

That didn't tell her anything. They could just be strolling the Strip for all she knew. But watching Rafe while he read the paper, Ari realized she didn't care what they did. This wouldn't be a business function or some event where she was commanded to be the perfect mistress — it would be a real date, where they spent actual time together having fun.

"Give me ten minutes," she said as she leaped up and practically ran off to dress. She didn't want to give him any chance to change his mind. His phone could ring at any moment with an emergency, and then their day would be over.

She emerged in nine minutes, feeling quite proud of herself. She'd simply tossed her hair back in a ponytail and thrown a baseball cap on her head. It was bright out, so she didn't bother with much makeup, and her jeans and shirt were the first in the pile she came to.

"I don't think I've ever seen a woman get ready so quickly."

"Then you're hanging out with the wrong women."

"I grew up with two sisters. I'm used to waiting on the opposite sex."

Rafe's referring to his sisters and not former mistresses put Ari in an even better mood. She was up for their mysterious adventures to begin.

"I can't do this. No way!" Ari said in a near panic as a man assisted her into a suit and tightly strapped her in.

"You can do it, Ari. Trust me, this will be a thrill you will never forget," Rafe answered with laughter.

"What if the cable breaks?"

"It won't break; I'll bet my entire fortune on it."

"That's an easy bet for you to make, considering I'll be nothing but a splash of blood on the cement below and unable to collect!"

"You can back out now, but I promise you will regret it if you do. I thought you weren't such a chicken," he said. Ari narrowed her eyes and closed her mouth. There was no way she was going to let him hold it over her head that she was too afraid to go on his thrill-seeking adventure, even if she did feel dangerously queasy.

"I swear that if I die, I'll haunt you the rest of your life. You won't know a moment's peace," she warned him.

"I'll hold you to that," he said as they stepped into the elevator for the short ride to the platform atop the Stratosphere tower.

"This is the highest controlled free-fall jump in the world. You need to follow the safety instructions to the letter. It is a thrill, but you have to use caution," the instructor said when the doors opened and another man began strapping cables to Ari's suit.

Was she really going to do this? Danger was *not* her middle name. Heck, she was even afraid of roller coasters. How could she have let Rafe goad her into jumping from a tall building and plummeting 855 feet to the ground below — the equivalent of 108 stories? She had to be crazy.

"Just take a small step and you'll have the thrill of your life," said the man next to her. It was easy for *him* to tell her to leap; *he* wasn't the one about to plunge to his death.

But it wasn't going to get any easier. Ari closed her eyes and walked off the little platform. Ooof! Whoa! As the wind was knocked from her lungs, and she began plummeting toward the hard cement far below, she said a quick prayer.

She must have got her breath back because she heard screaming, and the screaming was coming from her own throat. Blood was rushing through her veins and her heart was pounding so hard, she worried that it might rip right through her chest, but as she flew toward the ground, she forgot most of her fear.

She slowed as the ground rose to meet her, and allowing her eyes to take in the Las Vegas Strip, she felt an odd sense of freedom. For one small instant she was jealous of the birds.

Before she knew it, she was landing — on her feet, thankfully — and a man rushed up to assist her out of her straps.

"Did you have a good fall?"

"No. I'm afraid I'm happier that it's over than I am excited to have done it. Please don't tell the man who's coming down behind me, though," she said with a relieved laugh.

"This is something you either love or hate. There's not a lot of in between for this ride."

Ari agreed with him on that. As she stepped out of her suit, she heard a shout and looked up to see Rafe roaring toward her. Pure joy suffused his face.

To see him wear such an expression completely canceled out her earlier fright. He so rarely ever did something for pleasure alone — with the exception of sex — that she was grateful to be sharing this moment with him.

"What did you think? Was it great?" he asked her even before the attendants were able to unstrap him.

How could she disappoint him? "It was terrifying, but a little thrilling too," she admitted.

"Want to go for a second trip?" he asked eagerly.

"No!" she answered quickly, then gave her heart a moment to calm down before continuing. "I'm glad I jumped, but once is plenty for me. If you have anything else like that planned for the day, I'm going to have to decline."

"I promise that was the worst of the daredevil stuff. The rest of the day is all about fun," he promised.

What frightened Ari was that his idea of fun and hers seemed completely opposite. As they left the Stratosphere and caught a cab to an area closer to their hotel, Ari enjoyed the warm air and the sight of all the tourists.

When they entered the Mandalay Bay and she discovered a large shark tank, she turned an incredulous eye on Rafe.

"I promise you won't have to come near the sharks; there's a great water park where you can go down the slide if you want and look at their beautiful collection of marine life."

"Are you going?"

"Not on that one. If you don't mind, I'd like to dive. You could sit in the observation room and watch if you wish." The hopeful tone of his voice was refreshing. He wasn't telling her she had to sit and wait for him; he was asking if she wouldn't mind. It made a huge difference in how she felt about it.

"I'd love to see you play with the sharks. One of them may eat you," she added with a wide grin.

"Are you really so ready to get rid of me?" he growled as he pulled her into his arms.

"Mmm, not today," she offered before he silenced her with his mouth, leaving her breathless in a matter of seconds. His hands moved down her back and gripped her backside, pulling her tightly against him for a moment.

"I think it's far more dangerous to be standing here with you than to enter the shark tank," he said before squeezing her hips, then letting go and pulling her toward the scuba room. "This isn't nearly as great as diving in Mexico, but I haven't had the chance to get down there for a while, so it's better than nothing."

"Do you do this kind of thing a lot?"

"Yes and no. I like to dive every chance I get, but I'm usually too busy."

"That seems very sad to me, Rafe. Why don't you take more time for yourself?"

"I think I will, Ari," he said, while pausing to look in her eyes.

Something seemed to be changing in him — maybe, just possibly, they had a chance.

Ari watched him get ready; he looked pretty spectacular, she thought, in the skin-tight wet suit. She was led to an observation area, where she was able to watch him float around as he caressed the terrifying sharks. She could barely watch. Most of them were far bigger than Rafe, and though she was sure the hotel had ample precautions in place, all it would take was one good snap of their jaws to rip his head off. A shudder passed through her.

"The hotel has seven different species of sharks — sand tiger, nurse sharks, gray reef, and more. Also, there are a variety of fish and a few different stingrays inside. It's a thrilling experience, but it can be dangerous at the same time."

Ari turned to find out who was speaking — it was an employee standing right next to her. Why in the world would he tell her Rafe could be in danger? Was he trying to keep her blood pressure at an all-time high? Was she supposed to thank him for the information? She kept silent.

When Rafe gave her a thumbs up, then made his way to the surface, Ari let out the shallow breath she was holding and went to meet him by the changing area. She didn't yet know whether she'd survive the day.

Luckily for her, the rest of the afternoon was a lot more mellow. They went to The Mirage and entered Siegfried and Roy's Secret Garden and Dolphin Habitat, where she picked up a picture painted by the dolphins with their noses. She'd treasure those memories forever.

As the day wore on, she was finding herself fading. The hours of shopping in the forum shops left her barely able to make her way back to the hotel. Nobody could say that Rafe wasn't generous, and it made her incredibly uneasy.

When — if — she wasn't with him anymore, she wouldn't ever have a need to wear the abundance of fancy gowns and jewels he'd insisted on buying her. If and when that day came, she'd just have to leave it all with him. The thought of another woman having the items choked her up, but the guilt of keeping them would consume her.

When they finally entered their hotel and made their way to the elevator, Ari couldn't even muster up the energy to smile in relief; she just blindly followed behind Rafe.

"I'm falling asleep standing up," Ari said with a sleepy laugh as they entered the room. Her feet felt as if they were going to fall off, but the day had been more than worth it.

"Take a nap. I want you refreshed for part two."

"There's more?" she asked.

"Yes, and I want you rested."

Rafe didn't have to say anything further to convince her. She was so tired, she didn't know whether she'd make it to the bed, but a couple of hours' nap should refresh her. Ari lay down and nodded off immediately, but she did so with a smile on her face.

CHAPTER TWENTY-EIGHT

*Put on the dress hanging in the closet and
meet me by the front desk at eight.*

- Rafe

ARI LOOKED AT the note and forgave the ringing of
the phone that had jolted her from her restful sleep.
She hated wake-up service. The jerks didn't stop ringing until you answered the dang phone. She'd been sacked out
for two hours, and as she crawled from the bed and stretched,
she felt rejuvenated. It was only six-thirty, so she had a little
time to spend on making herself beautiful for an evening out.
There was something about being in Vegas that made her actually want to dress up and put on makeup. She hoped she got
back to her normal self once they returned to California.

When she opened the closet and saw the shimmering floor-length gown hanging before her, she couldn't contain her pleasure. Nothing was going to get in the way of her enjoying all this attention to the fullest. When they returned to the real world, things would go back to the way they'd been before, but for this one magical day, she would feel as if she were in a real relationship and the man she was with wanted to make her feel like a princess. It was sadly funny, of course, that she had to be in a fairy tale to be in that *real* relationship.

Leaving the closet open, Ari put her hair up and jumped into the shower to rinse off the grime from their busy day traipsing through the city. She used her favorite coconut body wash, knowing that it was Rafe's favorite, then rubbed herself from head to toe with its companion lotion. She now had costly French perfumes, but she chose this, knowing that the scent enveloping her would ring a little bell in his brain, starting a chain of reactions that would lead him to ravish her the instant they returned to their suite.

Not that their sex life was lacking — he was a magnificent lover, and she was more than satisfied in that department, even if some of his requests tended to frighten her. She still hadn't been pushed into doing anything that had struck her as less than fulfilling.

Fear kept her from wanting to try new things, but Rafe was such a considerate lover that only escalating anticipation flowed through her veins whenever they set foot in the bedroom. She was starting to want to learn some new tricks of her own.

Maybe if she kept things exciting, they'd both get to enjoy each other a while longer. Hard as she tried to fight it, she couldn't squelch that thought. She was enjoying Rafe's presence more and more — when he acted the way he did today.

Taking extra time with her hair and makeup, Ari made it back out to her closet at seven-thirty. She'd barely have time to get into the dress and delicate shoes and still make it down to Rafe in time. But hey! If she happened to be a few minutes late, he'd survive. Wasn't it a man's *job* to wait on a woman? According to a popular country song, it was. The thought made her smile. Again.

Slipping into extra-sexy lingerie, Ari looked at herself in the mirror and shook her hips slowly from side to side, dipping lower in mid-sway. She'd never before considered doing this sort of dance for a man; now her nipples hardened and her stomach clenched at the thought.

When she'd lost another five minutes moving her body in seductive circles, Ari frantically abandoned her dance practice and grabbed the dress. It fit her as if it had been tailored specifically for her body. *How does he do that?*

Sliding her shoes on last, she looked in the mirror again and decided she was as ready as she was going to be. She felt good — who wouldn't in that dress and those shoes? Grabbing her small clutch, Ari headed for the door and walked quickly to the elevator. She was ready to see what else Rafe had in store.

*****

"You look even more stunning than I imagined. How can that be?" Rafe asked as she approached. Seeing her face glow at his praise made his heart race. She was so easily pleased — another shocking attribute. Though he was proud to have such a beauty on his arm, her company was what captivated him. He greeted her with outstretched arms that gracefully moved up to her face where his large hands tenderly cradled the sides of her neck and his thumbs caressed her soft cheeks. He tilted her head back and kissed her with a passion that nearly made her breathless and she felt all the way to her toes.

"Thank you, Rafe. I have to admit that you're incredibly dashing in your black suit. That red tie is my absolute favorite."

Warmed by her honest compliment, he placed her delicate arm through his and led her out the front doors to their waiting limo.

"The day has been adventurous already. I can't imagine what else you have in store," she said as they settled down in the back seat and he pulled out a bottle of chilled champagne and a small bowl of strawberries.

"Ah, the night is young," he said as he handed over the glass. He wanted to keep pleasing her, see excitement shining in her eyes. To give to someone who asked for nothing was a real gift.

"If I don't get a chance to say it later, thank you, Rafe. Thank you for giving me such a perfect day."

Rafe didn't know what to say as he looked into her eyes, so he chose to say nothing, but instead bent forward and gently connected their lips. The soft feel of her kiss tugged at his emotions, but he suppressed them as he took her glass and set it aside so he could pull her onto his lap.

Their kiss deepened as the limo made its way through traffic toward the intimate rooftop restaurant. Just when he was getting ready to cancel their evening plans and take her back to the room, the car stopped.

With reluctance, Rafe gently eased Ari off his lap and took a moment to adjust his pants. Even after months of sinking deep within her flesh, he still couldn't get enough. He was beginning to think he never would. What if no other woman would be able to replace her?

He refused to think those thoughts right now.

Rafe made his way out of the car first and held out his hand. She took his fingers and emerged, and then, with his palm resting on the small of her back, he led her inside the hotel and up into the restaurant on the strategically covered rooftop. The maître d' greeted them as if they were familiar guests and escorted them to a private area.

"Oh, Rafe, this is stunning," she whispered as she walked to the railing, drinking in the picturesque landscape of the distant mountains. Below them was a man-made waterfall, its sound swallowing up the noise of the bustling city on the other side of their small paradise.

The soft light of the setting sun falling over Ari seemed to uncover a window to her soul and the exquisite beauty within. In that moment Rafe made up his mind to take her to Italy — he had to show her his home, to explore the countryside with her next to him. Viewing it through her appreciative eyes would surely renew his jaded soul. She had such a love of new experiences that it humbled him, stirring emotions inside him of how truly lucky he'd been in his youth.

"Back home, we'd take a lot of picnics. My mother's country is beautiful with water everywhere, and the land filled with green. I look out at the desert here and I can appreciate its peculiar beauty, the deathly traps it holds, the amount of survival it takes to live in such a barren area, but I need more where I choose to live. I need the fresh blooms of spring and the feel of soft grass in a park. I need seasons."

"I'd never been outside of California before meeting you," Ari said, "so it's all beautiful to me. I love the way the land changes as you move across it. It fascinates me how on one side of a mountain there can be thick, lush greenery and streams of flowing water, and then on the other side, dry, crackling ground and minimal plant life. Yet each area, no matter what it is, serves its purpose, and different people find beauty all around them wherever they choose to live."

"Do you ever have a negative way of looking at something?" he asked with a laugh.

"Well, I had quite a few negative thoughts of you when we first met," she replied teasingly.

"Do you still?" he asked, all laughter suddenly vanishing from his features.

The smile dropped from her face, too, as she tilted her head and looked at him as if really thinking about her answer. Rafe was unsure whether he wanted to hear what she had to say.

"You're not the monster I thought you were, Rafe. I can see the amazing man beneath your tough shell — but I also know our time will come to an end. I just hope we both walk away feeling as if we've gained something — as if our time spent together wasn't a waste."

The tightening in Rafe's chest became almost unbearable as he watched a bit of the light wane in her expressive eyes. Could he ever forgive himself if he permanently snuffed out her inner light of joy?

Rafe shook off the unwelcome thought. He'd promised himself he would let it all go for one night.

"Tell me about your home," Ari asked, as Rafe took her hand and led her back to the table, where dishes Rafe had ordered earlier were laid out for them. While she waited for his reply, she bit into a piece of roast duck, closing her eyes for a moment to savor the myriad flavors. "This sauce is amazing."

Rafe was silent as he enjoyed Ari's pleasure — her eloquent face fascinating to watch. When she looked up with raised brows, he smiled before he began to speak.

"We all led such a double life — no, not in that sense. We had two homes, two countries, and it's reflected in a split in each of our personalities, I think. Life was different in Italy. In my younger years I didn't like the time spent in the States — it seemed too driven, too focused, too…lonely, perhaps. When we were back in Italy, my father was home more, would take time to go on hikes with us, and take us on boat rides. When here, he worked long hours and we didn't see him as much. As I got older I realized he was only trying to make a comfortable life for his family, but I felt a lot of resentment during my teenage years."

"When did you meet Shane?"

"Here, in then States. He was unlike anyone I'd met before. My truest friend has a natural ability to draw others to him. I learned early on that most people wanted something out of me, whether it was my money, connections or the status of being friends with such a wealthy kid. I started to become bitter, I think — it goes with the territory. None of those things mattered to Shane. Even though he doesn't act like someone with an impressive balance sheet, the man is probably wealthier than I am. We got on immediately, and I know he needed someone. He hated his family with a passion — they were enemies, not allies, infected with intense hostility — and he refused to follow in his father's footsteps."

"What happened to make him hate his dad?"

"That's a story for Shane to tell. Let's just say that if I had been in his shoes, I'd most likely have ended up in prison for murder." As Ari cringed, Rafe shuttered his emotions. This was no time to display rage.

"He seems like such a carefree guy," Ari said, furrowing her forehead.

"Shane learned early in life how to mask what he was feeling. He had to in order to survive. His father was the *true* definition of a monster."

"Is he still alive?"

"We need to change the subject. This night is about relaxation and romance.

"Romance?" Ari asked with a twinkle in her eyes.

"Yes, romance. We'd better get on with our evening," Rafe said as he stood and held out his hand.

Soft music was filtering out to them, and Rafe pulled Ari into his arms, inhaling her unique scent as she leaned her head against his chest and the two began a slow, reverent dance.

"I could do this all night," she whispered.

"Then we won't leave." He found himself not wanting to deny her anything.

The waiter brought out their next course, and Rafe reluctantly released Ari so she could eat. Though the dishes were prepared to perfection, Rafe had no desire to sit across from Ari at a table. Too much distance. He wanted to hold her, feel her body pressed against his. And for the first time he could remember, that was good enough. Tonight, he wanted nothing more than to caress her smooth skin, run his fingers through her hair and whisper his dreams in her ear.

So dangerous. But one night of letting go wouldn't harm him. One night to feel more than lust wouldn't break him.

When their meal was finally finished and forgotten, Rafe took Ari to a smoky jazz club, where he held her in his arms as the sweet sounds of music drifted through the room. Cradling Ari's delicate hand in his, he gloried also in the warmth of her cheek as she rested her head on his chest. It was so easy to lose himself in the moment. He was in deeper than he'd ever planned — but he couldn't make himself feel regret.

By the time they arrived back at their room, Rafe knew he should leave her at their bedroom door and take a walk, but instead, he gently pulled her into his arms and slowly removed her dress in the dim light seeping through the curtains of the living room.

"Do you have any clue how ravishing you are, Ari? I'm a jealous man and I see the way you attract the attention of every male in a room. I also see that you don't even notice. I could spend all night and day doing nothing but worshipping your body."

He bent down and ran his lips along the delicate skin of her neck, delighted when a shiver ran through her.

"I can't think straight when you speak to me like that, Rafe," she whispered as her head fell backward.

"Then don't think. Just let go." Rafe lifted her into his arms and carried her to their room where he made slow, sweet love to her until the early hours of morning. When pure exhaustion took over, he fell asleep with her body atop him.

CHAPTER TWENTY-NINE

L
IA WOKE UP in Shane's arms and couldn't keep the smile from her face. They'd finally made love. The night out had done the trick, and she felt pretty proud of herself at seducing the incredibly suave Shane Grayson, even if it had taken help from her little sister and a very sexy burlesque show.

"What are you smiling about?"

Lia jumped as she tore her gaze from Shane's magnificent chest and met his stunning dark chocolate eyes. She loved the gleam in them, the way they mesmerized her — turned her to liquid heat.

"I seduced the lady-killer Shane Grayson, my body is exquisitely sore from a few rounds of earth-shattering sex, *and* I plan on repeating the night all day long," she answered with a satisfied grin.

The first sign of trouble came when the window shades came over his eyes. *No. No. No.* She absolutely wouldn't allow him to retreat. The sex had been better than she'd imagined it possibly could be, and he wasn't going to make up some lame excuse about her being Rafe's little sister and about how wrong it was for them to have slept together. She would have to kill him.

Lia glowered at him, letting him know she could read his thoughts, and that he'd better think twice if he were contemplating trying to sneak away from her. Never before had she been this bold with a man.

Yes, Lia was self-confident. She took care of her body, working out five days a week, eating healthfully, and going to the spas. She bought nice clothes and took time with her hair and makeup. She wasn't vain, but she knew she wasn't the worst catch in the world. Yet when it came to Shane, her confidence sank to an all-time low.

Her long-time unrequited love would be a blow to anybody's ego. Growing up in a wealthy, loving family didn't spare her from heartache.

If Shane walked out on her, she'd never forgive him — not after the night they'd spent.

"Lia…"

"I swear, if you spout off again about this being wrong —"

"Give me a minute here," he insisted.

She didn't relax her glare, but waited in silence for him to continue. When he raised an eyebrow as if asking whether it was OK to continue speaking, she nodded her head the barest inch.

"I'm not running. I just have to speak to Rafe about this. He's my best friend, and I won't sneak behind his back and sleep with his little sister."

"No."

"What do you mean, *no*? You can't just tell me *no*," Shane said with an outraged scowl.

"I don't want him to know. It's none of his business. Plus, I like the thought of a secret affair — at least for a little while. We can sneak off to one of the spare rooms at my parents' house during a family dinner, make love in the back of the car on the way to your office, meet for lunch and have only *dessert*," Lia whispered as she bent down and began kissing his chest.

Her hand reached down and she felt his obvious pleasure at her words. He was thick and hard and she couldn't resist slipping the covers down and climbing on top of him.

"We need to talk," he gasped as she positioned herself over him and slowly sunk down on his staff. The groan at the end of his words effectively shut him up.

"You fill me so full, Shane. I could ride you like this all day long," she moaned as she lifted herself nearly free of him before pushing down against his hips, enjoying the sound of their bodies connecting.

Shane gripped her hips and started thrusting up inside her, taking over their movements as pressure began building. One hand moved forward and he began rubbing her in just the right spot with the flat of his thumb, speeding up her heart, and bringing her to the brink of orgasm.

Lia reached up and gripped her breasts, squeezing her nipples in her hands as he plunged quickly inside her while still rubbing her swollen pink pearl.

It didn't take long before she shattered around him, and only a few more thrusts and he joined her, draining them both. When she could breathe easily again, she lifted her head to look into his eyes, but refused to budge from lying on top of him.

"See how good this can be? It's just our secret," she said, loving that she'd won in their little disagreement.

"You can easily distract me, Lia, but eventually we'll have to drag ourselves out of this bed, and the first chance I get, I'm talking to Rafe."

It took a moment for Shane's words to get past her euphoria to the rational part of her brain, but when they penetrated, her temper rose to the surface. She climbed off him and grabbed the sheet.

What should she say next? He wasn't listening to her. If Rafe got involved, it would make their relationship complicated, and she didn't want that. She just wanted *easy*.

"This discussion was held and now it's over. What man doesn't want no-strings, no-holds-barred, repeatedly orgasmic sex?" she asked in disgust.

"Lia, I plan on taking you over and over again. I plan on doing all sorts of very wonderful things to your body that I won't tell Rafe about. But I won't keep our relationship secret from my best friend."

Shane sat up next to her, pulling the blanket up over his lap, thereby shielding her favorite part of him from view.

"What is wrong with having a secret affair? No one has to know and no one has to get hurt."

"That may be OK with strangers. It's not OK to carry on an affair like that with a woman I've known for over ten years."

"You're an idiot, Shane. *Fine*! I don't want to do this."

Before she could get up, he had her flat on her back as he looked deep into her eyes and his hand slid down her body. Her traitorous nipples instantly responded to his touch, contradicting what she'd just said.

"You do want to do this — and we will. You chased me — now you're stuck. We'll continue this argument after I've spoken to Rafe," he promised as his head descended and he latched onto a peaked nipple.

Lia groaned as he ignited her once again. But before she could get lost in desire, she pushed him away and jumped from the bed, taking the sheet with her.

"If you decide to pull your head out and keep this between the two of us, you can join me in the shower," she offered before dropping the sheet and turning around. She put a little extra wiggle into her hips as an added incentive.

When Shane didn't join her after a few minutes, she glared at the door before angrily scrubbing her skin until it was red.

"Stupid men and their ethics," she grumbled before trying to thrust any and all thoughts of Shane from her head. She had more important things to do.

She decided she'd gotten what she wanted out of Shane, and she was done with him anyway. If only her aching body hadn't disagreed...

*****

Shane paced the hallway, taking deep breaths as he passed Rafe's door for the tenth time. What was *wrong* with him? He didn't run from a fight — he wasn't afraid to speak his mind, and he certainly wasn't afraid to tell his best friend anything.

He and Rafe had been through hell and back together. Rafe was the one who'd put him back together when the pieces of his life had completely fallen apart. It would all be fine, and later the two of them would have a good laugh over an exceptional bottle of single-malt scotch.

Drawing in a deep breath, Shane stopped on his next pass and knocked on Rafe's door. Standing there felt like an eternity as he waited for his friend to answer.

"Shane, I thought we were meeting downstairs. I'm not ready," Rafe said as he opened the door wider for Shane to walk through.

"I need to talk to you privately."

"Are the girls all right?"

Rafe's immediate concern reminded Shane why he had so much respect for him. Under his hardened exterior, Rafe was truly one of the good guys.

"Yes, everything is fine. I just need to let you know what's going on with Lia and me."

As Rafe's eyes narrowed, Shane knew he'd been too optimistic. This wasn't going to be a pleasant conversation. He thought back to the limo ride and the way Rafe flipped out over Rachel's teasing comments.

"I thought *nothing* was going on between the two of you," Rafe said as he made his way to his liquor cabinet and poured himself a shot. Shane noted that his friend wasn't offering him anything, so he walked over and helped himself. He needed a bracer to get through this conversation.

"Nothing *was* going on then, but…" Shane didn't know how to finish that sentence. He certainly didn't want to tell Rafe about last night.

"I have the feeling I'm going to have to kick your ass."

At Rafe's words, Shane's shoulders stiffened and he looked his friend boldly in the eye. Lia wasn't a child anymore. She had a right to date whomever she wanted, and Shane had no reason to be feeling guilty.

"I like your sister a lot, Rafe. We've decided to give a relationship a try."

Rafe returned the stare. Refusing to back down even an inch, Shane held his gaze, and silently let his friend know he wasn't going anywhere.

"We both know you're a screw-'em-and-leave-'em type, and one-night stands are your well-known M.O. Hell, Shane, a week with a woman is a major accomplishment for you. So if you don't stay away from Lia, our friendship ends right now."

Fire shot through Shane's blood at the assumption that he'd just back down. He loved Rafe, would take a bullet for the man, but right now he was fighting the urge to plant a solid right to his cheekbone.

"It's not that way with Lia," he said, his voice dangerously low.

"Bull! Like you can be any other way," Rafe thundered.

"Look who's talking, Rafe. Where in the hell do you get off telling me *I* mistreat women? Do you even know how to respect one? You are so good to your family and friends, the few of them you allow in your life, but when it comes to women, it's as if they're no better than wild animals to you — you tame them for your sport, and move on. I've never belittled even *one* of the ladies I've been with, or treated them with indifference or contempt the way you do — and I never would."

"I give the utmost respect to my mistresses. They are very comfortably taken care of and walk away with far more than they brought in to our relationship. I haven't had any complaints."

"You don't give them the option to complain, because you make damn sure that you own them from the second they enter a relationship with you. I don't even know why I'm calling it a relationship; it's a business agreement, damn it. Lia cares about me, and I care about her. I didn't come here to ask for your permission. I'm here because you're my best friend and I won't go sneaking behind your back. I have nothing to be ashamed of, and I won't hide in the dark when it comes to Lia. I said care about her, and I meant it!"

Shane turned to leave, fed up with talking. He'd known how it was going to go. When it came to his family, Rafe was completely unreasonable, but maybe, in time, he'd come to understand. Then again, Shane didn't know how long this…thing with Lia would last — it wouldn't be forever. So maybe he *was* making a mistake.

"Wait!"

Shane stood at the door with his hand on the knob. He knew he should go, but if there was a chance they could come to an understanding, maybe he wouldn't lose his best friend. Slowly, he turned around, his protective shield firmly in place.

"I'll listen, Shane, but I'm telling you, I don't like this at all."

"I know that anything beyond your control is hard for you to handle. I can accept that, Rafe. I don't want to give up what we've cultivated for the past fifteen years."

"How did this happen?"

"Hell, Rafe, you know Lia's been pursuing me since the first time I stepped through your door."

"She was a kid," Rafe accused.

"Like I was even looking twice at her back then!" Shane thundered. It pissed him off that he had to say that.

"Sorry. I know."

Shane accepted Rafe's apology, then walked to the cabinet and poured himself another shot. They could turn this around.

"You know about the time last year when Lia and I ended up at the hotel together. But I swear *nothing* happened then. Ever since, however, I've seen her in a new light. I've fought it like mad, but your sister doesn't give up. This trip, I just stopped fighting it."

Rafe let out a laugh, which astonished Shane enough to stop him mid-drink. Had his best friend finally gone off the deep end?

"Yes, I know how persistent my sister can be. Hell, I'm impressed it took her this long to get what she wanted."

Just like that, the tension evaporated and the two men sat down and discussed Lia for a few more minutes, then dropped the subject in favor of the upcoming UFC fight.

Shane was both relieved and surprised to have come to an understanding, but now that he had Rafe on board, he had to convince Lia to let go of her anger. When he'd left her room, she'd been furious. A smile came to his face as he imagined all sorts of ways to put her in a better mood.

CHAPTER THIRTY

SHANE WALKED INTO the event center and was over-whelmed with pride. The stage was set and people buzzed about as they made last-minute preparations. This was the season finale of *The Ultimate Fighter*.

It might have been a reality television show, but the kids who were in this competition had chosen to take the higher road in life — and he knew how hard that was.

"Where's your kid?"

"He'll be down shortly. I got him a room upstairs."

"That's a change for him," Rafe said with a smile.

"Don't be a smart ass, Rafe. You know what he's gone through."

"I know. You've done a great job with him, and the other dozen kids you've helped."

"You've been right there with me helping these kids, too."

"I'm not the one who got involved with this. You are, and we both know why," Rafe said as he patted Shane on the shoulder.

"Let's not talk about that. Today is a day of celebration. Seth gets to see where he'll be in a few years."

"I still don't get how his beating the crap out of somebody in a ring is any different than doing it on the street."

"I can't believe you're saying that, Rafe. You love to box."

"Yeah, boxing relieves stress for me, but these kids go beyond boxing."

"If my kids fight on the streets, they're out of the competitions. No exceptions — you know that. Giving them this control changes everything about how they act in life. They get an outlet for the frustrations their circumstances threw at them."

"Hey, Shane. That room is out of this world!"

"So you made it down here, Seth. Just in time to get to our seats." Shane turned around and gave Seth a hug.

"Rafe, I wasn't expecting you here. It's good to see you, man." Seth gave Rafe a hug next.

"It's great to see you, too, kid. You've grown about a foot since the last time."

"It's only been a couple of months," Seth said with a smile as he shifted on his feet.

"Well, you're seventeen now — and I hear you graduated from high school with honors. What college are you attending in the fall?"

"I just want to keep fighting and focus on that, but Shane won't let me unless I enroll. I'm starting at Stanford in the fall thanks to Shane's connections," he said with a sigh. Though he was pretending to protest, Seth didn't seem unhappy about attending such a prestigious school.

"It looks like Shane has your best interests at heart. You'll enjoy school there. I hear a lot of great-looking women attend."

"Nice! I can dig that! Hey, I can smell someone barbecuing and I'm *so* ready for a burger. Do you guys want anything?"

"We're good. Just meet us back down here when you're done."

Seth took off and Shane and Rafe sat down.

Shane reflected on when he'd first met Seth. He'd been at the beach swimming one day in San Diego. He'd left his shirt on his cooler and when he got back it was gone along with the cooler and everything in it. Since Shane had suffered through a difficult few years of his own, he knew it was most likely a street kid who often stole from tourists.

Normally, Shane would have just let it go, but it was one of his favorite shirts, so he took a stroll down the beach and was amazed to see a scrawny kid wearing his clothing. The kid wasn't even trying to hide the fact that he'd stolen Shane's things. To make the insult worse, the kid was sitting on Shane's cooler drinking a bottle of Shane's water.

Shane approached the young man and calmly told him he wanted his shirt back. Seth had looked at Shane and denied knowing what he was talking about; the shirt was his. But then a policeman passing by asked whether there was a problem, and when Shane saw the panic in the kid's eyes, he'd said no — everything was cool. Shane took Seth to dinner and didn't let up on him until he learned the boy's circumstances.

It took a while, but Shane found out Seth was living with a group of homeless kids, all between ten and seventeen. Seth was only thirteen at the time, but his eyes showed the evidence of years of hard living.

The group did what they had to in order to survive, including theft, prostitution, consuming and selling drugs — whatever it took. By the end of that dinner, which Seth practically inhaled, Shane earned enough trust that the kid agreed to meet him again.

Shane gave him a few dollars, enough to tempt Seth to come back, but not enough that he could get into too much trouble. They started meeting for lunch in a nearby park each

afternoon, and Shane learned more and more of his story —
that's when he'd decided to help his group.

He'd gotten them involved at a gym his friend owned, set
them up in a home where they could all stay together and
helped them get back into school. Four of the kids left, too
hardened to change, but six of the ten stayed, and out of those
six, four were still there. One had graduated from high school
last year and was in his first year of college. Seth had just graduated high school last month — a year early! — and the other
two boys only had one year to go.

Seth was the only one in the group who'd taken to fighting.
It was a way for him to channel his rage — anger from his
father's abandoning him, his mother's overdosing on drugs,
and his losing everyone he'd ever loved in his life. He'd picked
up on martial arts quickly, and within a couple years, he was
becoming the guy to beat in the ring.

Shane thought the kid had a real chance of making it in the
UFC. The day Shane knew Seth was going to be OK was the
day Seth broke down in Shane's arms. It was the boy's fifteenth
birthday and Shane had surprised him with a cake.

His heart had broken when he found out it was the first
birthday cake Seth had ever had. And that night, when Shane
gave him a brand new pair of Nike shoes, Seth had given Shane
an appreciative hug, then sobbed in his arms.

Shane couldn't hold back a few of his own tears as this tough
street kid allowed himself to show real emotion for the first time
in years. Shane couldn't save them all, but even one kid — just
one — was gratifying.

When Rafe had found out what Shane was doing, of course
he had jumped in, donating funds, spending time at the gym,
and letting the kids know that not everyone was against them.
Rafe had been the one who saved Shane's life when he'd run
away at the tender age of fifteen.

Shane would die for Rafe. But he didn't want these kids to
idolize him — he knew he was too far from perfect to deserve

that. But idolize him they did. They'd given up, and the unaccustomed kindness he'd shown toward them earned their adulation.

Seth returned to the two men well fed and with a smile of anticipation on his face. This is where he wanted to be someday — in that ring, fighting for the championship. There was a chance he just might make it.

The stadium began filling up, and music pumped out from the speakers. Seth was practically jumping in his seat. When the first fighters were introduced, he jumped up shouting as he waited for one of his heroes to walk through the tunnel on the far side of the stadium, where they'd walk along a narrow path to the ring in the center of the theater. Cameras followed the fighters, so before they emerged from the tunnels, the crowd was fired up as they saw them on the big screens approaching the opening.

"Did you see that?" Seth yelled as he turned around. The fighter had passed by and slapped his hand. Would the kid refuse to wash it over the next month? Shane wondered.

"You want to know what's even better?"

"There's nothing better than getting to high-five one of the fighters!"

"How about getting to meet a couple of them?"

Seth said nothing as he gazed wide-eyed at Shane, trying to decipher whether his mentor was telling him the truth. Trust still didn't come easy for the young man.

Shane pulled out the backstage passes and handed one to Seth, who looked at the card as if he were holding treasure. Tears filled Seth's eyes as he looked at Shane, then Rafe. He turned around to choke down the sob threatening to bubble up, and he refused to turn back until he was under control.

"I don't even know what to say, Shane. *Thank you* seems so lame," he said so quietly, Shane could barely hear him.

"*Thank you* is always good enough when it's meant," Shane replied, speaking with difficulty over what felt like a golf-ball-sized lump in his throat.

All conversation ceased as the fight began. Seth instead cheered so loudly that by the halfway point, he was losing his voice. By the end of the fight, he was down to only a whisper. And when Shane and Rafe took him backstage, the kid nearly passed out.

The fighters were amazing with him, though, encouraging him to keep up the fighting so they could one day stand in the audience and cheer him on. Shane knew that this was one of those life-changing events that Seth would never forget.

For that matter, it was pretty life-changing for Shane as well. As he and Rafe left the building, they were both silent as they thought about the way their lives had turned out. Rafe had grown up privileged, with a loving family, but he'd still gone through his periods of darkness.

Shane was lucky to have risen above his grim circumstances. Now, he was in a place where he could help kids like Seth. The rest of the world had given up on these "throwaway" kids, making them want to give up on themselves, but when people like Shane stepped up, some of them could be saved.

"Do you think you'll be able to talk again, Seth?" Rafe asked as he ruffled his hair.

"Who cares? This has been a dream come true," he squeaked as they made their way from the coliseum.

"I have no doubt you'll be in that ring soon, kid. But, seriously, don't ever think you have to keep fighting if you don't want to. You may find that you love college even more than being in that ring," Shane told him.

"No way, Shane. I love you, man, but right now you're just plain crazy. What could be better than stepping into that ring with thousands of people cheering your name?"

"You know, being a great fighter is important, but being a great person is what makes the audience love you. As long as you stay true to yourself, you'll always have fans. Someday, you'll inspire some kid who needs a break."

"And I owe it all to you."

"Hey, none of that. Why don't you enjoy some movies and room service before you fly home?"

By the time Shane and Rafe made it back to their hotel, both of them were ready to part. Shane needed to hold Lia, assure himself that he really had the right to pull her into his arms — after making sure she didn't bash him over the head.

Rafe didn't know what he wanted. OK, that wasn't entirely true — he knew what he wanted — he just didn't know how to go about getting it.

CHAPTER THIRTY-ONE

WHAT HAD HAPPENED in Vegas stayed with every one of them during the trip home. But their thoughts were not the sort to be shared. Even Lia kept quiet, for once uninterested in trying to antagonize either her brother or her lover.

"What the heck happened with you and Shane? You haven't looked at him once since we left the hotel." Ari finally whispered when they were halfway home. Lia shook her head quellingly and looked away.

When they landed, Ari learned that Rafe's plans for now didn't include her.

"Ari, my father's in town and I need to meet with him. Head back to your place. I'll call you." With that, Rafe led her to a waiting car, helped her inside, then shut the door.

Before this moment, Ari had hoped to have some time all to herself; she wanted to be able to sort through her thoughts and feelings about Rafe. But his manner of dismissing her so coldly and easily tore at her. He could be so caring and intense one moment and then businesslike and unfeeling the next. Now was the time to decide on her next step.

Three months had passed — her original agreement with Rafe was over, and she was living in limbo. She needed to lay it all out there, either offer up her heart or walk away and move forward with her life. But how to choose?

Ari opened the door to a condo that felt like a tomb. The silence hung heavily over her, dead, oppressive, and the familiar rooms suddenly felt airless and stale. The solitude she'd so often welcomed had become a cruel isolation, suffocating her, making her eyes sting.

Was Rafe an anchor or just a heavy weight upon her heart? Ari hoped for a chance to gauge her reaction when he next walked though her door. And so she waited. And waited.

When the ornate clock struck ten, Ari shook off her cobwebs and went off to prepare for bed. Rafe wasn't going to join her on their first night back.

*****

"How was your trip, Rafe? You're not usually one to take a four-day weekend to play."

Rafe downed his double shot of scotch, then poured another.

"It was a work trip, Dad. Shane and I are partners on a hotel and casino down there, and we were able to check in on the progress."

"If it had been a work trip, you wouldn't have brought along the extra passengers," Martin Palazzo said with a laugh as he sat down and waited for Rafe to join him.

Rafe had never been able to lie to his dad. Maybe his old man could actually help him. Without giving himself time to change his mind, Rafe sat down and tried to open up.

"I don't know what to do, Father. I do care about Ari — I think you know that." When his father remained silent, Rafe looked out the study window for a moment, and then continued. "There are things about me that you don't know — things I'm ashamed to admit to you. But it's how I've coped."

"I know more than you realize, son. What Sharron did to you was unconscionable — she took something away that isn't easily regained. I have waited for you to talk to me — for you to realize you were on a self-destructive path that can only end in heartache. Has that day finally arrived?"

"What do you know?" Rafe was aghast, horrified even to think about what his father might have discovered.

"I won't go into details here, but I know you've been less than honorable. I know that women are little more than candy for your arm, and a warm body for your bed. You weren't raised that way, Rafe. A woman is never to be used — never to be treated with disrespect. It's a privilege to earn their love and a responsibility to keep it."

"What if they don't deserve it?" Rafe thundered, frustration making his words to his father unusually harsh.

"No woman deserves to be treated as little more than your toy. If you feel she is nothing more than a cheap hooker, where is your self-respect in spending time with her at all? And if you know she's better than that, where is your decency? You owe it to such a woman to walk away," Martin scolded.

Rafe knew his father was right, but to admit that would mean he'd have to let Ari go. He couldn't do that — but he also couldn't give her his heart. He no longer had a heart to give.

"I'm good to my women, Father," he contended.

"You can put diamonds on their necks, but it's little more than a leash when the gems aren't given out of affection. You can tell yourself you treat them well, but do you really? I've watched you with Ari. Does she get your love — or does she simply get your body? How long do you think a woman like her will settle for less than she deserves? Even if she loves you,

Rafe — and I think she does — she will eventually respect herself enough to walk away from you."

No!

Rafe wasn't ready for Ari to leave him — or for him to leave her. But there was really no way forward with her. A woman had held his sanity in her hand once; it wouldn't happen to him twice.

"I can't tell you what to do, Rafe, but you came to me wanting advice. The only wisdom I can give you is to either give her your heart — or set her free."

Rafe slumped down in the chair, his father's words echoing in his head. Set her free? No. She didn't want to go. Ari had never had trouble telling him what was on her mind. Already, Rafe had bent his rules — made accommodations for her that he'd never made with any of his other mistresses.

He was in the right to keep their relationship safe — free from burdens like love and affection. Yet if he truly felt that way, why did his heart feel so hollow? Why did he want to listen to his father and run to her, tell her he cared? Was he falling in love with the woman?

If he was, it would only end tragically. She could never love him after the way he'd treated her. And if she did, she was a fool. This couldn't end well for either of them.

The thought tore through him. He needed just a bit more time — then he would listen to his dad. Then he would do what he should have done the moment he'd met her in his office all those months ago.

Even then, he'd known she was all wrong for him. His emotions had clouded his normally cool head. He'd chased her, something he never did. He'd won — but at what cost? The price may have just been too high for both of them.

"I just don't know, Dad."

"Go somewhere and think. You are surrounded every day by people whose only desire is to please you. If you give yourself some time alone, you can sort all of this out. You can come to grips with yourself and what's best for you — and for her. I think you'll be surprised by the answers you'll find."

Rafe rose and walked over to his dad, slinging his arm around his shoulders and giving him a warm hug.

"Thank you, Father. I'm sorry I've shut you out. I'm sorry I've disappointed you. I think time alone is just what I need."

With that, Rafe left the room and called his pilot as he climbed in the car. Telling no one of his destination, he left the country. It was past time he figured out what he wanted.

CHAPTER THIRTY-TWO

ARI INHALED DEEPLY, reveling in the evocative scents of her mother's flower shop. She'd been coming here since before she was able to form lasting memories.

Her mom had told her about the brightly painted basinet that had sat in the corner until it was replaced by a playpen, and then eventually a school desk. In that corner she'd learned how to make beautiful bouquets for weddings and create corsages for girls at their first prom.

"Hi, Mom," she called out when she spotted her mother at her beloved workstation.

"I wasn't expecting you in here today," Sandra replied as she wiped her hands, then quickly stepped around the counter and rushed over to embrace her daughter.

"I came to help and spend quality time with my mom."

"Well, you certainly picked a good day. I have a small wedding I'm preparing flowers for. I have to drop them off in the morning, so it was going to be a long night for me. But with two sets of hands we might get out of here in time to grab a bite to eat."

"I'm a bit rusty, but I'm sure you can refresh my memory in record time."

"It's just like riding a bike. It will all come back to you — besides, we're working with roses and it's hard to mess up a bouquet with such a beautiful flower in it. Come on and I'll put you to work while you catch me up on what's been keeping you so preoccupied these days."

The stress from the last few months evaporated as she stood by her mother's side and started bunching flowers together and tying ribbon around the stems. Turning nature into art was very soothing — therapeutic even — and soon Ari relaxed.

"Have you registered for classes yet?"

"Not yet, Mom, but I'm thinking about going back next term — I promise," Ari answered with a wince. Without her mother pushing her so hard, she might have given up on going back. Nerves and Rafe's insanely demanding schedule kept sidetracking her.

"I will go with you just to make sure. I want to see my baby girl receive that diploma."

"OK. I promise I'll do it. How about we make it a date and go in next Friday?" Ari asked with a laugh. If Rafe thought Ari was pushy, he obviously hadn't spent much time with her mother. Not that Ari wanted him to — she was too deeply involved with his him and *his* family, and adding her mom to the equation would make parting with him so much more painful.

"Now that we settled that, how is work going?"

"It's fine. I enjoy the Palazzo building. It's beautiful inside and out. The only real negative is that I hardly ever see Amber, Shelly and Miley from my old job anymore. Rafe has a crazy traveling schedule; we leave on a moment's notice. And then sometimes we're at the office until midnight. It's a little exhausting," Ari admitted. She didn't add that his demands in the bedroom were the most exhausting of all — very satisfying, but exhausting nevertheless.

"Ari, you have to make time for your friends. When a man starts to dictate too much of what you do and demand all your time, that's your cue to back away. I like Rafe, honestly I do, but I worry that he's taking too much from you. I'd have no problem with stepping in and letting him know he needs to back off," Sandra threatened.

"That means the world to me, Mom, but I can take care of it. He's not a bad guy; he just… makes the wrong decisions sometimes. However, he treats me well. When he tries some of his demanding crap, I don't allow it. I promise you that if I ever feel as if I'm being taken advantage of, I'll walk away from him so fast, his head will spin."

Sandra looked at her for a long moment and Ari began to squirm. She didn't know how her mother did it, but the woman just seemed to know things. She knew how Ari was feeling sometimes before even Ari knew. It was creepy and comforting all at the same time.

"I won't lie to you and tell you I think everything is perfectly OK, but I will respect your decision and take comfort in the fact that I raised you to be a strong woman. I hope I've taught you enough that you'll never accept less than what you deserve."

Ari felt tears fill her eyes. She was so grateful that her mother had pulled through the accident and the cancer. Never had she been more afraid than when she thought she wouldn't see her mom again. How could she lose the one woman who would always be her life preserver?

"Although I do make mistakes, and I will mess up, I was raised by a remarkable woman and I won't ever forget the values that you taught me. Rafe does get to be too much at times, but when he does, I hear your voice in my head telling me not to stay down when I get in over my head. I promise you that I will be OK."

"I think you will, darling. I see so much strength in you — more than I've ever seen before. You had to do a lot of growing up over the past year, but it's only made you stronger. You need to be very proud of that. A lot of women would have just sunk to the ground and felt sorry for themselves, but you've risen above and chosen to make do with the circumstances handed to you. I don't know when it happened, but you've gone from a little girl into a woman. Hmm. I don't think I like this," she teased with a sniffle.

"Thank you, Mom. I needed to hear that."

"Well, we've covered work, school and your personal life. Now you get to hear about something new in my life." Sandra's tears faded and she practically glowed.

Ari looked at her quizzically. Her mother was such a person of routine; what could she possibly say?

"I've started dating a really wonderful man."

"What?" Ari didn't mean to stand there with her mouth hanging open, but in the entire time she was growing up, she didn't remember her mother dating once.

"Hey, sweetheart, I still have needs…"

"Please, I'm begging you," Ari gasped in horror at the visual of her mother's *needs*.

"OK. I'll take mercy on you, but I have been seeing a wonderful man for the past month, and a woman my age doesn't want to waste too much time, so I'm giving you a heads up."

"What does he do?" Ari asked with suspicion. Her mom had been through enough — she didn't want some man taking advantage of her.

"He owns a beautiful restaurant downtown."

"Not to sound shallow, but is he financially secure? I don't want you being used for your flourishing floral shop," Ari joked. Her mother was doing well with her shop, but because of all the medical expenses, it would be a while before she had a decent amount in savings again. Ari was trying to work on that. She hated owing Rafe, even if her mom didn't know about it; she wanted him paid off and her mother's life back in her own hands.

"Actually, his place is very successful. He has a large celebrity following. To tell you the truth, I normally would never eat in a place like his, but the food is mouthwatering. I've never had such incredible pasta in my life."

"He's not a snob, is he?"

"No, he's a wonderful man. I would like to take you to dinner to meet him. If we get done early enough, we could go tonight."

Ari wasn't eager to go, but the excitement shining in her mother's eyes prevented her from refusing. Her own eyes took on a steely glint — *this man had better be treating Mom like the Queen of England or he's toast.* Nothing but the best for her mother.

"If we get done in time, then, I'd be pleased to have dinner with you and this man," Ari said with a forced brightness.

She found reason to regret her words as her mother kicked their pace into overdrive, and Ari felt as if her hands were going to fall off. Still, as she looked at her mother's youthful joy, she couldn't be too negative. This man was obviously giving her mom the happiness she deserved.

"I can't believe how nervous I am," Sandra said as the two of them approached the exclusive Italian restaurant.

"Wow, Mom, you are *really* glowing," Ari commented, almost agape at the sight. Her mother was beautiful in her long blue dress and with her hair put up. This new relationship seemed to be knocking years off her life.

Sandra looked young and almost carefree. Ari had to admit that she'd never seen her happier. But she'd never been forced to share her mother before, and a selfish part of her wanted to stake her claim, tell this man he had no rights to her mom. It was stupid, but she knew she would have battle this absurd surge of emotions.

"Marco makes me feel like a teenager again," Sandra said with a giggle.

"Then I'm very happy for you, though perhaps the tiniest bit jealous," Ari admitted with a smile.

"Ari, you should know that no one ever will or ever could replace you. You're my little girl, no matter how old you become. I never had a desire to date while you were growing up, because you were my first priority and I didn't want to risk your being hurt. After your father... Well, let's just say, it was hard for me to trust that a relationship would last, and I didn't want to put you through the turmoil of having men coming and going from your life. I still wasn't looking for a man, but I met Marco and it just...well, it just sort of happened."

"I think that's wonderful, Mom. I have a feeling I will love your Marco, even if I want to bring out the claws and make sure he knows you're mine first," Ari admitted with a half grin and an exaggeratedly furrowed brow.

"He's a charmer. I think he'll have you under his spell within seconds."

"I don't know, Mom. I'm quite hard to charm," Ari told her with a twinkle in her eye.

The two of them stepped into the restaurant and the maître d' glanced up and gave Sandra a beaming smile.

"How lovely to see you this evening, Ms. Harlow. You are more gorgeous each time you bless us with your presence."

Ari's mouth dropped open as the man approached them, took her mother's hand, bringing it to his lips and giving it a kiss, and then turned his twinkling eyes on Ari.

"Oh, this must be the stunning daughter you've spoken so fondly of. I can certainly see the family resemblance. Welcome to Il Mio Cuore," he said as he took Ari's hand and kissed it as well.

"Thank you, Gene; you are too kind, as usual," Sandra said with a light laugh.

"Let me take you to your table. The world should wait on beautiful women, but never make them wait," he said with a flourish as he gave Ari and her mom his full attention. He led them straight to a private room glowing golden in candlelight and smelling of something savory and delicious wafting to them from their table.

"Ah, it looks as if Benny spotted you and has brought out something to keep your hunger at bay until Marco joins you."

"Whatever it is, it smells ambrosial. Tell Marco to take his time. We don't need him to rush right out," Sandra offered.

"How could I attend to anything else when I know such a beautiful woman is near?"

Ari turned and her jaw dropped as she assessed the man standing behind them. Her mother giggled as she rushed to him, and his arms wrapped around her as he pressed a sweet kiss on her lips.

The man was arrestingly handsome, standing about six feet tall and wearing a dark navy blue suit that matched his eyes to perfection. His olive skin and salt-and-pepper hair gave him a refined appearance. Age had been good to Marco, and the laugh lines around his eyes attested to a good sense of humor.

"I am being so rude; I apologize," he said as he turned to Ari, while leaving one hand clasped around her mother's fingers. "I am Marco Giannini, and it's such a pleasure to meet you, Ms. Arianna Harlow," he finished as he leaned in and kissed her cheek.

Ari wasn't used to men being so touchy or flirty, but she found herself standing there tongue-tied and smiling. Finally, she pulled herself together enough to speak.

"The pleasure is all mine. Please call me Ari."

"A lovely name for an exquisite woman, Ari. And do call me Marco."

"You are quite the flirt, Marco. I can see why my mother is fond of you," Ari said with a chuckle as she sat in the chair he pulled out for her.

"Ah, being around beautiful women brings out the romantic in me. I hope you don't mind if I order for us. My chef has incredible talent and exquisite taste, and your mother hasn't found fault yet with any of his dishes."

"That would be perfect; thank you."

Marco helped her mother to her seat, and then the waiter stepped in and poured a fine Italian red into their lovely crystal glasses. The evening started off quite pleasantly, and soon Ari was laughing and enjoying herself immensely.

"Ari, your mother tells me you're soon to graduate from Stanford."

"I have one semester left, so I hope I'll be graduating soon," she said with a bit of an uncomfortable laugh. She really didn't want to talk about her education.

"What are your plans after you're finished?"

Ari barely managed to hold back the sigh. "I don't know, yet. My dream was always to get my doctorate and work as a college professor in history, but things change…" she trailed off. She hated even speaking of that dream because it seemed further and further away with each day that passed.

"Do you not want that anymore?"

She knew he was just trying to get to know her, but she needed to change the subject.

"Oh, life never stands still for any of us. Please, I want to hear the story of how you and my mother met."

Her words did the trick — Marco and her mother looked at each other with identical besotted looks on their faces.

"It's actually a bit of a Cinderella story…" Sandra started saying with a wink and a sly giggle.

"It's a complete modern fairy tale come true," Marco took over. "I was down at the docks picking fresh seafood for the day's specials when something shiny caught my eye. I turned and there was your mother arguing with man over how fresh his fish was, and her bracelet was sparkling in the sun. I was amused at first that this tiny woman was going head to head with Albert, who weighs at least three hundred pounds. I know he's a gentle giant, so I wasn't worried, but Sandra didn't know that. Finally, she turned and her heel caught in a gap on the dock, and she went flying into the water."

"Oh my gosh, Mom. You never told me you hurt yourself!"

"I didn't get injured — well, my pride got hurt a bit, but Marco dived in after me, and I was so mesmerized, I couldn't take my eyes off him."

"Luckily for me, your mother was wearing a white blouse that day, too," Marco said, wiggling his eyebrows and rolling his eyes. Ari couldn't help bursting into laughter at the way these two supposedly sophisticated people were acting like children.

"That's a great story! You were her knight in soggy amour," Ari said between fits of laughter.

"Ari, I thought I recognized that laugh."

Ari turned to find Rafe standing in the doorway wearing her favorite black suit with a teal dress shirt beneath, and a midnight tie. His eyes zeroed in on her and her breath caught mid-laugh. She'd been apart from him for only a few days and yet seeing him brought an extra beat to her heart. Why did he have to be so enthralling?

"Hello, Rafe. I'm having dinner with my mother and her friend."

"It sounds as if you're having a good time." He didn't move from the doorway and she hoped he wasn't going to expect her to leave. Her day with her mother wasn't over, yet.

"I'm sorry, I've been rude. Rafe Palazzo," he said as he approached Marco.

"I've heard a lot about you in the business circles. I'm Marco Giannini. Would you like to join us?" Marco asked as he stood to shake Rafe's hand.

"It would be my pleasure." Ari was a bit peeved that he'd tracked her down while she was with her mother, especially since he'd been gone with not a single word for almost a full week. What had he been up to? What was going on in the hidden depths of his mind? Suspicion caused her eyes to narrow.

"How do you know Ari and Sandra?" Marco asked.

"Ari and I are seeing each other. I met Sandra while she was in the hospital," Rafe replied as he took his seat and accepted a glass of wine from the server.

"Then you are a fortunate man, indeed, to be dating such a lovely woman. I know I have counted my blessings every day since meeting Sandra."

"Yes, the Harlow women have a certain sparkle about them," Rafe said with a secretive smile.

Ari was afraid the evening would become uncomfortable, but Rafe fit right in, and soon they were all bantering back and forth. When it was time to say goodbye, she felt assured that her mother was being treated properly. It wasn't a hardship for her to hug her mother goodbye and arrange to come back soon to dine with her and even Marco.

Ari had agreed to let Rafe take her home, but she thought about insisting that he drop her off and not come in. It was her right. But, as he assisted her into the passenger seat of his car, she knew that to pretend she didn't want him there was absurd. She'd be hurting only herself.

They both remained silent as he moved through the bustling streets of San Francisco. Though it was close to eleven at night, there was much traffic on the road. Ari preferred taking the bus, feeling safer than when she tried to navigate the freeways or the narrow roads through town, where the fear of a wreck was always in the back of her mind.

At least while Rafe drove, she felt secure. He was confident and sure as he steered his way through the city streets. She really had nothing to fear, well, nothing on the roads, at least. Once they arrived at her home, she had a lot to worry her.

When he pulled into her garage, she reached for her seat belt, but sudden weariness made her move in slow motion. By the time Rafe parked and stepped around to her side of the car, she was still fighting the blasted clip.

"Let me help." The soft sound of his voice made her stop fidgeting with the clasp as she turned to look into his shining eyes.

"Thank you," she managed when he unclasped her belt and assisted her from the car. Placing his hand behind her back, he led her to the elevator and pushed the button. Now was the time to speak up if she didn't want him to stay. Well, she wanted him to, but she didn't think it was the best idea with the way her emotions were scattered all over the place.

"I don't want to sound ungrateful for the ride, but I'm actually pretty worn out, Rafe. I got up early and was hoping to get to bed soon."

"Then we will." When he didn't elaborate, Ari followed him into the elevator without another word, then waited while he pushed her floor's button. He was in a strange mood that she couldn't quite figure out. She decided it best not to push *his buttons*. Soon, he'd reveal whatever was on his mind.

Rafe led her straight to her bedroom, where he tossed his jacket over the back of her chair and then started pulling his tie down. When he began unbuttoning his shirt, she unfroze and closed herself in her bathroom. Still at a loss, she showered and changed, then stepped into the bedroom to find him lying in her bed shirtless with only a light blanket covering his lower half.

Since he normally didn't stay in her bed unless it was for sex, she was baffled by his actions. He was reading one of the books that had been resting on her nightstand. He looked in no hurry at all to have sex. She was unsure whether he expected her to follow him or not — even if it was her own bed. This was all new territory for her. She stood there fidgeting for several moments.

"Join me, Ari." The husky quality of his voice sent a shiver of anticipation down her spine. With no further thoughts, Ari floated across the room and climbed into the bed. Her stomach quivered as he reached an arm out and pulled her against his side.

When Rafe continued to read the book while holding her tightly against him, Ari didn't know what to think or what to do.

"Relax," he whispered. He must have felt the tension vibrating through her. Between her eventful day, and Rafe's strange mood, Ari was exhausted. Still, though she closed her eyes, she didn't think she'd be able to nod off. But it didn't take long.

With Rafe holding her tight, she fell asleep with her head cradled against his chest.

CHAPTER THIRTY-THREE

R AFE LOOKED DOWN as Ari slept peacefully in his arms. He was letting her go; it was the right action to take. He didn't know how he was going to do it, but as he gazed at her while she slumbered so deeply, he knew he couldn't continue holding her against her will.

Yes, she'd chosen to stay, and she was developing feelings for him, but wasn't it the same as a victim developing feelings for a captor? He couldn't trust that what she was feeling was true, because he'd never given her the chance to refuse him.

He'd forced her hand.

Somewhere in the middle of all of this, he'd fallen for her. He didn't even know whether he believed in love anymore, but what he felt for her went far past just sex, and far past mere affection.

He cared about how she was feeling, about what she did during each day. He wanted her to be happy. There were many emotions that he felt for Ari, and he knew he couldn't make her do anything she didn't want to do any longer — so he would let her go.

He promised himself just one more day. He needed the chance to say goodbye so he could move on with his life.

"Rafe?"

"I'm here."

"What are you doing?" Through the dim light shining in through the open windows, the moonbeams lit her face just enough for him to memorize her features, and for her perhaps to see the worry he must be wearing in his eyes.

"I was just getting up. You need to go back to sleep," he said softly as he brushed back the loose strands of her hair.

"My throat's dry. I think I'll get up and get a drink of water. It's just so hard to move when I have my own personal heater." As she spoke the words, her body edged even closer to his as her arm held on tightly to his waist.

"You stay warm underneath the blankets; I'll get your water." Though she groaned her disapproval, he managed to slide from the bed and walk across the room, unconcerned with his nakedness.

Stepping into the bathroom, he filled a glass, then stood there for just a moment before turning and walking back. Ari was leaning up against the headboard, the blankets pulled up high.

His first instinct was to pull them away so he could gaze upon her. After a thousand times of touching and tasting almost every inch of her ivory skin, he found that she still took the breath right from him.

Rafe handed her the glass, and then climbed back into the bed. He knew he should leave her alone, get up as he'd told her he was planning, but as she quickly snuggled against his side, he couldn't.

If he had only one more night with her, he wanted to make it last. There was nothing wrong with that.

"You seem down. What has you so worried?" The soft sound of her voice drifted to his ears. He could hear genuine concern. But how could she care for him when he'd been nothing but an ogre with her — demanding his own needs be met while expecting her to sacrifice everything?

"Ari, I think it's time for me to release you from our agreement." As the words came from his mouth, he wanted to take them back, tell her he was a fool and he couldn't let her go, but he knew it was the right thing to do. She must be free to live her life the way she was meant to live it. The way she deserved to live it.

"What are you talking about?" she barely whispered, her voice so low, he had to lean toward her to understand.

"We've been together past the three months we originally agreed upon. It has become clear to me that we are at the end of our journey. I've enjoyed my time with you, and I want to thank you for all your sacrifices, but I have to be honest, and this relationship has run its course."

Each word he spoke pierced him as it emerged from his throat. He didn't want to do this. What had happened to the strong, decisive man he'd been only a few months ago? Hesitation wasn't in his makeup. He would not hesitate any more that night.

"Have I done something wrong?"

Ari's voice was no longer a whisper, but hollow, emotionless, flat.

"No. Of course not. I've been quite pleased with the way our affair has played out. You've been one of the better mistresses I've had."

Watching Ari's body flinch at his words, Rafe berated himself for his cruelty. Why had he felt a need to say such a thing? Was it because he was hurting, and he wanted her to hurt a fraction as much? Instead, she simply sat there and spoke as if she had no feelings whatsoever.

"I understand. I think it probably best if you go home for the rest of the night. Tomorrow is Sunday, so we should talk about my employment before Monday morning. I'm sure it would be too uncomfortable for both of us to have me working in your offices."

Still nothing but unemotional words.

"I have no objection if you want to keep your current position. You're doing a fine job."

Rafe wanted to kick himself. Why had he said that? How was he expected to reset his brain if he had to look at her each and every day knowing she wasn't his for the taking?

With agitation filling him, he left the bed and walked to the chair draped with his clothes. He *would* be fine because he always was. Even if Ari did work at his offices still, he wouldn't pine for her.

Ari was just a woman — one of many — who had graced his life. The emotion he was feeling was most likely due to the soul-searching trip his father had suggested. Rafe hadn't found any answers by himself, and he certainly wasn't going to while looking at Ari as she sat against the backboard, her eyes trained on the shadows behind the window.

Well, he'd thought he'd found an answer, he corrected himself as his hand ran along the left side of his jacket. But that had been a mistake, a foolish, impulsive moment...

"I think it's best if I try to get my old job back. I enjoyed working there."

He barely heard her speak over the pounding of his heart, but her words registered and he wanted to instantly deny her. Why? Getting her from his offices is what he'd just decided was best. He opened his mouth to agree, but that's not what came out.

"We'll discuss this more tomorrow. Get some sleep; I'll come by after dinnertime." Rafe turned and walked from the room before he could convince himself he was a fool and climb back into bed with her.

As he opened the front door and started to step out, he thought he heard the sound of a sob, so he stilled as he strained his ears. When he heard nothing further, he knew he must have been mistaken. Ari was obviously relieved to have him out of her life.

He firmly shut the door behind him as he made his way down the hall. He'd have her come to his place tomorrow to discuss employment. He never wanted to enter, or exit, this building again.

CHAPTER THIRTY-FOUR

"**Y**OU'VE BEEN AVOIDING me."

Lia jumped at the sound of Shane's voice directly behind her. Slowly she turned around, then froze as she waited for him to continue. When he didn't speak further, she placed her hand on her hip and narrowed her eyes.

"You didn't respect what I had to say before; now I have nothing to discuss with you. I'm trying to work, so if you'd kindly leave, I'd appreciate it."

With that, Lia began walking away. Should she have known that wouldn't keep Shane from speaking his mind? Probably.

"Do you want to talk about our affair in front of all your co-workers, or would you like to speak with me in private?"

Several heads whipped around as the people in the office gazed from her to Shane and then back again in delighted disbelief. Lia could feel her cheeks heat as the spotlight was pointed straight at her.

"Follow me," she growled at him, then moved with as much dignity as she could muster toward the closest private room she could find. It happened to be the copier room — great, just great.

Shane shut the door behind him, sealing them in the small room together. The temperature rose a few degrees as he stared her down.

"That was unbelievably rude, even for you, Shane. Let's get this over with so I can get back to work." She tried to keep her tone calm, but he was flustering and frazzling her and making her grind her teeth.

"I've been trying to call you, and you're avoiding me."

"Wouldn't that tell you that I don't want to speak with you?" she said, tapping her fingers violently on the sorting table beside her and with an elaborate sweep sending a ream of paper flying.

"You chased after me for months, years, even —"

"Stop right there. I didn't exactly chase after you. I liked you; you liked me. I just found you being typically stubborn, so I didn't allow you to shut me out. But right after a great night of making love, you felt the need to go squeal like a little girl to my big brother. That ended the very brief affair."

As Shane's lips turned up in a smile, Lia felt like stomping her foot. He wasn't listening to her, and as this was only her second week on the job, she really didn't want to mess up. Although she was employed at her brother's company, she had to work much harder than the rest of the people to prove she was there on her own merits.

"What are you doing here, anyway?"

"That's none of your business."

"You can stop acting like a pouting child and answer my questions. We'll get through this a lot faster if you do." He crossed his arms and leaned back against the door, not only blocking her exit, but letting her know he had all day if she wanted to take it.

"I'm the new Public Relations Specialist," she answered and thrust up her chin.

"Oh, really?"

"Don't give me that snarky tone of voice. I did graduate from college with honors. In communications sciences from the world-renowned University of Bologna, then went on to get my master's degree in world politics. I'm not the spoiled little heiress you believe me to be. I'll be very good at my job if you let me get back to it. As a matter of fact, I'm currently working on a big press release and need to do some research. I'm done talking. Don't let the door hit you on the way out."

Lia was quite proud that Rafe had faith in her abilities. She'd done similar work in college and graduate school and knew she'd do a good job for her brother's company — that was if she wasn't constantly interrupted.

"What project are you working on?"

"Why do you care, Shane?" The room was either rapidly increasing in temperature, or she wasn't as unaffected by Shane as she'd hoped to be when he'd left her room. As mad as she'd been in Vegas, she was even more mad now seeing him standing there looking beyond scrumptious.

"Let's just call it idle curiosity." The gleam in his eyes worried her.

"Fine. I'm working on the Gli Amanti Cove project."

As a huge smile spread across his cheeks, she got a sick feeling in her gut. Surely he couldn't be involved with that project. It would require her to spend a heck of a lot of time on a small island off of her beloved Italy. She could possibly be there for months.

"Why are you looking at me like the cat who got the cream?"

"I have no idea what you mean, Lia. I simply came here to remind you of what you've been missing the last few weeks."

As Shane pushed away from the door, all thoughts of work fled Lia's mind and she nearly panicked. She couldn't allow him to touch her — she'd melt into his arms. No! Not gonna happen.

Burn her once, shame on him; burn her twice, shame on her. She took a step back and found herself trapped between his rapidly approaching steps and the massive printer behind her.

"Look Shane, we had a great night. I'm not saying it wasn't fun, but it's over now. You need to respect that and move on to your next victim. You have left a slew of women flopping around in your wake, after all. And more of the poor saps are lining up."

"Tsk, tsk, Lia. Are you trying to make me mad? It isn't working. Now that I've had a taste of you, no other woman will do. It looks as if you're stuck with me. Since you're the one who was in hot pursuit, you should damn well be pleased about it."

"You're just a bit too overconfident, don't you think?" Lia had intended her statement to sound far harsher, but the effect was undermined by the breathlessness of her voice.

"I think you just want to be chased." With those words, he pulled her into his arms and forced her head back as he pressed his lips against hers.

Stubbornly refusing to open her mouth, Lia pushed against his chest. If she melted into him, it would all be over. Her blood would ignite, and her will to resist him would join the flames — she'd been in love with him for too long.

Shane nipped her bottom lip at the same time as he gripped her backside and pulled her up against his hardening body. An involuntary groan escaped her throat, making her open her lips to him. He didn't hesitate as he plunged his tongue inside her mouth and reminded her how great a kisser he was.

After a couple of minutes, Shane pulled back just enough that he could see into her eyes.

"Are you so sure you don't want to continue where we left off?" he confidently asked.

The arrogant sound of his voice managed to snap Lia from her sexual high, and with an unknown strength, she found she pushed hard, making him take a step back.

With a fingernail poked into his chest, she looked him in the face. "You can go...*please* yourself, Shane Grayson. I'm done with you."

With those words, Lia managed to skirt around him and flee the room. Just before she was out of earshot, she heard his parting comment.

"Nothing attracts me more than a fiery temper, Lia. We'll continue this later..."

She turned the corner and ducked into the women's bathroom, grateful it was empty. As she looked at her flushed complexion, and noted her dilated eyes, she knew she was in trouble. She'd wanted him for so long; she didn't know how to turn that emotion off.

What if she never could?

Rafe hadn't said a word to her about his conversation with Shane, but that wasn't even the point. She'd asked Shane to keep their relationship private and he hadn't respected her enough to do the very first thing she'd asked of him.

Worse, she knew Shane didn't stay with women long. She'd forgotten that while she chased after him. All she'd wanted was for him to want her — need her — have her as his only one. She'd obviously been more infatuated with him than he with her. But, typical male that he was, he'd gotten a taste of sex, and now he wanted more.

Enough! She had work to do, and it was important.

In about ten minutes she was meeting with a committee for the project she'd mentioned to Shane and she wanted to look her best. This was going to be a beautiful, exclusive, very high-end resort for those who needed privacy, but still valued the ultimate in luxuries.

It had taken Rafe years to get the go-ahead because that area of the island was breathtaking, and the residents hadn't wanted tourists to come in and ruin the balance of the island. With Rafe's designs, the place would have everything a spoiled multimillionaire would want while still using and respecting the island's natural gifts to maximize the resort's appeal.

Nonetheless, this project would take a lot of effort on her part because there were still many against it getting started. Protesters had already started lining the beaches, camping out and refusing to back down. When Rafe had hired her, he hadn't been joking when he told her he hoped she had a strong backbone.

Time to get ready. Lia washed her face, then groaned when she realized she didn't have her purse to at least reapply her makeup. Giving up on her appearance, she made her way to the conference room. As she walked through the doorway, with her shoulders back and a smile on her face, she looked around, giving a nod of her head to her brother before approaching the front of the room.

That was when Shane walked in the door and moved to stand beside Rafe. Her stomach turned over as the pieces came together.

"Thank you for meeting us here, today. It seems Ms. Palazzo has a plan of action for us as we move forward with the Gli Amanti Cove project. The floor's all yours, Lia."

"You're part of this project, Shane?" She knew she shouldn't ask, because she was certain she didn't want to know the answer.

"Yes. I'm surprised Rafe didn't tell you. I'm the lead on this one. It looks as if we'll have plenty of time to catch up."

The wicked glint in his eyes left no doubt he was very much looking forward to being stuck on a nearly deserted island with her. Lia had two options. She could either suck it up and do her job, or she could cry about her misfortunes and walk from the room.

Never had Lia been a quitter. With a small glare sent Shane's way, she addressed the rest of the partners involved.

"First, I'd like to start by saying…"

Lia missed the determined glint in Shane's eyes, and the way Rafe looked at both of them. If she had known what she was about to get into, she might have taken this opportunity to run.

CHAPTER THIRTY-FIVE

I T WAS ALL or nothing. Ari knew he cared — he was just
afraid of being in a real relationship. That's what his family
members said. He wouldn't have said the things he'd said,
made love to her. She knew it wasn't just sex. Perhaps he wasn't
in love with her, but he had feelings.

What he'd said the night before had been him protecting
his heart. That was her hope. She knew he could really be finished with her, but if there was even the slightest chance of
him loving her, she had to give it a try. So much for her fine
words to herself about walking away!

Slipping into the nightie she'd splurged on, then sitting at
her vanity as she carefully applied her makeup, Ari couldn't
help the fluttering in her heart. The night was going to go either very well, or horribly wrong.

Yet it ultimately didn't matter how the night turned out.
She needed to tell him the truth, and more important, she

needed to know whether he did have feelings for her. If not, it was better for her to know now.

He'd summoned her to his home for the employment talk. He'd had a full night and day to think about what he'd said. Was he rethinking his feelings? He surely wouldn't bring her there just to let her go, would he? Wouldn't it make more sense to meet at a neutral place, such as a café? She'd known from the beginning not to fall in love with him, but how could she not?

She'd gone from loathing him, to understanding him, to caring. Now, she had no doubt she loved him. She couldn't explain when it had happened, but somewhere in the middle of their battles, a door had opened, and over their time together, that gap continued widening until she was at the point that she couldn't stand back and hide the way she felt anymore.

Putting on her long coat, Ari stood from her vanity and cast a final look in the mirror. She wasn't trying to be a seductress, but she needed to feel good about herself. She needed to take her destiny into her own hands.

If he denied her love, then at least she would know she wasn't a coward, at least the door could have a chance of shutting again. Ari refused to give up on love. Never. Even if she wasn't destined to be with the man she loved, she knew love was real, knew the emotion was strong and pure.

Ari knew *she* wouldn't turn into a bitter soul, blaming every man out there for the actions of one. That was a fault that Rafe had to live with, and until he realized that the heart wasn't something to abuse or toy with, they didn't have a chance. She only hoped he'd managed to heal what had been broken before he'd ever met her.

Grabbing her purse, Ari slipped on her stiletto sandals and made her way to her front door. She smiled as she thought about her beautiful red lace nightgown. She felt sleek and feminine, even sexy, underneath the soft fabric, giving her that boost of confidence to say to Rafe what she needed to say.

Feeling almost like a teenager sneaking out into the night, Ari made her way to the elevators, then pushed the lobby button. Rafe's trusted assistant, Mario, was picking her up, and she was grateful — she was too nervous to be behind the wheel of a car.

As she stepped outside, the cool wind blowing in off the bay gave her instant goose bumps. The nightie was sensual and sleek, yes, but it offered no protection as the wind climbed beneath her coat and instantly chilled her.

"Good evening, Ms. Harlow. How are you tonight?"

"I'm very well, Mario. I'm sorry to have you dragged out on such a cold evening."

"It's never an inconvenience to pick up such a lovely woman," he answered with a smile as he held the door open. "It's nice and warm inside."

"Thank you, Mario," Ari said after he climbed into the driver's seat. The two of them chatted for a few moments, and then Ari turned to look out the window and collect her thoughts.

The closer they came to Rafe's home, the more nervous she became. Could she do this — lay her heart on the line? There was a good chance he'd reject her love, not because he didn't want it, but because he was too stubborn to accept it.

Then again, maybe all the emotions were simply in her head. Maybe he didn't really care about her the way she thought he did. What if she were just wrong about it all?

After they'd pulled through his security gate and Mario came around the car to open her door, Ari nearly asked him to drive her back home. She wondered if he would do that — it was almost worth asking just to see his face.

But no. Ari accepted his hand as he assisted her from the car.

"Have a wonderful evening, Ms. Harlow. I'll be waiting if you need me."

His words engendered more nerves than relief. Mario knew more than anyone that Rafe didn't spend the night with his mistresses. Mario had been the one to take her home in the middle of the night once when Rafe was through with her.

The ugly thought had her again wondering what she was doing. How many times did she have to be a fool before it sank in that he was incapable of love?

As she stepped through his doorway, noting the dim lights on throughout the house, she drew her shoulders up. If it was a fool she had to be to either gain love or set herself free, then a fool she'd be.

There was no sign of Rafe downstairs, so she made her way up his wide staircase, her heart racing. Why wasn't he there to greet her? She was too agitated to feel the full force of his rudeness, but a glimmer of his neglect penetrated her brain.

Having been to Rafe's home only twice, she was a little unsure of the way, but there was a single door open on the floor, with a soft light shining from within. She slowly made her way toward it.

Peeking in the doorway, Ari discovered Rafe sitting in a chair by the window. Unwilling to hurry, she took a moment to look around; yes, it was his bedroom. He seemed so solemn as he gazed out at the stars that she wasn't sure whether she should say anything. But he'd been the one to call her over, so he must know she was coming.

"Rafe?"

His shoulders stiffened at the sound of her voice — not a good sign. A couple of seconds passed before he stood and turned to face her. The blank look on his face showed her nothing of what he was thinking. Her nerves jumped another level as he stepped toward her. It felt as if her knees weren't going to hold her up any longer, so without being asked, Ari walked over to his large bed and sat on the edge.

He stilled as if uncertain what to do about her sitting there. It wasn't as if she hadn't spent many hours in various beds with him. Was he really so opposed to her sitting on his?

"I'm sorry, Ari. I meant to meet you downstairs. The time got away from me," he said in an expressionless voice that sent a shiver of apprehension down her spine.

"That tends to happen to me at times, too" she tried to joke, but in the ominous atmosphere her attempt fell flat.

"Thank you for meeting me here. We need to finish our talk from the other night."

"Yes, Rafe, we do. I've been doing a lot of thinking —"

Rafe interrupted her before she could say what she needed to. "I don't want to drag this out, Ari. Our time is up. I'll have you reinstated at your old job with no questions asked. I agree with you that it would just be too awkward to have you working right in the Palazzo building here. As for your home, it's yours. You have no need to move. Monday morning I will have my attorney start the paperwork to transfer the title. Also, I already have a bank account set up for you with a substantial fund that should take care of you for many years to come."

Ari sat there as she received blow after blow from his words. She didn't care about any of this. She wanted neither his money nor his condo. She'd made it just fine her entire life without him, and she would make it again after he was gone.

What she wanted to do right now was make a dignified exit from the room. She stood up and nearly did just that. Wasn't it more than obvious that he wanted her purged from his life?

No. She'd come there to say something, and she'd always regret it if she didn't get the chance. He might be saying goodbye to her, but if this was her last night seeing Rafe, then she needed him to know how she felt.

"Rafe, I love you. I know you warned me not to care. I know I broke the rules, but I can't help it that my heart has opened to you. I can't contain what I'm feeling. I understand that you're telling me goodbye, but I have to say this. I have to let you know that somewhere in the middle of all this madness, I fell for you. I don't want to let you go, not today, tomorrow or ever. I want you to let me love you."

Never had Ari said that to a man before. Never had she opened herself up so far. He could rip her in half right now, and there would be nothing she could do to stop it. She had never imagined how frightening it would feel to be so vulnerable.

Rafe stood before her, not showing a hint of what he was feeling. As he quietly gazed at her, Ari's heart stopped. She didn't know whether his silence was a good or bad thing. Would he accept what she was offering him?

Finally, his lips turned up in the smallest hint of a smile, and hope surged through her. He didn't seem angry — that was a positive sign. If he truly gave them a chance, she knew they could be happy together.

When he remained silent, a shimmer of fear tried crawling in, but she suppressed it. He was just surprised, that was all. He'd been trying to tell her goodbye, and she was telling him she loved him. That would give anybody human pause, wouldn't it?

"Ari…"

Without realizing she was even doing so, Ari felt her body stiffen. She'd laid it all out there and she could hear the sound of rejection in his tone. With one word, she knew it was over. How could she have been so wrong?

"You don't need to say it, Rafe. You told me from the beginning that this would never be more than an affair. I was the one who broke the rules. I apologize for that." Ari was relieved when her voice came out sounding just about as cold as his did.

"Do not presume to know my thoughts, Ari. I can speak for myself," he snapped, real emotion appearing in his tone for the slightest moment before he once again made his expression blank. He took a step toward her.

"I'm going to leave now." Ari turned as his hand reached for her. She looked at his grasping fingers, then up into his chilling eyes.

"It doesn't need to be this way. I've planned on ending this, but I've been satisfied with you as my mistress. We can forget all about this emotional dilemma and go back to the way things have been."

Again, his voice sounded almost dead, as if he didn't care what happened, or what she did.

"Is it so much easier for you to keep screwing the girl you're familiar with than to go through your application process all over again? Contrary to what you may think of me, Rafe. I'm not a whore, and I'm no longer for sale. Take what you want from me and my mother — I just don't care about any of it."

Ari was done with his game. She was done with his brutal ambivalence toward her, the way he blew hot or cold but nothing in between. She'd fallen in love with him, though she didn't see how, and now she was standing before him completely disillusioned.

"Would you like to see something, Rafe? Look at what I wore for you." She tore off her coat and revealed the nightgown beneath, the lacy fabric skimming her curves, hinting boldly at her womanly treasures. The only treasures from her that he'd seemed to value throughout their months of intimacy. "Look at it. I paid a fortune for this frivolous confection of lace. And why? To speak to you in the only way you seem to appreciate. Sex... And submission."

"Ari, please..."

"No, Rafe. I am finally able to tell you my feelings, and they're not the ones I would have thought. Here they are. What I did disgusts me. And you disgust me. We are both better than our actions suggest, but I'm not sure I can forgive you, or myself. Still, I will walk away with my head held high because I loved you honestly, and because I am leaving you honestly. I am leaving you so I can do what I should have been doing all along. I refuse to submit to you or to any man who does not submit to me. Openly, honestly, and lovingly."

Ari picked up her long coat and shrouded herself in it. Rafe still sat there unmoving, silent and grim. She knew somewhere inside, she was hurting, but she pushed that away. Too many women allowed a man to upend their lives — abuse them — neglect them — treat them as if they were beneath them. That was over for her.

When Ari resumed speaking, her tone had changed from defiant to sad. "And you, Mr. Palazzo? As long as you continue to blame all women for the wounds inflicted by one, you'll never be the man you should be. You'll never truly live your life. And I pity you."

"Ari. I'll say it again. It doesn't need to be this way."

"Yes it does, Rafe. Goodbye."

This time when she pulled her arm, he released her, and Ari walked from his room with as much dignity as she could muster. She knew that pain would eventually set in, but for now she felt an odd sense of numbness protecting her shattered heart.

She was free to go. To her greatest surprise, she realized that she didn't want that freedom she'd so coveted more than three months ago. She wanted him to be somebody that he wasn't. She wanted the man who had danced on a quiet balcony with her, laughed at a stupid joke, and made her stretch her wings and fly. He was in there...somewhere, but she now realized she couldn't reach him. Holding her head high, she walked through the door and straight down the steps, making her way outside, where she found the car still waiting.

Rafe must have told Mario not to leave. He'd known she wouldn't be there long.

"Ms. Harlow, I wasn't expecting to see you again so soon," Mario said with surprise as he came jogging out from a side door. "I was just getting ready to park the car for the evening."

"Please take me home," she said in a firm voice. She didn't wait for him to open the door, but gripped the handle and flung it open.

"But, Ms. Harlow —"

"Please, Mario. I want to leave now. You can either drive me, or I'm walking." She didn't care how she left, but she was getting the hell out of there.

"Yes, Ms. Harlow," he said before shutting her door and going around to the driver's side. He started the engine and the car rolled forward. Ari thought she heard her name, but ignored it. It was time to pick up the pieces of her life and move on.

She didn't notice Rafe running down the stairs after them. Soon, she was pulling farther away from him…too far for him to catch her.

EPILOGUE
Six months later

"I THOUGHT I'D FIND you here."

Rafe slowly turned around and gave Shane a semblance of a smile. Of course he was at Ari's graduation. She hadn't spoken to him in six months, but he couldn't get her from his mind. This was a momentous occasion for her, and he had to be there.

"Why are you here, Shane?"

"Because I knew your stubborn, opinionated, stealthy sister would be here and unable to run from me."

"She's still refusing to talk to you? I find that amusing," Rafe said, smiling for the first time in months.

"You know I got called back to South America. She's refused my calls, and for the past week since I've been home, she's managed to avoid me at every turn. I know how close she's become with Ari, so I've finally cornered her. It was either this or wait until next year, when I have her trapped on a private island during the Gli Amanti Cove groundbreaking. I'm not that patient."

"Good luck."

"Has Ari spoken to you?"

"Not a word. After the first month, I decided to give her some time. She refused her old job, moved from the condo, and went back to school. I may have to admit I was wrong about her. She hasn't even touched a dime of the severance money I set up for her, though she's a fool not to."

"Why? She seems to be doing just fine on her own."

"She's been working at a small café for the past six months. It's ridiculous! A woman like her, with her talents, her intelligence, her beauty…"

"And her integrity? Not everyone is as greedy as your ex-wife, Rafe. Haven't you figured that out by now?"

"I'm beginning to see that. It may just not be enough."

"I know the feeling. Man, you do *not* want to defy Lia. That girl holds a grudge."

Rafe laughed at the desperate look on his best friend's face. Rafe knew more than anyone how stubborn both of his sisters could be.

The two men sat in the back row as Ari walked to the podium and accepted her diploma. Rafe could hear her mother's cheers all the way from the front row. His sisters were just a decibel level quieter than Sandra.

As Ari turned toward her cheering section, she graced them with one of her award-winning smiles and Rafe's gut clenched.

He missed her — far more than he could have ever imagined missing someone.

As he watched the diplomas being bestowed, he sat in a comfortable silence with Shane. Once the ceremony was over, he tracked Ari with his eyes, making sure not to lose sight of her. Finally, when she was alone, he made his approach.

"Congratulations, Ari." The stiffening of her shoulders was his only clue that she'd heard him above the many voices surrounding them. Slowly, she turned, for one brief instant with a slight smile upon her lips before it melted away.

"What are you doing here, Rafe?"

"I had to see your big moment. I'm proud of you." Silence greeted his words as the two of them stood there awkwardly. Rafe couldn't remember ever feeling so like an intruder.

"Thank you. I have people waiting," she said as she tried to brush him off. Rafe reached out and grasped her arm, refusing to let her leave until she heard him out.

"I need just five minutes," he said as he began steering her through the crowd. Surprisingly, she didn't fight him, and soon he found an empty hallway for the two of them to talk.

"Say what you need to, Rafe. But please get it over with." The new coldness in her eyes shook him more than he cared to admit.

"I've made mistakes, Ari. I know that now. I shouldn't have judged you on mistakes from my past. I miss you, and would like for us to give a real relationship a try." After several moments, Ari's lips turned up and Rafe felt relief fill him. This had been easier than he'd thought it would be.

"No, Rafe. You are in no way ready to be in a committed relationship. The way you treated me was abhorrent, and even worse was that I fell in love with you anyway. You're completely lacking in self-awareness, think you always have to be in charge, and deem women as the weaker sex. What I've discovered about myself in the last six months is that I'm a good person. I don't need to hide behind fake glasses or baggy clothes the way I did before I first met you. I don't need to cower in the corner afraid of someone judging me. I'm strong and intelligent, and I won't ever let myself be mistreated again. I know there's a good man beneath your hard exterior, but you need to find him. If you ever do, call me — I might even answer."

With that, Ari turned and started to walk away from him. Rafe stood there not knowing what to do. Should he once again chase after her? Should he let her go? Was their time over? For someone who always had the answers, he simply didn't have any.

"Ari," he called out without having any idea what he was going to say. She stopped and turned, looking at him with pity, which instantly had his anger rising to the surface. He was not a man to be pitied – not ever!

"Goodbye, Rafe." With that she turned and started walking away again.

"There are no goodbyes, Ari. We will see each other again." Her shoulders stiffened, but eventually the crowd swallowed her up as her feet carried her away, and like that she was gone from his life.

Walking away from the courtyard with the sounds of happiness filling the air, Rafe was at a loss. Picking up his phone, he dialed his assistant, Mario.

"Have the jet fueled and ready. I'm going home." Rafe moved with purpose to his car. It was time to go back home to Italy, back to his home and maybe even back to the heart he had somehow lost along the way.

If you enjoyed Submit, continue reading for an excerpt from the third book in the Surrender Series:

SEDUCED

Book Three in the Surrender Series

PROLOGUE

"**M**Y, MY, HOW the tables have turned."

"I swear, by all that's holy, that if you don't wipe that smart-assed smirk off your face, I will pound you to a bloody pulp!" Rafe thundered as he looked at his best friend, Shane.

"Wow. Aren't you cranky? Did you wake up on the wrong side of the bed?" Shane wasn't the least bit intimidated by Rafe's outburst. Of course, part of that could be because his best friend was securely behind bars.

"Yeah, you've had your fun, Shane. Now pay the damned bail and get me the hell out of here!"

"I don't know if I can afford it, since this *is* the second time in two months…"

"Shut up, Shane! This isn't the time to be a jackass. They won't let me pay the bail myself, and I want to go home!"

"Maybe if you stopped picking fights at clubs, you wouldn't get locked up," Shane said as he came closer to the bars.

Rafe's hand snaked through the opening and grabbed hold of Shane's shirt in an iron-tight grip. "Get — me — out — now!"

"OK. OK. There's no need for violence," Shane said, unable to control the laughter spilling from him. "We wouldn't want you to be thrown back in jail before you even get out."

Once Rafe released him, it didn't take long for Shane to post bail, and then he was leaving county detention with a very irate Rafe. "That wasn't amusing the first go-around, Shane, and certainly not this time," Rafe growled as he climbed into Shane's sleek silver Porsche.

"I seem to remember that you found it quite amusing when the shoe was on the other foot and *I* needed to be bailed out."

"That was different," Rafe muttered, rubbing his eyes. He hadn't slept in forty-eight hours, and he smelled like stale tequila and sweat. He didn't want to analyze the other odors drifting from his clothes.

"We need to get out of this town. One month in Italy wasn't long enough for Ari to forgive you, and you've been back for two months doing nothing but causing trouble. I think the best thing you can do is give the woman space. I'm scheduled to leave next week for South America because your unbelievably stubborn sister still won't speak to me. Let's take the hint and get away for a while."

Rafe stewed silently as he considered his best friend's words. The Gli Amanti Cove project was on hold because of environmental disputes, so they were stalled there. Rafe felt like crap, and for the first time in his life he had no motivation whatsoever to find the next big acquisition. Maybe he *should* just leave for a while. It would give him time to pull himself together. He didn't even know who he was anymore.

He hadn't seen Ari in three months and it was taking its toll on him. Every time he tried to speak to her, she would hang up the phone. He'd had gifts delivered to her new place, but she just returned his packages. The one time he'd cornered her, she'd coolly told him *he* wasn't ready yet.

Yes, he'd screwed up, but didn't people make mistakes? What was so wrong with liking sex? Was he that bad a man because he knew what he wanted and wasn't afraid to be with women who weren't intimidated to explore their sexuality? He didn't see it that way, but Ari apparently thought his actions were unforgivable. He'd even tried to enter into other satisfying sexual liaisons — not romantic, of course — but those had fizzled before they had even started.

He couldn't seem to forget one bright-eyed blond woman who'd stolen his breath away.

"I'll go with you."

Shane turned in surprise; his car swerved slightly into the next lane and almost clipped a station wagon. If Rafe had been in a better mood, he would have chortled at the look of terror on the father who was driving the old Volvo. The poor man had probably peed himself.

"Seriously?" It was obvious that Shane had never expected Rafe to walk away from the business world so easily.

"Yes. I need to get away before I do something incredibly foolish."

"Like you already haven't," Shane said with a laugh.

Rafe glared at him before replying. "I'm serious. I'm ready to do this."

"What about work?"

"I thought you were the one trying to talk me into this in the first place," Rafe said with a frustrated sigh.

"I am. *Really*. I just want to make sure you aren't going to get there and then turn around and leave in two weeks. These people are really counting on us."

Rafe knew that Shane was right. The homes and businesses they built in Third World countries changed lives. Rafe was surprised by how much he wanted to be a part of it. He'd grown anxious, bored, and frustrated with his life.

"I'll make some calls. My manager can run things from here. I'm ready to leave."

Assessing Rafe for several moments, Shane finally spoke. "Good. Pack up, because we'll be gone at least six months."

"What if you get called away?" Rafe asked.

"We'll cross that bridge," Shane said. He was used to being yanked away, and he always came back as soon as the task was finished.

This was a brilliant idea. Some hard physical labor was sure to take Rafe's mind off of Ari. He just needed to get away from this mess for a while. His infatuation with one woman was out of character; hell, it was completely insane. But it was all in his head and he'd be over Ari before he knew it!

CHAPTER ONE
Two Years Later
Ari

"ALL RIGHT, CLASS, I want you to take out your books and turn to page one hundred and four." Ari took a deep breath as she looked out at the sea of students before her. *Don't let them see your fear. They will eat you alive.*

No matter how many times she chanted this in her head, she could feel the sweat beading on her brow, and what felt like ten-pound weights sitting on her chest. What if she messed up? What if she *threw* up? What if everything just went black and she face-planted in front of the entire room?

You will not psych yourself out! You are Arianna Harlow, a strong, independent woman who just completed a master's degree. That takes guts, determination, and stamina. Not everyone is cut out for a higher education, but you did it in the face of everything you'd gone through. This is nothing in comparison. A class of fifty students will not intimidate you.

OK, she was feeling a bit less faint as she dimmed the lights and turned on the screen projector. This was her first job and she was grateful to be teaching.

The last two years hadn't been easy for Ari, but she'd worked hard, studying longer, jogging for miles upon miles to try to relieve the constant ache in her body, and spending what little free time she allowed for herself with her mother and friends.

The most difficult of times was being with Lia and Rachel. She loved them both so much, but they were a reminder of what she'd never again have.

Rafe.

It seemed that not a single day could pass without a thought of him fluttering through her mind. Time had lessened the ache but hadn't removed it altogether. Love for a man like Rafe didn't disappear overnight — apparently, not even after two years. She didn't regret her decision to walk away — it was what she'd had to do — but still, she missed him. Missed his smile and his laughter, missed the way his hands had caressed her body.

The few dates she'd attempted since leaving him had been a joke. No man could measure up to Rafe Palazzo. Yes, he'd been controlling and had pushed her in ways she still couldn't believe — he'd had her doing things she'd never thought she'd enjoy — but he'd also changed her forever.

She could never go back to that innocent girl she'd been. Rafe had opened her eyes to a new world, and it was a place she'd enjoyed. She would never settle for less than love, but she did miss the excitement the man provided. Missed the hunger that swelled into desire from deep within whenever he touched her.

Rafe was many things, but boring wasn't one of them. No man had stirred her the way he had, and she missed him desperately, though she never admitted that — not even to herself. What good would it do her?

Shaking off the melancholy thoughts, Ari focused on the meticulously written out notes in front of her as she began her carefully planned-out lecture. Too nervous to focus on the students, she was relieved when class was nearly over and it came time for them to ask questions.

Please, someone have something to ask was her only hope in that moment. The next few minutes passed with several questions, and the stiffness eased from her body. Only a couple of minutes more to go and she could call her first class a success.

"Are there any more questions?" This she would soon regret asking.

"Yes. Will you join me for dinner tonight?"

Ari's body stiffened and her face flushed. She would never, ever forget that voice — it haunted her in her dreams, making her wake up aching and empty. It trailed her as she walked the streets and heard a man's laughter. It caressed her body when she lay in bed at night and ran through the various conversations they'd had.

Ari's ears were ringing too loudly for her to hear the chuckling in her classroom as she lifted her head and her eyes locked with Rafe's purple-and-blue gaze.

Sitting comfortably in the back of the classroom, he took her breath away with his confident grin. Two years since she'd last laid eyes on him, and he still looked deliciously perfect. Several students turned his way, the girls batting their eyelashes, the guys wanting to *be* him. It was obvious to anyone present that he was a man who would always get his way.

Some people you were drawn to simply because of their confidence. Rafe was one of them. There was nothing about him that shouted insecure. His command was obvious from his very demeanor.

No! She reminded herself. He didn't always get his way. He'd wanted her, and she'd had the courage to walk away because he hadn't been willing to give her what she deserved. He might have been a man in charge, but that didn't lessen who she was. She'd stood up, been strong and hadn't stopped her forward momentum for a single instant once she'd finally gained the courage.

Yes, her heart had shattered that day she'd left his home, then shattered again when she walked away from him at her college graduation. However, she hadn't let it stop her. She'd accepted the pain, had felt it to the utmost, but she hadn't let it define her. She'd moved on.

When she'd come to the realization that, yes, love could be magical but that magic was still only an illusion, her pain had eased. It took time and effort to make love last if you wanted it to go beyond that illusion, that vision. Rafe had expected to get what he wanted without putting in the effort. It was his loss.

Looking him straight in the eyes — showing him she wasn't afraid — she spoke. "Are there any questions pertaining to the lecture?" Only the slightest bit of breathlessness entered her words as she forced her gaze from his in a deliberately measured way.

The room was silent, apart from a few remaining snickers.

"Very well, then. On Wednesday, upon your return, I want the questions at the end of the chapter done and turned in. We'll be discussing the Civil War all semester, and I expect you to learn a heck of a lot more than who fought and the dates it happened. By the time you move on to your next subject, you should have a basic understanding of why this war took place, and the lives that it affected. Thank you. Class is dismissed."

Ari turned back to her desk and sat down, her knees shaky. Her hope was that Rafe would rush from the room with the rest of the students, but Ari wasn't a fool. Rafe was there for a purpose and that she'd ignored him didn't mean he'd simply turn and walk away. That wasn't *who he was*.

Rafe would have his say, and she'd just have to bear up while he did it.

Be strong, she commanded herself as she heard the din of students' voices fading. She greatly wished at that moment for another class to be entering, but it was the end of the night and she was teaching only one class a day, Mondays and Wednesdays.

Toying with the thought of running from the room, she knew she'd never make it. Plus, Rafe would get the satisfaction of seeing her try to escape. She refused to reveal how much he still affected her. She absolutely rejected the thought of showing weakness in his presence.

"I've missed you, Ari, more than you could possibly imagine."

The familiarity of his voice stimulated every cell in her body while his scent swirled around her, draining the strength in her knees even more, and she was grateful to be sitting. How could he still have such power over her? How could she have such strong feelings about a man who had shattered her heart, leaving her to pick up the pieces of her life, alone?

"You are wasting your time, Rafe. I would have thought you'd have moved on by now. Have you had trouble hiring your next mistress?" Finally, Ari peered up at him, prepared to see irritation on his features.

When a smile formed on his lips instead, she was taken aback. What was this new game he was playing? She hadn't read the textbook on this one. Was he still upset that someone had walked away from him, even after so much time had passed?

Not even Rafe could be that determined to win.

"I want no other woman but you, Ari — and I've given you enough space. I made mistakes, and now I'm here to prove I'm a new man."

Ari's mouth dropped open. Rafe Palazzo was admitting to being *wrong* about something. Had the world stopped turning? She had to be dreaming — this was just another of her fantasies, and she was going to wake up at any moment, alone in her small room. And then she would have to fight the pressure in her chest as she took deep breaths and once again banished him from her mind.

No. She hadn't had an anxiety attack in a long time, and she wasn't going to start with them again. She was a college instructor, something she'd dreamed about for a very long time. A man wasn't going to unravel her — not even a man she had fallen hopelessly in love with.

"This is ridiculous, Rafe. We had our fling. It was great, but it's over and done with. Nothing good can come from us even attempting to come together again," she told him as she started to gather her possessions together.

She had to get out of that large classroom. Suddenly the walls felt as if they were closing in on her. She must get away from him before she did something foolish — such as actually believe what he was saying. Or, even worse, jump from her chair and wrap her body around his just to experience one more taste of his lips.

She wanted so badly to envision a happy ending with him that her heart was thudding at the possibility that he had changed — that his interest in her was now more than just *really* great sex.

"Ridiculous or not, I've decided to woo you."

For the second time in sixty seconds, Ari's mouth dropped open. Did he actually just say the word *woo*? Who was this man and what had he done with Rafe Palazzo? It couldn't possibly be the same person who'd forced her into an affair with him. She needed to remember what he'd done — what he'd demanded from her.

"I hate to disappoint you, but I'm not that same desperate girl who allowed you to make me go against everything I was brought up to hold important." *There, that would show him.*

Rafe came around her desk, turning her chair and boxing her in. She leaned back, but he followed, his face only inches from hers.

"I did some things I will forever regret, but I've had a lot of time to think since then. Yes, I forced your hand, but the night you walked away from me, you told me you loved me. I'm here to prove I'm worthy of that love."

Ari couldn't speak. Her eyes lowered as they took in the fullness of his lips, her ears straining to hear more of the enticing words coming from them. Of course, he was saying what she wanted to hear, but that's what Rafe did best. He got his way — by any means possible. She couldn't be so foolish as to actually believe him.

"No witty comebacks, Ari?"

Leaning in even closer, Ari breathed in his masculine scent and felt her heart race, the sound of her blood rushing through her veins echoing in her head. Finally, snapping out of her trance, Ari lifted her hand and pushed against him, shocked when he responded to her unspoken request to stop and pulled himself away.

Hoping her knees would work, Ari grabbed her briefcase and stood. So far, so good. She'd resisted kissing his full lips, and when she'd risen from her chair, she hadn't face-planted in front of him. Thank heavens for such small mercies.

"The girl who professed her love is long gone, Rafe. I'm following the path I want to be on, and I don't have time to date. I appreciate that you thought of me, but it's best if we both just move on," she said over her shoulder as she began ascending the steps to the back door of the classroom.

She could feel him right on her heels as she reached the top of the stairs and walked into the quiet hallway. It was late, the school quickly emptying as most of the kids had finished their last class of the day. Summer terms had fewer students attending the school, anyway, and the campus was almost a dead zone when evening classes met.

Ari began walking toward the parking lot; Rafe moved silently beside her. There was no use in telling him to stop — he wouldn't allow her to walk on her own, even though there were security guards patrolling the area. It was dark, and he was a man who insisted on escorting a woman to her destination, even if she hadn't asked him to do so.

It should irritate her, but it was one of those old-fashioned actions that she actually liked. A gentleman should ensure the safety of a woman he cared about. Not that she was going to get ideas into her head that he actually cared for her.

Yes, she would admit that she was confused. How was she supposed to respond when he so suddenly popped back into her life? She obviously needed time to think. She certainly couldn't keep a clear head with him right by her side.

Rafe had a way of causing her body to short-circuit. It was one of the things she both loved and hated about him. How could she trust what she was feeling when she couldn't think straight? She was intelligent — far above average — but she felt like a ditzy schoolgirl when she was around him.

Hunger was good — she would admit to that. But with Rafe, it wasn't just hunger, it was an all-consuming passion that took over your mind, body and soul. That wasn't healthy. It couldn't possibly be good for you.

When they reached her car, he put his hand on the door, preventing her from opening it. Her will was wearing thin, and she needed to remove herself from his presence, immediately.

"I've had a long day, Rafe. Please let me leave." Her voice was firm, except for only the slightest shake, but she felt like a cornered animal, and instinct had her wanting to lash out by kicking his leg. That might have made him move.

"I want to talk to you. I think you owe me that much," he said.

She looked at him incredulously. She *owed* him? Oh, she didn't think so.

"That is the most ridiculous thing I think I've ever heard you say, Rafe. I *owe* you nothing," she snapped as she thought about reaching for the scissors she knew were in her bag and poking them into the offending hand that was keeping her door closed.

"You owe it to *us* to listen to what I have to say," he said.

"I owe it to *myself* to do what makes me happy."

"Fine," he replied, that easy smile back.

Her suspicions rose as she looked at him. He still hadn't removed his hand. With a bow, he stepped away and as she opened her door, thinking she'd actually gotten off quite easily, he spoke again.

"I'll be back on Wednesday — and Monday — and Wednesday — and when are your office hours again?"

"Fine!" she interrupted. "What will it take to make you go away?"

"Dinner and a conversation."

Simple and to the point. Now *that* was the Rafe she remembered well.

"I guess you'll be enjoying history, then. Have a nice night, Rafe." As she slid swiftly into her car, she couldn't help but glance back. Instead of seeing anger or frustration on his face, she saw a huge grin.

That couldn't be a good sign.

CHAPTER TWO

Lia

"ARE YOU KIDDING me?!" Lia slapped her arm as another bug landed on her, hell-bent on doing horrendous things to her tender flesh. What in the world was she doing in this tiny cabin in the middle of nowhere?

Once the resort was finished, this area would be breathtaking, with carefully designed spa retreats, luxury cabins, and private getaways for couples wanting exclusivity, romance, and the ultimate in indulgence.

Right now, it was hard to picture what the resort would become, because the area was untouched. Some found this beautiful just as it was, and many thought it a shame Rafe's company was building the Gli Amanti Cove, but she was a firm believer in the project.

She'd witnessed first hand what Shane and Rafe could do. There was a reason the two of them were so successful. They didn't just throw buildings together. They made dreams come to reality, and they had a line of customers anxious to enter their next paradise.

Never before had she really thought of herself as spoiled, but as she swatted another bug trying to land on her, she admitted that she *was* used to nice things. That didn't make her shallow or unfeeling; it made her sensible. Had she been born in a different time, then she'd expect…less. She'd heard of people who shunned air conditioning, but she had no interest in meeting crazy people.

"Troubles, Lia?"

Speaking of crazy people… Her entire body tensed as she heard the laughter of his rich voice. She turned slowly, and there was Shane, only ten feet away, leaning casually on the rickety railing of her steps.

Even knowing she'd be seeing quite a bit of him didn't lessen the reaction her body was having at the sight of the man. Though she wanted this project to succeed, since it was her first one with the company owned by her brother, Rafe, she'd been relieved by the delays, needing that time to build up her armor against Shane.

She'd wanted him for so long that she couldn't remember a time she hadn't. Then he'd had to go and ruin it all. Now, she couldn't even remember why she was so angry with him, but she felt justified in accepting that he was the enemy. It was a girl's prerogative to be irrational, wasn't it?

But of course that wasn't true. She remembered quite well, and she'd ended her incredibly brief affair with him for a good reason. She'd made a simple request — that he not tell her brother about their new relationship. True, it hadn't been simple to Shane. He always told Rafe everything, and he felt he had to tell him about the two of them.

In short, Rafe meant more to Shane than she did. And Shane's own feelings mattered more to him than hers did. No, they hadn't discussed marriage — hell, they'd just been to bed once. But what Shane had done didn't follow her rule book. It didn't count as forsaking all others. It counted as thinking that men in general mattered more than women, and in particular that everyone he knew with testicles mattered more than she did.

Here's what really pissed her off — Shane hadn't had enough respect for her and her brain to wait and consider carefully what she'd asked. No, he'd run off and squealed to her brother while the sheets were still warm.

She didn't need another man like that, another man who dismissed her, thought of her only as a nice, warm body, useful at night, but not a friend and a confidante. Maybe she couldn't do better; maybe all guys were insensitive louts. Just look at Rafe. But she could try, and she could hope to find a man who really knew how to treat a woman, really knew how to love her.

She didn't think it was too much to ask to be put first.

"No troubles at all, Shane. Why are you here so early?"

"I couldn't let you have all the fun on your own, could I?" As he spoke, he took a step toward her, and it took all her will-power not to retreat. She couldn't back down even an inch, or he'd pounce. That was who Shane was.

"The first two weeks here is a lot of surveying, and you could have been relaxing on the beach while we do this part. Don't worry, though. It's not too late. Why don't you hop into your boat and go flirt with the locals across the channel?"

The thought of him doing just that had her stomach turning, but there was no possible way she'd admit it. Eventually she would will herself to get over her extreme lust and infatuation with her brother's best friend.

Shane wasn't fazed. "I would rather stay right where I am and flirt with you."

Why had he decided too late to say everything she'd always wanted him to say? Men! They never did what they were supposed to.

"You're wasting your time, Grayson. Go find something to do. I'm going for a walk." Lia brushed past him and bounded down the steps. There was little hope that he would listen to her and disappear, but she had to give it a try.

"Good. I was in the mood for an evening stroll. Where are we off to?"

Lia sighed and made her way in a leisurely manner along the trails she knew so well. She'd been across the entire island and back again so many times, she could probably map it out. That's what it had taken to place the resort in just the right location. There was so much more involved, too, such as not disturbing the natural appeal of the island while still making the resort a place that big spenders would be willing to come to.

"I don't recall inviting you, Shane." Though she knew he wouldn't listen to her protests, she had to give it a valiant effort. If she didn't, she would soon be falling into his arms, and that would only lead to disaster, as she'd so quickly discovered while in Las Vegas. Falling into his bed had obviously been a mistake.

What the two of them had shared had been nobody's business but theirs. Even after over two years, her blood boiled at the thought of what he'd done immediately afterward.

"The invitation was in your eyes," he said with a grin. It took her a moment to realize he meant an invitation for him to walk with her, which she hadn't issued, and not an invitation to her bed, which she didn't want, either. "Besides, someone has to protect you," he continued. He grabbed her arm and wound it through his. She tugged for a moment, then gave up, unwilling to show him that he was, in fact, affecting her.

"Believe what you will. I just want to finish this job and get back to the real world."

"How can you turn your nose up at such natural beauty? Besides, we're going to be here for a good six months...at least," he said.

The excitement in his tone had her pulse racing.

Lia had no doubt that Shane expected them to pick up where they'd left off in Vegas. For so long she'd chased him, trying to prove she wasn't the little girl he'd first met when her brother had brought him home on a break from college.

But Shane was no different from any other boyfriend she'd had. He was intimidated by her brother, or worse, he cared more about her brother than he did about her. She was the odd woman out in a cozy bromance. Whatever the reason, he hadn't been willing to be with her without Rafe's permission — he hadn't even listened to her objections. Shane had just run off to Rafe, even though she'd told him what that meant. That just pissed her off all over again every time she thought about it.

"I spoke with the designer last week and we're on schedule. I don't expect you to be here the whole time," she said. She really hoped that was the case. Nobody could ever describe Lia as weak, but when it came to Shane, she didn't trust herself to keep holding out against him, especially if he decided to be charming. She'd seen the man in action through the years, and he was good at making women trail after him. She didn't want to be another in his long line of heartbreaks.

"Yes, the project is on schedule, and we have a wonderful crew to run it. Yet the problem is that I don't trust anyone to see it through. I've decided this task needs me here until the end," he said, stopping so he could turn her to face him.

The light in his eyes left no doubt that he was more than happy about their situation. Her stomach clenched as she fought her rising hormones. As Shane lifted his hand and removed a piece of hair that was clinging to her cheek, she knew she was in trouble.

Her breath quickened, and she was hot and hungry. She hadn't been with another man since Shane in Vegas, and her body was going through withdrawal. It wasn't easy to keep her distance, but she cared about herself enough to do so.

"Shane…" She attempted to warn him off, but there wasn't much heat behind her words.

"Yes, Lia?"

Oh, the man knew how to seduce, knew exactly the power he had over her. She'd just have to be that much stronger.

Lifting her hand as if she were going to caress him, she saw triumph flash in his eyes. When she slapped his forehead instead, his shocked expression made a giggle escape her previously pursed lips.

"You had a mosquito about to attack." With that, she pulled from him and turned back toward her small cabin. She felt victory at resisting him, even knowing she had a long way to go.

"This is only the first day, Lia," Shane called out to her, making her shoulders stiffen. Yes, it was only the first day.

So he'd snatched away some of her victory. She certainly wouldn't let him get another piece of it, or her, by sticking around. Not slowing her pace, she made it back to her cabin in record time, and she locked herself safely inside.

Yes, it was only their first day, but she'd still congratulate herself. If she took it only one day at a time, she might get through this unscathed. *Might* being the key word.

36170437R00196

Made in the USA
San Bernardino, CA
14 July 2016